# The Eastern

Book One: The Early Years

# The Eastern

## Book One: The Early Years

**A NOVEL**

# Deborah Gould

**Maine Authors Publishing**
Rockland, Maine
www.maineauthorspublishing.com

THE EASTERN *Book One: The Early Years.*
Copyright 2015 by Deborah Gould.
ISBN 978-1-63381-053-2

Cover art: "The Eastern," by Ginger Brown. Oil on board, 18x12.
Map of Eastern River District by Ginger Brown. Pen and ink.

Rising in East Pittston, Maine, at the confluence of its east and west branches, the Eastern River flows fourteen miles through Pittston and Dresden to Merrymeeting Bay, where it empties into the Kennebec River.

This is a work of fiction. References to people once living are used to provide historical realism; all characters, however, are used fictitiously and all non-factual events, descriptions, and conversations are of my own imagination.

Book Design by Lindy Gifford for Maine Authors Publishing.

Produced by
Maine Authors Publishing
558 Main Street
Rockland, Maine
www.maineauthorspublishing.com

Printed in the United States of America.

*There are still Thompsons, Blodgetts,*
*Crockers, Calls, and Stilphens*
*living on or near the Eastern River.*
*I extend my deepest respect to them all.*

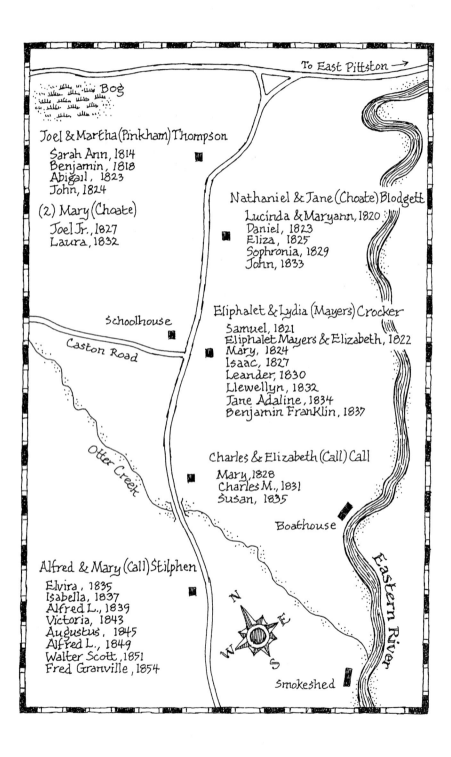

To East Pittston →

Bog

Joel & Martha (Pinkham) Thompson

Sarah Ann, 1814
Benjamin, 1818
Abigail, 1823
John, 1824

(2) Mary (Choate)

Joel Jr., 1827
Laura, 1832

Nathaniel & Jane (Choate) Blodgett

Lucinda & Maryann, 1820
Daniel, 1823
Eliza, 1825
Sophronia, 1829
John, 1833

Schoolhouse

Caston Road

Eliphalet & Lydia (Mayers) Crocker

Samuel, 1821
Eliphalet Mayers & Elizabeth, 1822
Mary, 1824
Isaac, 1827
Leander, 1830
Llewellyn, 1832
Jane Adaline, 1834
Benjamin Franklin, 1837

Otter Creek

Charles & Elizabeth (Call) Call

Mary, 1828
Charles M., 1831
Susan, 1835

Boathouse

Eastern River

Alfred & Mary (Call) Stilphen

Elvira, 1835
Isabella, 1837
Alfred L., 1839
Victoria, 1843
Augustus, 1845
Alfred L., 1849
Walter Scott, 1851
Fred Granville, 1854

N
W E
S

Smokeshed

# PART I

# 1820–1830

# Chapter One

To make hay in the very best manner, you should cut in the forenoon, after two or three days of dry weather, and rake it before the dew falls, putting it into cocks of 100 each. At ten, next day, open it; at eleven, turn it; at twelve turn it again; at two put it on your cart while the sun shines clear. Then your hay will look bright, and keep sweet...

*Cold Water Fountain*
Gardiner, Maine

THAT NIGHT, they lay close and lazy, talking softly in the darkness between first and second sleep.

"I'd like for us to have a cow," Martha said.

"A cow?" he repeated, shifting closer to her on the bed, reaching out for her, quick to rise.

"Yes." She touched his mouth with her fingers, to pause him, to slow him down. "Not only for Sarah Ann and Benjamin, but also for the one I'm carrying now."

"A milk cow?" he asked. "No, not yet, although I'd like to oblige." He put his hand out, found her.

"I'll milk it myself, Joel; thee needn't bother with it," she assured him, her fingers light against his arm, his chest.

Not yet, he thought. Next spring would be soon enough; the small field he'd stubbed up behind the house—rocks and stumps cleared, fences staked and started—would have grass then, would have enough to feed a cow.

"Next spring," he said, moving his palm along the curve of her hip. "I can then pasture it in with its calf, feed the two together." He turned onto his side, facing her, eager now. "Next spring."

"So, it is set," she said, and moved closer to him on the bed, sealing the agreement.

———

Late June, and the heat rose from the small field of English grass he was scything, rose and clung to his arms and face, caught all morning under the brim of his hat and pressed the sweat up against his brow.

This was good enough timothy, Joel Thompson thought, for the year's first cutting; a second in August, if as plentiful as this first, would yield enough to feed the oxen and horse for the winter.

He reached the end of a pass, turned, and eyed what was left: only two more sweeps if he made them both broad, three if his shoulders gave way.

He stretched, set his feet, and started in again, moving across the slope of the field that led down to the river. His muscles pulled sharply across his neck, the length of his upper arms.

Three, he thought instantly. It will have to be three.

He reached the end of the row, turned, started back across the slope. The scythe sang through the grass, through the timothy and red clover that fell back over the blade—*swing forward, swing back, step left and right, balance, swing forward, swing back…*

Martha watched him from the side of the road, paused for a moment on her way to Nathaniel and Jane Blodgetts'—to get milk for the children, to tell Jane she was carrying again. The sunlight was hot on her back and shoulders, Benjamin heavy on her hip, Sarah Ann wandering, out of sight, perhaps, but not far away—always hiding, that one; lovely to look at, to be sure, but not quite right.

She jounced the baby, turned to set his face toward the field.

"See?" she engaged him, pointing down the slope of the meadow to Joel. "There's yer pa!"

Benjamin stretched out hard, pushed his heels against her as he grinned. Far down the hillside, the sunlight flashed on the blade of his father's scythe.

Sarah Ann, almost six; Benjamin, nearly two; the one she lost in between, in the winter of 1816; now this one, coming, she thought, in February.

There was a rustle, a quick movement behind her, and Martha turned, found Sarah Ann close by, arm extended, offering a stalk with a bruised yellow flower.

"A buttercup," she said, smiling down. "For me?" She took it from the girl's fist, twirled it in her fingers.

Sarah Ann nodded, then moved back through the bushes into the grass, back into those yellowcups, humming, droning.

Not quite right, Martha thought, our Sarah Ann; not an imbecile, thanks be, not bidgering and flailing, not tied to the bedstead or barred into a back room like that Davenport child over to King's Mills—Judith, was it? Judith Davenport?

At first they thought it to be God's damnation for something they might have done—something she herself had done, or Joel might have done, or something they might have done together—although they'd lived lives of consideration, they thought; they had done no wrong.

They examined it endlessly; they wore themselves out with it. Finally, they turned their backs on the possibility that they had been at fault. They put Sarah Ann's imperfection down to the will of a God they both acknowledged less and less in the face of her undeserved deficiencies.

And that was that, she thought, for along came Benjamin, and he was fair right, so penance paid, if there had been, in fact, any due.

Martha kissed the top of Benjamin's head, then turned back to the field. Joel was nearly done, making what looked to be his last pass across the slope of the meadow, arms long and easy, swinging, swinging, and she remembered last night, the rhythm of it.

Sometimes his grace overwhelmed her.

## Chapter Two

*Pittston Town Meeting*
*East Parish*
*April 15, 1821*

*Cattle should not run at large in the Eastern River district. Any person so letting their cattle run at large shall be liable to a fine.*

*Hogs may go at large by being yoked and rung according to Law.*

*Eliphalet Crocker*
*Hog Reeve*
*Eastern River District*

JANE BLODGETT arrived at dawn to be with Lydia Crocker in her labor.

She tended to Lydia all morning and, during those times Lydia had no need of her, did the work of the house—she washed and swept, kept the fire fed and the kettle hot—while Eliphalet, between his chores in the barns and sheds, came in and out of the kitchen, in and out of the bedroom, watchful and jumpy.

All morning it went like that, but by early afternoon, Lydia's discomfort increased, and Jane sat at the edge of the bed and mopped Lydia's forehead with a wet cloth she rinsed over and over in the bucket of water on the floor beside the bed.

She looked over her shoulder to Eliphalet as he stood in the doorway to the main room. "Fetch me clean water," she said quietly, "and go fetch Martha Thompson."

"Is there trouble?" Eliphalet whispered, his throat squeezed tight around the words. "Is this right?"

"It's her first," Jane said by way of explanation. "Just go for Martha."

Hog Reeve, he thought, pulling on the shed door. I'm the newly sworn Hog Reeve for the Eastern River District and I am running like a shoat from the sound of my wife, who lies in the front room, the air in there thick with pain and determination. She sweats, grunts like a sow, her eyes first shut in a daze then wide with the ripple and roar of another push as this baby tries again and again to be born.

He braced a foot against the jamb, dragged the door outward against the push of the wet spring wind, then slipped inside and let it slam shut behind him.

The oxen breathed, shuffled their feet, restless in this drizzle and wind. There was just enough light to see them by, two brindled shapes close together in their places, secured by nose ring and chain.

"Noah," he said. "Ham."

They swung their heads, opened their eyes to the whites. He ran his palms down their huge haunches, not so much to settle them as himself—their stolid presence eased his discomfort at what he had done to render his wife such suffering.

"'Tis just the wind," he assured them.

The horse, too, was on edge; he sidestepped lightly, danced between his ties. Eliphalet, clumsy in his urgency, fumbled some on the halter, but Ned took the bit easily, accepted the saddle.

"There now," Eliphalet murmured, "there now."

He put his back to the shed door, forced it open, and led the horse out into the wind and wet. He held him tightly as he closed and rebraced the door, and then he was up on Ned's broad back and around the corner of the house to the road.

He thought he heard Lydia yelling as she bore down, thanked God he was a man, and then tucked his heels into Ned's sides and headed north, moving through the muck of the road up past Nate Blodgett's and on to Joel Thompson's.

———

This was the first year they'd had glass in all the windows, and Martha Thompson could see outside her house from anywhere within it for the first time in the nearly five years they had lived on the Eastern. The light lifted the gloom from the inside corners and drew her eyes to the outside—east and south from the front of the house, west and north from the back.

The shed was still windowless, but Joel had put true glass in the east and west gable windows of the barn, and now he did morning and evening chores in real light. The chickens were laying more; she'd been finding three or four every day.

"Gratitude," Joel said when she told him how many. "They are thankful for our improvements to their coop and their welfare."

Martha laughed, shook her head at the fancy of that.

They do not have the sense to dodge the rain, she thought, let alone to be grateful for window glass.

She leaned up against the south window and watched the rider come up out of the trees past Blodgett's yard and along the road. She saw the muddy water splash out to either side of the roan and knew he was in a hurry.

"Joel," she called out. "It's Liph, coming at us full chisel!"

He left his tea and came to stand beside her.

"Lydia?" he questioned, never taking his eyes off Eliphalet, who was now swinging into the drive and approaching the house, his hair stuck long and wet to his forehead, his legs dark with rainwater.

"No doubt," she replied. She turned away, gathered her things: her kit bag with herb pockets, strong thread, small knife, scarf and cape.

"I'll carry John with me," she said, lifting the baby from the cradle, "should I be there for the night." She folded him tightly in a sling against her chest, then wrapped her cape about them both.

"'Lo, Thompson!" Eliphalet shouted from outside, and Joel opened the door.

Martha passed through, stepped up on the mounting block and, as Eliphalet Crocker extended his arm to give weight and counterbalance, swung up on Ned. She put both arms around Liph's waist and clasped her hands, leaned her cheek against the back of his rough coat, John burrowed safely between them.

"Go!" she said, and they were off.

Joel Thompson watched them go, leaned against the window frame and watched them leave the dooryard and turn onto the road, Eliphalet high in the saddle, Martha pushed up against his back, astride Ned's broad haunches. Her skirts, hiked for the ride, filled out to the sides, rising and falling like a wake with Ned's even gait.

He watched them up the muddy road until they were past the front of Nathaniel Blodgett's house and over the top of the rise, then they dropped over the edge from his view.

The moisture fell slowly, more of a heavy mist than a true rainfall; the maples and oaks along the road were slick with it.

He pushed away from the window.

With Martha and the baby gone, he needed to keep an eye on the other two children, especially Benjamin, who ran and lurched about the house like a drunkard, knocking stools and chairs about, careening too near the tin kitchen on the open hearth. And there was Sarah Ann, as well, who was uncomfortable without her mother about the place and needed his attention.

He turned, swept his eyes across the room and found her sitting quietly in the corner, knees pulled up, arms wrapped tightly about her legs. His heart pulled inside his chest, and he squatted down before her, reached out for her chin and brought it up in his hand, met her eyes and smiled.

"Thee need not fret, girl," he said. "Yer ma'll be back home after the Crocker baby's born."

Her eyes changed, but she said nothing.

"Think of that," he said, more gently. "A new baby in the neighborhood, and one that might need yer tending when it's a bit older."

She looked over at Benjamin, sleeping in the trundle.

"Yes, thee's right, for sure—our Benjamin is first on the slate and yer ma needs thee to help with young John—but there will be times Miz Crocker will be needing yer assistance, as well."

He stood up, put his hands on his hips and stretched back, shrugged off some of his tiredness; a richer man would have others at his call, would have time to simply sit down, to rest.

"Would thee come out with me to the barn," he asked, "and keep watch on Benjamin for me while I do early chores?"

She nodded, her eyes on him, then rose and came near to him, leaned against his side. He reached down and slid his palm across the back of her shoulders for just a moment—a gesture of reassurance he and Martha had adopted by agreement—for a touch seemed to calm her, just as it calmed the livestock when the wind switched or lightning tricked across the sky or when the foxes prowled too near the woods side of the barn during an evening.

He checked the fire, found tight embers and a small flame. He leaned the fire screen across the front and propped it in place with the poker, then lifted the drowsy Benjamin and settled him on his shoulder, turned to his daughter.

"Set?" he asked, smiling.

She nodded, and opened the door for him, and, after he passed by, shut it carefully behind them.

They headed diagonally across the dooryard, Sarah Ann breaking into her slow, strange trot. The mist swirled, the wind caught at their clothes, but there was less of a bite to it, he noticed; there was even a slight hint of warmth over his face.

Time to put taps to the maples, he thought, and followed his daughter into the barn.

———————

The little side room burned with the heat of Lydia Crocker's labor; the stench of sweat and fluid and blood filled the space, wrapped tightly around the women, held them together.

Martha Thompson and Jane Blodgett were each to a side of the rumpled bed, their sleeves rolled high, foreheads and arms still slick with the effort of it all: Martha cleaning her knife, wiping out buckets and bowls; Jane gathering soiled sheeting and cloths for the copper boiler, singing just beneath her breath—

> O Father, look from heav'n and bless
> Where'er thy servant's labor be…

Not that God had much to do with this particular kind of labor, Martha thought, turning occasionally to keep an eye on Lydia, propped up in the bed, her back cushioned against the headboard, her long, slow hours of push and pain behind her, her hair all straggle and mat; Lydia, triumphant, holding her son.

Later, Lydia Crocker took inventory: traced a finger across the baby's cheek, then up to his forehead and between his eyes and down along the slope of his nose—My nose, she thought, *my* nose—ten of each, fingers and toes; ears tucked neatly against the side of his head like Eliphalet's.

Samuel, from the Hebrew: an answer to prayers.

"God forgive me for saying this," she said, looking up at her husband, "but I have made something perfect."

"Perfect he is," Eliphalet answered, sitting down on the edge of the bed, "but ye're not to forget that I, too, had a small part in creating his perfection!"

"Very small," Lydia responded, smiling. "A second or two, as I recall."

"More than that," he protested, his pride nicked, she thought; he then saw the tease in her eyes and grinned at her.

She handed him the baby. "Mind his head," she cautioned him. "Keep it in yer crook."

*Pittston Town Meeting*
*East Parish*
*June 17, 1822*

*Fence Viewer     Joel Thompson*
*School Agent     Nathaniel Blodgett*

*Now comes Eliphalet Crocker of Pittston to Register the follow-*
*ing, born to him & Wife Lydia*
> *Samuel, March 5, 1821*
> *Eliphalet Mayers & Elizabeth, born May 19, 1822*
> > *Recorded by me, Eli Young, Town Clerk*

*Now here comes Nathaniel Blodgett of Pittston to Register the*
*following, born to him & Wife Jane*
> *Lucinda & Maryanne, both born February 4, 1820*
> > *Recorded by me, Eli Young, Town Clerk*

*Notise of Deaths in the Town of Pittston, East Parish*
> *Eliphalet Mayers, son of Eliphalet Crocker & Wife Lydia,*
> *Departed this Life June 10, 1822*
> > *Recorded by me, Eli Young, Town Clerk*

# Chapter Three

Receipt for Soap
Mix soda and lime. Pour on boiling water. Let it stand until
perfectly clear, then drain off. Put in clean rendering, hog or
steer is best...boil until it starts to set, thin with limed cold
water. Set it to a trencher. Wet a tub to prevent sticking; turn
in the soap and let it stand.

*Cold Water Fountain*
Gardiner, Maine


JANE BLODGETT opened her eyes at first light, stretched just a little,
then turned on her side.

Nathaniel stayed still.

He sleeps like a stone, she thought, like a stone dropped into a dry
well; has a few moments of twitchiness before falling off, then hardly
moves all the night long.

She watched him for a while—handsome as he was, with his eyebrows full and brown, the stubble on his cheek and chin thick. But handsome is as handsome does, and she'd known what he did for some time
now; he'd strayed from their bed on occasion, she knew, taken what he
wanted at will, and she'd no recourse.

She let her eyes drift across and down his profile, heard the first birds
outside, crows and robins, mostly, heard the squirrels chattering in the
oaks and maples in the woodlot.

She began to plan the course of her day: stir up the kitchen fire, start
the kettle for tea, start the oatcakes, start the stew to warming, start the
washing, start...

15

She reached out, laid a hand on his shoulder, and tapped him with her fingertips.

"Nate."

He stirred.

"There's light," she said, then stretched herself out of bed, stepped into her skirt and pulled it up over her chemise, added a top blouse, moved out of the bedroom, and headed to the kitchen, barefoot.

Later, after she had yoked four buckets of washwater from the spring to the kitchen, she lifted the kettle to the crane, poured the water in, swung it back over the fire to heat.

Jane eyed the pieces of washing—their other sets of daywear, mostly—and worked with a stiff brush to scruff away most of the dried dirt, then dropped them into one of the soaktubs; in the other, some table and kitchen linens, all their small clothes.

She set the washboard into the tub, reached into the water and pulled free one of her aprons, slapped it against the board, and scrubbed it up and down. She leaned hard into the motion, watched the water churn and run through the fabric and over the grooved face of the oak board and back into the washtub; she watched the dirt wash away.

She looked down at her hands, roiling the graywater, then raised them, stood straighter, and rested her fingers against the washboard; the water slipped over the grooves, back into the tub.

It's in the swirling, she thought, looking down at her hands again. It's the churning of the water that makes things clean; it's the water, pushing through the weave of the clothes and pulling the dirt away.

"Nathaniel?" she called out, crossing the backhouse floor, wiping her hands dry on her apron, excited now. "Nate?"

And when he appeared in the shed doorway, his arms full of firewood and his head cocked, questioning, she asked him for the use of a barrel.

"No," he said directly, and pushed past her into the kitchen.

She looked away, pursed her lips and blew air out. No; again and always it was no; he was not even listening: no.

"Ye're goin' to Jonathan Young's this morning with that first load of barrels at any rate," she said, following him, "so why not?"

He had twenty-one new oak barrels in the part of the backhouse he used as a cooperage—his winter's work lined up and stacked neatly against the north wall—and Jonathan Young was willing to pay him in coin for them.

He dumped the firewood into the box, turned to look at her. "You want me to ruin a barrel?" he gruffed. "I'd find a hundred ways to use that money."

She put her hands to her hips, leaned against the doorjamb. "It's not much I'm asking," she said.

"For yer washing?" he challenged, his voice hardening. "Ruin a barrel for yer washing?"

She wiped her face with the back of her hand, then looked him square on. The skin around his eyes and the corners of his mouth pinched tight.

"Why not try it," she said, "as ye're goin' anyway."

He shrugged.

"As a kindness to me," she added.

She watched him struggle with that, knowing he couldn't think of how to refuse her—his guilt about his philandering was workable. She was asking for a single barrel only, and if she proved right, it would be a great ease.

"I'll pay for that barrel from my egg money," she offered, to add some sweet to the deal.

He gave in.

"I'm willing to give one over to you," he said, wagging his forefinger, "but just one. It leaves me with an even twenty to sell, and evens are better luck than odds."

She wasn't sure about that part of it—the better luck of even numbers of things—but this was a gift from Nathaniel, and she didn't care to risk questioning it.

He rolled the first barrel up into the wagon for her and secured it upright with a length of rope, then harnessed and hitched the horses while she transferred buckets of warm water across the kitchen, through the shed, and into the dooryard to the wagon, up into the bed, up again into the barrel. She lugged the clothes from the soaktubs and dumped them in as well, added a handful of softsoap, and swished it all around.

Nathaniel tapped the lid down with his fist, then loaded the rest of his barrels—seven more, for a total of eight; two across, four deep.

An even load.

He climbed up into the seat.

"I'll be home for dinner," he said, "and we'll see if ye're as smart as you think."

He turned to the horses, flicked the reins lightly.

She crossed her fingers behind her back, stood in the doorway, and watched him turn out of the yard, the wagon already tipping and bumping. She imagined the water sloshing and churning inside the barrel, imagined her washing, coming home clean.

I am, she thought. I'm as smart as that and then some.

---

*Town Meeting*
*East Parish*
*June 28, 1824*

*Fence Viewer    Joel Thompson*
*Field Driver    Nathaniel Blodgett*

*Now here comes Eliphalet Crocker of Pittston to Register the following, born to him & Wife Lydia*
*    Mary, May 20, 1824*
*        Recorded by me, Eli Young, Town Clerk*

*Now here comes Joel Thompson of Pittston to Register the following, born to him & Wife Martha*
*    Abigail, January 20, 1823*
*    John, February 27, 1824*
*        Recorded by me, Eli Young, Town Clerk*

*Now here comes Nathaniel Blodgett to Register the following, born to him & Wife Jane*
*    Daniel, October 5, 1823*
*        Recorded by me, Eli Young, Town Clerk*

## Chapter Four

Receipt to Cure the Cholera Morbus
Take a porter bottle Cork, lay it upon a clean hearth so nigh
a hot fire that it will burn to a coal; put the coal into a teacup, add thereto a common spoonful of the best Cognac
Brandy…peppermint tea, loaf sugar, grated nutmeg…

*Eastern Chronicle*
Gardiner, Maine

HE FELT the sudden weight of the quilt fall across his chest, felt her leave the bed.

He pushed himself up and, in the quiet light of the spring moon, caught faint sight of her as she hurried from the room. And then, just as he lay back down, he heard the slap of the shed door against the jamb and knew she was outside, on her way to the outhouse.

She is unwell, he thought, something she ate.

He turned onto his side and dropped away again.

When he next opened his eyes, it was just past dawn, and Martha's place was empty—still or again, he did not know. So he rose, pulled on his trousers and overshirt, and crossed quickly through the kitchen, out through the shed door to the chilly outside, where the chickens were already hard at work, scratching in the dooryard, their yellow feet jumping in the early sunshine.

"Martha?" he called, and listened.

The cardinals whistled in the tree line, and he knew in his throat that something was not right. He started to run, barefoot, across the dooryard and down around the far corner of the shed toward the outhouse.

19

He found her there, on the ground, slumped against the outside wall, hands clenched to her belly within the curve of her updrawn knees. She was covered from mouth to foot with her own filth.

He stood in the sunlight and looked at her for a long moment, watched the flies circle around her head, crawl on her soiled chemise. Her eyes were wide open, fixed on a spot far off, high up above the trees.

He knew she was dead; he backed away.

———

He took the children from their beds.

"Yer ma's right sick," he told them, "and we need to leave her to her rest."

He wrapped Abigail and John in their bedclothes, carried them together. Sarah Ann and Benjamin were slow and reluctant, unsure of his manner, his tone of voice, but he herded them out of the kitchen and into the outside, then stepped in front of them and led them across the dooryard. He turned south on the road, toward Nathaniel and Jane Blodgett's, took them away from their mother, dead in the backyard.

He started walking, the two youngest each to a shoulder, Sarah Ann and Benjamin behind. As they passed the south boundary wall, he heard his older daughter crying, heard her sharp, shallow gasps; he turned and looked back at her.

"Come along," he said, gently, "just come along with me."

She came forward then, took Benjamin's hand in her left, took hold of Joel's hanging shirttail in her right, and followed him down the road.

When he was assured of their care, their safekeeping, he told them to stay with Jane Blodgett until he came back for them, then stepped out the door.

Nathaniel stepped out with him.

"I'll come along back up," Nathaniel said, looking Joel straight in the eye, "and do chores, help take care of things."

Joel looked back at him, nodded, then turned and started out. Nathaniel stayed a short distance behind him; they moved into the shadow of the woodlot, walked a few minutes under the oaks, then into the bright sunshine again.

"I've got the two horses and the ox," Joel said, finally.

"I know," Nathaniel replied.

"And the cow needs milking—"

Nathaniel reached out then, touched his shoulder to stop him; they stood, together, in the road.

"No need," Nathaniel said, "to tell me all that needs doing." He looked down at their feet for a moment, then back up at Joel. "I know yer barn as well as my own."

Joel turned his shoulder to Nathaniel, looked away, looked down to the meadow. The grass rippled in the breeze, rolled away down the slope to the Eastern River, all bright and shining on an incoming tide.

They took two of the ladder-backs from the kitchen. They carried them through the shed and side door and set them up in the yard at the edge of the apple orchard, then crossed over to the barn for a length of board, carried it around the back of the shed.

She was exactly as Joel had found her, slumped against the outhouse wall, her eyes still open, still searching for something above the long line of maples.

The flies buzzed about her head, scrawled along her body.

"Ah, Jesus," Nathaniel breathed.

Joel took her by her ankles and pulled her away from the wall, dragged her body away from the outhouse, and straightened her out on clean ground. Together they rolled her onto the plank, then, each to an end, lifted it and carried her over to the chairs, rested the ends of the board on the seats.

Her arms dropped away to either side of the plank, her curled fingers rested in the bright spring grass; pink and white petals dropped softly from the blossoms in the branches above.

Joel Thompson held his breath against the smell.

He leaned down and tore at her chemise, ripped it straight down the front of her and stripped it away, pushing one hand against her body while pulling the cloth from her with the other. He carried the shreds of it back to the outhouse and tossed what was left through the open door.

And then he went back to her.

He sluiced buckets of well water along her legs, her thighs, over her breasts and face, over her palms and her fingers, her knees, her soft hips; he cleaned the worst of her as best he could, weeping, choking all the while.

When he was done, he closed her eyes, his fingers brushing against the prick of her lashes. He covered her with a piece of sheeting, then went back to the house and sat in the sunlight in his doorway and waited for Lydia Crocker, who would, he knew, wash her anew, rub her with sweet oil, wrap her for burial; she would do the things for Martha that he did not know how to do.

Lydia stepped down from the wagon carrying a sling bag over her shoulder and a length of clean linen folded over her forearm; Eliphalet held the horses still as she stepped over the wheel.

She went directly to Joel, still sitting in the doorway.

"Can you take me to her?" she asked, her voice calm and certain.

He rose without a word, led her around the back of the shed to the edge of the apple orchard where the young trees stretched up beside and over the chairs, up beside and over Martha Thompson, green leaves bright and clean in the sunlight.

"Go now," Lydia said, putting her hand lightly against his chest, pushing him back toward the house, away from Martha. "Go on now, and I'll see to her."

---

"I'll get an ember," he said, turning away from Eliphalet and heading back to the house, "if ye'll braid a flare."

Eliphalet Crocker stepped into the shed for a moment, gathered a fistful of dry hay from the corner, and with two hands, stretched and twisted the stalks around themselves, over and over, added more lengths until he held a tightly bound torch. He frayed the top ends with his fingers, then stood in the doorway until Joel came out of the house, a hot ember balanced on a kitchen shovel.

Over by the outhouse, Joel touched the end of the torch to the ember, held it until it caught fire, then tossed it into the open door. It smoldered there for a moment, then caught with a sudden *whoosh;* the breeze funneled through the door and sucked the flames up through the top vent.

Martha's ripped and soiled chemise twirled in the flame for a moment, then disappeared in a spin of smoke and ash.

---

Later, after Lydia had oiled Martha's body, had shrouded her tightly in the linen, Joel and Eliphalet lifted the plank and carried her into the house, set the board on the full length of the table in the kitchen.

"I wish I had a proper parlor for her," Joel said, "but this will have to do; I don't want her scavenged during the night."

He buried her himself.

"In the orchard," he said, when they asked him, "where she can be under the apple trees; where she can see both the house and the river."

---

All four of our children, Joel thought, have Martha's eyes. John and Benjamin have her hair, Abigail her nose, but Sarah Ann carries the all of her.

At first, he could not bear the sight of them.

He walked them down the road each morning, pushing Abigail and John in a barrow while the two others followed like ducklings in a row, their feet slap-padding in the soft dirt on the road behind him. He carried his daughters to Jane Blodgett, who had attention to spare for Abigail and was gentle with Sarah Ann; he carried his sons one more house down the road to the Crockers, where Lydia blended them in with her own, kept her sharp eye on them.

Each evening he went back for them, oftentimes accepting at one house or the other a light supper of soup and bread or biscuit before walking them back up the road at darkfall.

They always stopped a moment to watch Nathaniel's draft horses wander and graze in their upper field. The children never tired of those horses. They leaned on the fences and extended their arms into the pasture, waved, called them by name, and the horses, curious and magnificent, lumbered over for a look; their soft lips closed gently over the tops of his children's palms, accepting their small bundles of grass and clover.

And in September, just as the trees threw hints of red and yellow along the edges of the woodlots, Jane Blodgett came to his door one midday, sat herself down on his step.

"Lydia tells me that yer boys are well recovered," she said, quietly.

He stood near the stoop, looking down at her, taking it in.

"And I can tell you that Abigail and John are too young to remember…"

He nodded, swept his eyes across his dooryard up beyond the back corner of the barn where the wood of the new outhouse showed golden, clean.

"…but that Sarah Ann," she went on, "is too old to forget."

At that, he sat down beside her, uncertain and, he realized, a little afraid.

"Joel," she said, "you cannot do it alone—you cannot work the farm without a woman to work the house."

She then held out the offer of her sister, Mary Choate, who could, she said, come from King's Mills to stay—to care for the children, to do the cooking and cleaning, the washing, the sewing; to keep the house, she said, in exchange for room and board.

"You cannot do it all," she said, "and me and Lydia's got our own to tend."

He looked down, studied the ground between his feet, then tipped his head back and looked upward; a small cloud passed over, pushing eastward over the Eastern River valley.

"It's time," she added.

"All right," he said.

She looked at him briefly, then stood up and walked herself back home without another word.

On Monday morning, he stood in the sunrise with his children and watched Mary Choate come up the road from Blodgett's, skirts and shawl fluttering in the morning breeze. She turned into his yard and approached him.

The oxen bellowed in the barn and the chickens scattered across the drive.

She picked up Abigail, who was not afraid, and smiled down at the other children; Sarah Ann clung to her father's leg, pressed up against his thigh, but the boys smiled back at her.

"I'm called Polly," she said.

Joel nodded, then held out his hand and she took it—the bargain offered and accepted.

Polly Choate had her own room for the very first time in her life.

In her father's house, on the west side of the Sheeps Cotte River over in King's Mills, she had slept upstairs with her siblings—the seven girls in the east room and the six boys in the west. They slept all together, two or three to each straw-stuffed mattress, sharing quilts and blankets; it was a jumble of knees and elbows, a symphony of snores and smells.

But here, in Joel Thompson's house on the Eastern, she had a room to herself—a real room, large enough for a single bedstead along the inner wall and a small chair at its foot, although what she might do with her own chair was a mystery to her.

It was, in truth, the pantry and house store, and so she shared her floor space with three large crocks—one of wheat flour, one of cornmeal, one of ground oats—along the other wall, two large jugs of molasses, and several smaller ones of Joel's own maple syrup. There were shelves above the crocks for various pieces of tinware, a few containing spices; spare jars and bowls; boxes of softsoap and candles (some store-bought, she was glad to notice, for it meant the farm was turning a profit); and a tin of loaf sugar, which felt so out of place to her, tucked in as it was with the soap and candles, that she moved it to a space directly over the crocks.

There was a small trunk, too, one with leather handles and a curved top with the initials *MP* hobnailed into the wood. She opened it tentatively; pasted on the underside of the lid was an inked sketch of a fancy love knot—for a quilt, perhaps—and a signature beneath:

*Martha Pinkham*
*This knotte drawn July 1809*

She found a small sewing box containing several spools of different threads, a packet of pins, two needles folded into a piece of leather, and one silverbright thimble. There was a collection of patches for a quilt, some yarn skeins, four whalebone knitting needles, and one complete wool mitten.

Under the yarn was a pen-box, with nibs and shafts, and, flat on the bottom of the trunk, some sheets of blank writing paper and a pair of soft leather slippers wrapped in a piece of muslin.

Dancing shoes.

She rested them on her lap.

Fancy that, she thought; Martha Pinkham Thompson had owned dancing shoes!

She held them together, sole to sole, wrapped them back in the muslin, and replaced them in the trunk, closed the lid and slid the whole thing under the bedstead beside the night pot to gain a little more floor space.

She could hardly get out of her bed in the morning without bumping into one of the crocks or banging her shoulders or head on the shelving, but it was worth every bit of the trouble.

It was her own room.

She moved carefully around him those first weeks, learning his sense of timing, his daily patterns, working her schedule around his.

It was the right thing to do, she thought, especially since he had insisted upon paying her in coin each week. It wasn't much, but it was enough to make it clear to her that he valued her service, and it astonished her to think she could earn money by doing for him the things she'd been doing for nothing all her life in King's Mills—cooking, cleaning, and washing, mainly, with additional hours caring for the never-ending litter of children her mother delivered.

Here, though, there were only four, and caring for them seemed as simple as breathing in comparison, except for Sarah Ann, of course. The girl never spoke, communicating instead with nods and glances, with drones and hums and the occasional smile. She could vanish in an instant, disappear like smoke whenever Polly took her eyes off her, usually to wherever it might be that her father was working—barn, field, orchard, woodlot—and spent a great deal of time beneath the table in the kitchen, sometimes to sleep, sometimes to sit silently, arms wrapped about her knees.

But even with that, these four children were easy enough to manage, and living down the road from Jane gave her a sense of family connection.

All in all, life on the Eastern was better than life on the Sheeps Cotte.

Simple as that.

They spent time together in the kitchen each morning, she and Joel, before the children were up. He oftentimes ate a small bowl of bread and milk before doing first chores, disliking, he said, working against the gnawing of his empty stomach.

She readied it for him. She ripped yesterday's bread into the bowl, then opened the trap in the floor and leaned down to retrieve what was left of the previous night's milk from the top cellar step. She poured it carefully over the bread, let it soak in before serving.

She warmed the milk one morning, heated it in a little tin dipper on the fire grate before pouring it into his bowl, then added some cinnamon to it all and set it before him on the table.

When he took a spoonful he raised his eyebrows in surprise, looked at her.

"You like it, then?" she asked, standing by the table, her hand resting on the chairback.

"Yes," he said, and scraped the bowl clean before going out to the barn to water and feed while she awakened and fed his children.

Sarah Ann had her own bowl and mug, her own spoon; she had her own place to sit at the kitchen table, and she checked when she passed by, tipped her head slightly to the side and looked to see if Polly had put something in her bowl for her.

No, not yet, so she looped through the house again—front hall, stairs, along the upstairs hall past the bedchamber doors, down the other stairs and back into the kitchen—and past her side of the table, looking down into her bowl again.

She knew there would be something there eventually; she knew that Polly would spoon something into her bowl.

Sometimes she made just one loop through the house before finding her breakfast, sometimes two or three on mornings when Polly was very busy, but hardly ever four. When she saw that her bowl was full—sometimes oatcakes with raspberry jam, sometimes biscuits with honey, or sometimes porridge with syrup, her favorite—she sat on the very end of the bench and kept her head down, spooned it into her mouth, and swallowed; spoonful after spoonful, exactly like that.

---

That fall was exceptionally fine.

The sun rose up over the valley each morning: all day the golden light spread over the tops of the trees, then disappeared each evening beyond the western wall; all day squirrels chittered along the branches of the oaks, their gray faces fat with acorns. They buried them all about the yard and under the apple trees where deer grazed at night, feeding on the falls.

One morning at table, while spooning thick oatmeal into the breakfast bowls, Polly Choate heard the first faint call. She gathered the children and drew them outside into the dooryard, put her hands on their shoulders to shush them.

"Wait, wait!" she whispered. "Listen!"

Louder, and louder still, and then, there they were—geese, hundreds of them—soaring high over the barn and spreading out wide across the blue sky, heading down the Eastern River to Merry Meeting Bay and beyond.

She lifted Abigail to her hip. "Look!" she exclaimed, pointing skyward. "They're heading south for the winter; they'll come back home to us in the spring."

Benjamin and John tipped their heads back, looked straight up into the long line of birds, and heard the passing of their wings in the air, their frantic singing in the cool, clean sky.

"Farewell!" Polly called out. "Safe journey!"

She waved her hand, and the boys, quick to pick up her enthusiasm, waved as well, then left her side and ran across the dooryard to the front fence, better to see them press south beyond Blodgett's field to the river.

Something caught her eye and she turned: Sarah Ann in the shed doorway, eyes fixed on the birds.

———————

By spring, there was no stopping them.

"We're as bad as rabbits," he breathed, backing her up against the pantry wall. He fumbled with his buttons; she lifted her skirts for him, laughing, then once he was inside her, let go and put her hands up around his neck for balance.

"Where are the children?" Polly whispered, her mouth close to his.

"Outside." He rested his palms against the wall, leaned into her, backed away, leaned in again. "The girls are in the coop, the boys cleaning stalls."

"That's too close," she said, but Joel was in a hurry now; she shifted her hips, fell into the rhythm of it all.

One evening, after the children were all in their beds—Sarah Ann and Abigail together in the side bedroom, Benjamin and John up the stairs—she wiped the supper table clean with a rag, then paused by his chair, rested her hand on his shoulder.

"I'm carrying," she said, and waited there for his reply. She heard the fire settling in the grate; she heard foxes yipping and yowling from somewhere beyond the barn.

He turned his head and looked at her, searched her face and eyes for distress and regret, and, finding none, smiled up at her.

"Well, then," he said, "well, then."

———

*Pittston Town Meeting*
*East Parish*
*October 12, 1827*

*Notise of Births in the Town of Pittston, Recorded by me, Henry Dearborn, Town Clerk*
    *To Nathaniel Blodgett & Wife Jane a daughter, Eliza, August 31, 1825*
    *To Eliphalet Crocker & Wife Lydia a son Isaac, September 9, 1827*
    *To Joel Thompson & Wife Polly a son Joel, Jr, May 18, 1827*

*Notise of Deaths in the Town of Pittston, Recorded by me, Henry Dearborn, Town Clerk*
    *Martha Thompson, Wife of Joel Thompson, Departed this Life on the twenty-second of May, 1826*

*This is to affirm that Mr. Joel Thompson of Pittston and Miss Mary Choate of King's Mills were united in marriage January 28, 1827*
          *Recorded by me, Henry Dearborn, Town Clerk*

# Chapter Five

"...the lumber, hay, shingles and other products found their way to the outside world by...the Eastern river...where the tide enabled boats to land and load with goods to be conveyed to the schooners at the Dresden landing..."

*Illustrated History of Kennebec County, Maine*

LATER, nobody would remember for certain when Charles Call first started talking about building a scow.

It might have been March of 1828, when he'd had some winter hay left over and some furs from his trapline to sell, when Nathaniel Blodgett had some sturdy oak barrels he'd built over the winter, and Joel Thompson had shaved nearly two hundred shingles. Everyone along the Eastern had something to sell, it seemed, but roads were so wet, so muddy that wagon wheels disappeared to the axle and nobody could get down to Dresden.

"You could lose a child in those ruts," Joel commented.

They'd need to wait until late April at the earliest, all the way into May if the weather stayed chilly and damp and the water continued to seep from the slowly thawing ground up into the cart tracks and walking paths.

"Too late for best prices," Charles complained, standing in Thompson's barn doorway, "and that coin would be handy."

"It would," Joel agreed. "As it is, I bought seed on my word from Jonathan Young." He toed his boot on the sill. "I can settle that debt when I market those shingles."

And that's when Charles had first mentioned building the scow; it was just a thought, a glimmer of an idea, nothing more.

Elizabeth, truth be told, never thought anything would come of it.

Charles was always chock-full of grand ideas, some so wild she would shake her head in disbelief when he spoke of them. But he talked about it all that spring and summer, only occasionally at first, but then more and more, especially in the evenings after chores were done and she set his supper before him on the table.

She never really thought anything would come together, never thought he'd make good about it, so when he began to whittle pegs every morning after first chores and drop the finished ones into a bucket he kept in the corner of the kitchen, she paid attention.

He means to do this, she thought. He means to build himself a scow.

"I'm thinking to go up to Eliphalet today," Charles said to her one morning, scraping his spoon over the bottom of the bowl to get at the last of the stew.

She ripped a chunk from the loaf and handed it to him across the table. "Mop that juice," she said, then poured herself another half cup of tea, settled back on the bench to show him she was listening.

"I'm going to ask to use his oxen to haul those logs up to Dudley's mill."

"What logs?" she asked.

"Some of the ones behind the shed," he said. "They've set long enough to cut for planking, and I can use some on the scow." He swiped the last of his bread around the rim of his bowl, then tucked it into his mouth.

"Take our horse," she proposed, watching him chew, waiting for him to swallow. He wiped his mouth on his sleeve.

"I'd have to make two trips if I use the horse—maybe three," he explained, "but his oxen can pull 'em all in one session."

He stood up from the table. "Come along with me," he said. "You can stay and talk with Lydia for a while."

She scurried to be ready—scour their bowls, bank the fire, wrap

Mary and sling her against her hip for the walk up the road—for the thought of a visit with Lydia lifted her.

———————

"Near ox is Noah," Eliphalet Crocker said, settling them into the yoke. "Off ox is Ham."

Charles Call stood back, eyed the pair. They were enormous; their beady eyes made him nervous.

"By God," he said, "they look just the same to me."

Liph snorted. "They might look the same," he said, "but they work different—each to his own side."

Charles Call was suddenly unsure; horses he understood, oxen he did not.

He looked at Eliphalet, pleading.

"I'll go with you when it's time," Liph said, and grinned.

They waited for a good snowfall.

When it came at the end of December, they levered and rolled the logs up onto the sled, hitched the oxen, and hauled the load up to Dudley's mill, both of them standing on the front lip of the sled, leaning back against the butt ends of the logs.

"Come back up for yer boards at the end of January," Aaron said. "They'll be ready then."

They went back on the twenty-eighth, on what was, Charles thought, the coldest day of the year. He and Eliphalet wound wool scarves about their heads and faces, wrapped themselves in thick buffalo robes; whenever they breathed, the hairs in their noses froze tight together.

The oxen lumbered through the snow, slow and steady, impervious to the dreadful cold. Bright sunlight danced along the drifts up against the side of Nathaniel Blodgett's barn as they went past; there was smoke pluming from Joel Thompson's chimney, drifting slightly toward the frozen river.

At the mill, a couple of men who lived in the village helped them load all the planks on the sled, then they enfolded themselves in the buffalo robes again and balanced atop the load for the return trip. They arrived at Eliphalet's house just before darkfall.

It was so cold they simply dropped the chains, let the sled sit in the dooryard overnight; they hustled the oxen into the barn and themselves into the house for warm cider and Lydia's bread pudding.

Charles stayed over the night, unwilling to walk the mile home in the dark, in the cold; Elizabeth would know, would expect him the next day.

In the morning, they yoked the oxen again and hauled the lumber down to Call's, unloaded the sled, and stacked the boards in the middle bay of the riverbarn.

They shook hands; Eliphalet was back home by midday.

———•———

Charles Call and Eliphalet Crocker built the scow in early April, the two of them cramped inside the main bay of the riverbarn.

It was chilly that first morning, but they opened the doors and let the sunlight stream inside; the rising sun thawed the rime from the floor, and the steam curled up into the doorway.

They squared up the boards with sledge and adze, then assembled the frame on the main floor, drilling the joints with bit and brace, pegging them together, then siding the whole of it with cured planking, setting hot tar to the edges of the boards before clamping and pegging them to the ribs. With both the tar and the swelling of the oak in the waters of the Eastern, they'd have a tight hull and a dry passage.

They worked the better part of the week, meeting after morning chores, working through the day and parting at evening, each to his own home for evening chores.

The last day, they had a couple of oatcakes with honey and a bottle of ale at noon. They ate just inside the doorway in a bright shaft of light, leaning against the jamb and watching the ice break and shift in the deeper parts of the river, watching egrets fish in the shallow open waters to the north of the cove.

The finished scow was twelve feet wide and twenty long; poled from either bow or stern, it could ride the Eastern without having to turn broadside. That S-curve just before the spread above Dresden might be tricky at dead low tide, but they figured an hour either side of that it was navigable, especially if they raised the sweep and relied on poling.

They made their first run to Dresden in mid-April of 1829, when the ice was completely out of the Eastern and the snowmelt gave an extra foot to its depth. They spent a morning tide riding the river upstream as far as Thompson's, where they loaded his jugs of fresh maple syrup and a large batch of shingles. When the tide shifted, they rode back down, stopping to load cargo along the way—Nathaniel Blodgett had some good winter hay and ten kegs; Eliphalet himself had spring shoats, and they used Blodgett's barrels to fashion a small pen for them near the stern.

By then, the tide was near to turn again, so they secured the loaded scow against the pilings at Charles Call's wharf and walked up their own meadows for chores and a meal, a good night's sleep.

They were back on the river the next morning, poling the scow down through the twists and turns of the Eastern, riding the sweep hard through the faster passages and hugging the shoreline when they dropped into the wider spread just above Dresden.

They tied up at the town pier just as the tide turned again.

To their amazement, they sold their entire cargo within two hours— the hay and syrup to a tavern owner, the shoats to a farmer who'd lost his own to his careless sow; the kegs to a trader bound first for Bath, then for Portland and Boston.

They bought four barrels each of flour and cornmeal, one keg of molasses and a smaller one of machine-turned nails, balanced the load on the scow, then started back up the Eastern with the incoming tide, running two hours before the water began to lull, shift. They tied up fore and aft to thick trees on the shoreline, then rested while waiting out the change.

"If we had sails," Charles offered, "we could sail against this tide."

Eliphalet shook his head. "Too much force, especially considering the scow's flat bottom," he said, "but with a good wind we could double our time running *with* the river."

The water whispered against the sides of the scow.

"Could we make the run down and back in a single change of tide if we had sails?"

"I guess we could," Liph said. "But we have to account for unloading, selling, then purchasing and loading again for the return trip."

"Not enough time for all that."

"Doubt it, but we could do it easily in four half-changes."

Charles rubbed at his stubble, dragged his hand through his hair. "We could tide over at the upper bridge," he said, "then make the rest of the run next day."

He watched the water for a bit, then turned to Eliphalet.

"Good enough," he said. "That's good enough."

When the tide shifted, the pebbles on the shoreline chittered against each other, rattled for a minute while the current dragged them over the larger stones to a new resting place. The ropes on the scow tightened, squeaked against the cleats as the weight of the hull shifted upstream with the pull of the Eastern.

While waiting in the half-light for Eliphalet to waken, Charles caught sight of a raccoon, picking its way carefully to the shoreline. It settled its haunches on a larger, flatter rock, then moved its delicate hands in the water, searching slowly in between the smaller stones for the small fish that hid there.

Patience, thought Charles, such strong patience.

He was short of patience, that he knew all too well. Elizabeth was often made nearly frantic by his constant agitation; he was forever stirring the proverbial fires, restless, always setting to move on. He was irritated now by the slowness of the tides, would have hurried them if he'd been able, not content to let things move at their own pace.

He clapped his hands lightly, and the raccoon, startled, splashed around and disappeared up over the banking into the woods.

Charles laughed, then stood, nudged Liph with the toe of his boot.

"Up, up!" he encouraged. "Time to run."

Five hours later they poled the scow into the space beside the short dock at the Board Landing at East Pittston. They sold all their provisions to Jonathan Young for twenty dollars, who, in turn, would resell them in his general store.

With four dollars each due Thompson and Blodgett, three more to Eliphalet for his shoats, and two for Charles for his own goods sold, their profit on transport was a stunning seven dollars.

Charles wanted to divide it equally with Eliphalet Crocker, but Eliphalet would accept only two dollars, giving the remainder to Charles.

"It's yer scow," he said logically. "I'm just yer hired man."

———

*Pittston Town Meeting*
*East Parish*
*November 14, 1830*

*Voted the Paupers be sett at auction, on condition who ever bid them off, should keep them in sickness and health and find their clothes—Doctors Bill to be paid by the town.*

*Fence Viewer   Joel Thompson*
*Hog Reeve      Charles Call*
*School Agent   Nathaniel Blodgett*
*Pound Keeper   Eliphalet Crocker*

*Notise of Births in the Town of Pittston, Recorded by me, Daniel Sewall, Town Clerk*
    *To Charles Call & Wife Elizabeth a daughter Mary, December 19, 1828*
    *To Nathaniel Blodgett & Wife Jane a daughter, Sophronia, October 29, 1829*
    *To Eliphalet Crocker & Wife Lydia a son, Leander, March 14, 1830*

# PART II

# 1831–1840

# Chapter Six

*Pittston Town Meeting*
*East Parish*
*June 17, 1833*

*Surveyor of High Ways    Eliphalet Crocker*

*Notice hereby given that wages for labor on town roads shall be established at half a dollar per day for a man and one dollar per day for a team of oxen until first day of November next.*

HE WORKED them only in the forenoons on hot summer days.

He put out three or four steady hours with them while there was still a trace of coolness in the woodlots and along the tree lines; later on, when the sun reached full height and the heat pressed heavy upon their necks and shoulders, he took the yoke from them and set them free, drove them down the long slope to the Eastern, where they waded up to their bellies in the shallow waters to cool, their dark eyes pooled and patient.

———————

They rode the stoneboat tight along the wall that separated their land from Nathaniel Blodgett's, the oxen keeping their peculiar pace on their own while Eliphalet Crocker and young Samuel, balanced in the bed of the sled, unloaded rocks onto the wall along the line.

Eliphalet handled the larger ones; he hefted those he could manage onto the wall, rolled the others crosswise off the back to angle up against the base. Samuel, his hands neither broad nor strong enough for heavier stones, worked the smaller ones, reaching out as the stoneboat passed by to toss them into the gaps between the larger rocks atop the wall.

It was a temporary measure. They would both come back over the late summer and fall, whenever there was an hour or two to spare, to set the stones more firmly into the wall—one rock over two, two over one—taking great care in balance and placement, setting wedge stones where necessary to keep both sides of the wall slanting inward.

Samuel could even come back on his own, Eliphalet thought; he was old enough to do that now. Not so tall yet, but sturdy enough to put in real work, and old enough to work alone as long as he was no more than a shout from the house and barn.

"It's good time that ye're giving me," Eliphalet said, grunting a little with the effort of throwing a granite stone, "and I appreciate yer effort."

Samuel dipped his head, pleased.

They moved down the length of the wall, Eliphalet on the back end of the stoneboat to give more lift and less drag to the front of the load, Samuel in the midsection, where his weight—such as it was—mattered less, until all the rocks were gone and they were near the kneelers at the end of the wall.

"*Whoa!*" Liph called.

Noah and Ham slowed, stopped, and shifted their weight from front to back, side to side to find balance beneath the yoke; the chain to the stoneboat slackened a bit.

"Enough?" asked Samuel.

Eliphalet stood straight, knuckled the small of his back; he heard the slight lilt of hope in his son's voice.

"Oh, I'd say." He stepped off the back of the sled, leaned over to stretch out his back, rocked from side to side a few times. "Let's go back to the house, see what yer ma and the girls have got in the pot for dinner," he said, turning to Samuel, "and then we can spend a little time this afternoon working yer team—show 'em the yoke, maybe."

Samuel's head came up. "Is it finished?" he asked. "Is my yoke done?"

"It is." Eliphalet pushed his fingers up through his hair. "But it's too big for 'em yet."

"So, I can't use it now?"

"Not now, but they'll grow into it by next spring. We'll let it hang in the shed to cure over winter; it'll be right dry and light by April." He paused, rested his palm on Noah's rump. "I've got an old yearling yoke that'll do for now," he said. "We'll try it on yer team for fit—not for long, though; it's too hot for those little fellows."

Samuel nodded.

"So, that sounds all right to you?"

"All right."

"Good," he said. He ran his hand over Noah's back and shoulder as he moved his way up alongside the ox.

"Ready now?" he asked, turning back to look at his son, still riding the sled. "Have yer balance?"

"Yes."

Eliphalet stood still for a moment, waited; the oxen waited with him, ears pricked, ready.

"Now, *git, git!*" he urged, moving forward.

They pushed their shoulders into the yoke; the chain tightened and the stoneboat slid forward, cleared the gate at the end of the wall.

"Now, *gee, gee!!*"

They swung a broad turn to the right, Ham taking smaller steps on the inside of the turn to accommodate Noah's longer stride on the outside. They swung around, returned through the gate and came back the other way along the wall, headed up to the barn.

Samuel, still riding the sled, watched the sway of their huge rumps as they kept time with his father, who walked about two feet off Noah's shoulder, talking softly—no switch, no rod—taking them all home.

---

Lydia Crocker, sitting on the side porch in the shade, pulled the strings off the dinner beans, listened to Elizabeth and Mary chatter in the yard as they switched over the clean clothes. They pulled them from the bushes and fence rails, turned them over, and respread them to finish drying in the bright sunlight.

Nothing like the smell of clean clothes, Lydia thought, that scent of sun and wind, sometimes of cut grass; the feel of them, too—a slight stiffness against the skin for the first day, then softer as they loosen.

She watched the girls turn the sheets, each to a side, working together, finally, after a few years of constant bickering and misbehaving. Not so much unpleasantness from the boys; perhaps the five-year spread between Samuel and Isaac was enough to spare them all that misery.

"Lizbeth!" she called out. "Keep yer pa's shirttails out of the herbs; remember how fussy he gets when he smells like thyme!"

"Needn't worry, Ma." She and Mary spread the last sheet up over the fence, straightened it along the rail. "We put Pa's shirts on the low honeysuckle."

"That's all right, then," Lydia said, and lifted a bean from the bowl. She'd as soon eat a bean fresh out of the garden than anything else she grew there; she'd as soon bend over in the row and pick a fistful, then rest here in the shade of the side porch and eat one atop of another on a hot summer day like this.

She smiled at the thought—but then, no time for that, for here come Liph and Samuel, back from working the walls; here they come, the oxen plodding up over the rise and into the barnyard; here they come, hungry for dinner.

"Mary!" she called. "Time to ready the table, quick now; and, Lizbeth! Find Isaac and Leander—they ought to be in the shed, filling the chip basket!"

Boil the beans for now, she thought; boil the beans and that old chicken will do for dinner; later, add what's left of the bird—bones and all—back into the bean water, throw in some onion, potatoes, carrots, let it simmer and stew up, and there's supper for tonight. Good; that's decided and done.

———

Samuel took them from their pen one at a time.

He fastened a slipknot and looped it over the first of the yearlings, then led it out to the center of the barn; went back for the other.

Eliphalet helped him cross-tie them across the alleyway, then moved away, leaned up against the side of the grain bin, waited, watched. This was Samuel's job to do.

Prince and King stood there, side by side, swinging their heads a little, moving their feet on the barn floor.

"Talk to 'em," Eliphalet said, "and touch 'em. They're nervous—they don't know what ye're doing here."

"Just like I talk to 'em every day?"

"Just like that," Eliphalet said. "They know yer voice now, and the sound of yer talking will calm 'em."

Samuel moved in then, moved up to Prince's shoulder, rested his hand on his neck. "Ye're my own near ox," he said, softly; Prince's ear twitched, turned back to listen.

He moved around the pair, hands slow, touching their shoulders and necks, smoothing their backs and haunches, talking, talking, until he came back to their heads. He rested his right palm on Prince's face, reached out with his left for King; he stood before them and tugged gently at their ears.

They settled eventually, the two of them, settled and grew patient, soothed by the sound of Samuel's voice, the touch of his hands. He groomed them, lifting away bits of hay and chaff, brushing his fingers against their hair.

"Keep yer talking," Liph said quietly, "while I get that small yoke."

He moved up the alleyway to where the training yoke hung against the wall. He lifted it from the peg, pulled out the pins, brought just the bow back to Samuel and held it out to him.

"Take this," he said. "It's real light; give 'em a chance to see it."

Samuel took a breath, then took the bow from his father's hands and held it before Prince and King; they eyed it cautiously, then nosed at it, their warm breath moving over his fingers and wrists.

"Talk to 'em," Eliphalet reminded him.

"This is yer bow," Samuel said quietly. "It won't hurt; it'll ride on yer neck and pull against yer shoulders." He let them sniff and push at it a little more, moved slowly around the pair, touching them occasionally with the bow, rubbing it against their necks and shoulders, talking, murmuring all the while.

Eliphalet backed away, left the boy to his work and busied himself in the back end of the barn. He raked manure from the stalls and shook out clean straw for bedding, listened to his son talk to his team.

"In school, I'm fair at addition," Samuel said quietly to the yearlings, "but I admit to a bit of trouble with division—I lose my numbers in the mess of it all."

Eliphalet smiled, took the wooden water buckets, filled them from the rain barrel just outside the barnyard door, and brought them back;

He's got a way with 'em, Eliphalet thought. He'll have 'em trained in two years; they'll be doing real work by then; listen to him, now, listen to him talk to 'em, so easy and conversational, so calm, so certain.

---

*Pittston Town Meeting*
*East Parish*
*April 22, 1834*

*Surveyor of High Ways   Alfred Stilphen*
*Field Driver              Joel Thompson*
*Fence Viewer             Charles Call*

*Voted to restrain all cattle from going at large this present year.*

*Notise of births in the Town of Pittston, Recorded by me, James Fletcher, Town Clerk*
    *To Charles Call & Wife Elizabeth a son Charles M., August 6, 1831*
    *To Joel Thompson & Wife Polly a daughter Laura, December 27, 1832*
    *To Nathaniel Blodgett & Wife Jane a son John, June 6, 1833*
    *To Eliphalet Crocker & Wife Lydia a son Llewellyn, March 22, 1832*
    *To Eliphalet Crocker & Wife Lydia a daughter Jane Adaline, May 23, 1834*

*Marriages Recorded in the Town of Pittston*
    *Mr. Alfred Stilphen of Pittston and Mary Call of Dresden on the twenty-first day of November 1833*
        *Recorded by me, James Fletcher, Town Clerk*

# Chapter Seven

*Pittston Town Meeting*
*East Parish*
*October 16, 1834*

*This is to give you notice that the mark of my sheep is a punch to the right ear and two notches to the left.*

*Alfred Stilphen,*
*Eastern River District*

HE LOVED keeping sheep, but he couldn't explain why.

It had something to do with his father, Alfred thought, and the soft sounds his father had taught him to make deep in his throat whenever he was around them—almost like singing, but closing his mouth around the sound of it, pushing it down inside—something to do with that.

The sheep calmed to it, bunched together and followed, bleating back at him as he led them from the lower meadows back up to the farm in the October afternoon, their small hooves clicking against the stones in the pathway. Once he got them up into the barnyard, though, they went to the pens on their own, skirting the sturdy fence Mary had insisted he build around the dooryard.

"I spent the first two years here trying to keep the sheep out of the house," Mary Stilphen told Jane Blodgett, "and one day, I just set my foot."

He remembered that.

He'd been mucking out stalls in the barn one morning and, hearing Mary's shrieks from inside the house, had thrown aside the pitchfork and run hard to the outside. Five or six dirty little lambs came leaping out of the kitchen doorway, scattering, bleating, and Mary right behind them, hollering, kicking her skirts and shaking her fists.

He'd laughed out loud at the sight of her, and paid dearly for it—he spent the next two days building that fence around the dooryard, keeping the sheep without and the peace within.

He herded them now into the pens: several mixed English breed, a cluster of blackface, the best of last spring's lambs that he'd kept within the flock—nearly twenty altogether—and went in after them, pulling the gate shut behind.

The blackface were bolder than the others; they bumped at the backs of his knees, hoping for the pieces of chopped root vegetables he oftentimes kept deep in his pockets, hungry for something other than the last of the aftermath they'd found in the meadows today.

Alfred, still humming, lifted the lid from the barrel beside the shed and scooped out pieces of dried beet and turnip; he set them in the curves of his hands and leaned down. They nuzzled his palms, their noses black as night, their eyes narrow slits in this bright afternoon.

There was something about that nuzzling, he thought, that suggested their satisfaction with his company, his care of them.

His father had taught him to go over them each night, to look them over for cuts, nicked hooves, mats of mud and weed. He kept his fields as clean as he could, but the burdocks were always a problem in the fall, catching easily on the fleece of their chests and thighs, soon tangling into thick mats that pulled uncomfortably whenever they moved across the hillsides to graze.

The blackface would improve that. The nine he had now were better grazers, cleaning out his bushy hillsides and improving his pastures; he ran them after the horses, for they ate the weeds the horses wouldn't touch, and the fields were cleaning up nicely. He admired their hardiness as well—they weathered even the coldest winters easily, protected from the snows and winds by their coarse wool. Each year they dropped sturdy lambs and surrendered thicker, denser fleece than his English breeds; those better fleece weighed more.

And more weight brought more money at the markets in Portland and Boston.

"We need more of those," Mary had said, "if thee's to build the best flock in the Eastern River district."

She'd been right, of course; he listened to Mary, paid great attention.

The month after they'd married, when the flush of it all was still fresh on their faces, he'd taken her with him to King's Mills to purchase his first blackface; he'd used some of the money her father had given as dower, and he felt obliged to include her in the transaction.

She leaned against the rail of the pen, scanned the sheep, and soon pointed out the two she felt the worthiest in the yard. The drover culled them from the others and took the coin from Alfred.

"She's got an eye," he said. "I'd be challenged to do better than that!"

They walked the sheep home and marked them after supper. Mary hiked her skirts and straddled their haunches, squeezing them still between her strong thighs. Alfred, in front of her, held their heads between his knees and punched the right ears with an awl, drew two notches to the left with his knife.

They bleated a bit, dropped some blood, but Mary greased their wounds and scratched between their eyes, cooing and calming them; once they quieted, she turned them into the shed with the others, fed them sweet beets, hummed to them in the evening light.

"There, there," she said softly, moving among them, "all's right; thee belongs to the Stilphens now."

# Chapter Eight

They come to us from heaven, with their little souls full of
innocence and peace; and, as far as possible, a mother's influence should not interfere with the influence of angels.

Lydia Maria Francis Child
*The Mother's Book*

"LOOKS RIGHT close, it does," Polly Thompson said, "but they're not
the same." She moved closer to the edge of the field, picked a stalk of bedstraw, and turned back to Sarah Ann.

"This one is a bedstraw," she said, holding it out to the girl. "See how it's
got yellow flowers all up and down a smooth stalk? And little, slender leaves?"

Sarah Ann came nearby, looked down.

"Hold it side by each with the parsnip," Polly said, "and look at the
difference in those flowers—the parsnip's are all growing off the top,
each to their own little stem, and they're thicker and fuller than the
bedstraw's."

Sarah Ann held them each to a hand; Polly could see her eyes jump
back and forth between the two, sorting the changes.

"So," Polly went on, reaching out to touch Sarah Ann's right hand,
the one holding the parsnip, "the 'snip's got a groove in its stalk, and
thick, yellow flowers, all stemming from the top."

A nod.

Polly took her hand away, moved it over to the bedstraw in Sarah Ann's
left hand. "This is the bedstraw," she said, "and it's got a smooth stalk, thin
yellow flowers all up and down, leaves that look like little stars."

She let Sarah Ann gaze at the bedstraw for a bit.

"This is the one we want," Polly said, patting the girl's left hand for emphasis, "the bedstraw."

Sarah Ann opened her right hand and dropped the parsnip; looked up at Polly, eyes clear and bright with sky and sunlight.

My goodness! Polly thought. We often wonder whatever goes on behind those eyes; I sometimes have a sense it's more than we ever acknowledge.

"Would you like to be gathering the bedstraw on yer own?"

A nod, a faint tugging at the corners of her mouth; Sarah Ann was pleased.

"That will be a great help to me," Polly said, handing over the larger basket, keeping the smaller one for herself. "I'll go up by the wall, do my other picking."

They moved across the slope of the field, the two of them, Polly concentrating on cutting the best of the yarrow that grew in broad swaths near the high wall, Sarah Ann staying lower on the slope, gathering bedstraw, loping from spot to spot, twirling occasionally in the sunlight, droning to herself—that low, single note that sometimes drove Polly near to foolishness.

Let her alone, she thought, cutting another stalk of yarrow, let her be; she's harming no one, it soothes her, helps her keep to task.

And speaking of task, she reminded herself, juniper berries for pessaries.

"Sarah?" she called. "Sarah Ann?"

The girl paused, lifted her head and turned. The breeze swept up the slope from the Eastern, spread the grass in waves that rippled across the field and pushed against her skirt. She looked, Polly thought, bedraggled.

"I'll be going across the wall to the juniper," Polly said, "but you'll still see me."

Sarah Ann watched her for a long moment, then turned back to the bedstraw.

All right.

Polly rested her basket on the top of the wall, gathered her skirts in both hands, and stepped up atop the stones and then over, down into the juniper that grew tight up against the far side. She settled into picking.

Let's see then: Lydia, Lizzie, Jane, me—that's six handfuls each; none for Mary Stilphen, for she's hoping for a child.

---

Lydia Crocker felt a strangeness about her all day Sunday. There was an ache in her back all morning, another stronger one in her belly all the afternoon and into the evening.

She kept the bed, had no supper for herself. Eliphalet ladled out simple gruel for the children, added bread and some cheese; it was enough.

During the night hours, she made two trips to the privy—nearly doubled over from the cramps the second time—but was slightly better by first light on Monday when she rose to stoke the fire and set the bread pudding to bake.

Later, as her family ate, she moved carefully about her kitchen, making small fussings, measuring out the tea and pouring steaming water into the pot.

"I do like yer ma's bread pudding," Eliphalet said to the children, "'specially when she's got raisins in it." He scraped his spoon along the bottom of his bowl, grinned at his oldest daughter, then licked it clean.

"Raisins and cinnamon," responded Elizabeth; Mary and Isaac, swallowing their last spoonfuls, nodded.

"I like mine with molasses," Samuel offered, "lots of molasses."

"Do you now?"

Lydia came to the table with the teapot, passed by the back of her husband's chair, and sat at her own place, just cat's-corner from his.

"Off to chores!" she said, smiling at her children. "Off to yer chores now while yer pa and I have morning tea."

They pushed back their benches, scrabbled out through the shed to the dooryard, out into the morning light, the girls out to feed the chickens and collect the eggs, the boys out to the woodshed—Samuel to chop kindling and young Isaac and Leander to basket up the woodchips for the kitchen fire.

When they were gone, she turned to Eliphalet, rested her palm on the back of his hand, patted him gently.

"I lost the baby," she said quietly. "During the night."

He caught her fingers, ran his thumb across her knuckles. "I thought things were amiss," he said. "Are you all right now?"

"I think so," she answered.

"Will you go up to Polly today?"

She looked over at him quickly.

"Just to be sure," he said. "And she might have something to ease yer discomfort."

She nodded, then took away her hand and poured the tea into their cups, placed the pot back on the table between them.

"There'll be another," he assured her.

The sunlight streamed through the eastern window, pooled on the table. They sat together, looking down at their cups, looking at the tea within, shimmering, shimmering, at the leaves nesting on the bottom.

"When I birthed the last," she began "and he fair ripped me apart?"

She waited for his nod of acknowledgment.

"I thought I might die from it all."

She took a quick sip of tea, then looked over at her husband.

"I'm not certain I will live through another."

---

Elizabeth Call waited until Charles began his soft snore of contentment, then lifted his arm from across her belly and slipped out and away from the bed.

Gentle man, she thought, glancing back at him, then smiling her way through the doorway into the dim light of the kitchen. Too quick in the bed, oftentimes, but at least gentle and considerate of her pleasure— unlike Nate Blodgett, if there was truth to Janey's tormented confidences during their sewing at Mary Stilphen's last week, and she had no reason to doubt Janey's accounts.

She took the jar of Polly's yarrow prevention out of the brick oven— still warm from the fire, thank goodness—and the long-necked bottle beside it, uncorked the first and poured a two-finger measure into the second. On the smooth floorboards, she settled herself on her back, lifted her gown above her raised knees, and inserted the long neck of the bottle as deep as she could go, then lifted her hips from the floor, bracing her hands beneath her for support, feeling the warm liquid spread within her.

She'd used it unheated the first time; the clench of her womb against the cold had ripped her breath from her chest, and she now tucked it into the oven every evening after supper—ready and warm whenever she needed it, and if she did not, it went back into the shed in the morning.

Oh, she'd be willing to have another child all right, but not so soon, not until Charles reined in his restlessness and constant searching; not until there was a bit more money coming in from the running of the scow and they could pay off more of the land mortgage.

Then it might be time.

She nearly fell asleep in the kitchen, lulled by the night sounds outside the house, soothed by the warmth of the kitchen hearthstones and the spreading heat in her belly.

She rose eventually, rinsed the long-neck in the bucket of graywater and returned it and the corked bottle back to the shed. She wiped herself with a damp rag, and then went back through the kitchen into the back room, back to their bed.

———

Nathaniel approached her in the kitchen while the older children were outside in the yard, came up behind her as she leaned over to put John into the trundle for his sleep. He ran his hands around her hips and pulled her back, pressed himself against the curve of her buttocks.

"Nathaniel!" she protested. "Not yet, not now!"

"Ah, Janey, Janey," he whined, thrusting at her a few times. Even through his trousers and her skirt, she could feel the stiffness of him. "Give a man his due, won't ye?"

"Yer due?" she challenged him, rising, spinning out of his grasp, turning to face him. "I've given you six children and you want yer *due*?"

He slapped her then, quick and hard; slapped her once across the cheek with the flat of his hand, then grabbed her by the shoulders and shook her once, twice.

"My due," he whispered, his face tight. "Like it or not, ye're my due, and I'll take you whenever I want."

But he let go her shoulders, turned, and left her.

———————————

Evenings, Mary Stilphen thought, sitting in the shadow of the kitchen doorway after supper, my favorite times are evenings: when the last of the sunlight rolls away down the near meadow and the sheep are still grazing, their soft bleating rising back up the slope to the house; when Alfred shakes clean straw in the stalls for the horses, closes the chickens into the coop for the night, and then walks across the dooryard to join me for a moment on the step; when together we watch the sky over the Eastern grow first purple and then black, and when the very first star shines clear and bright out over the valley; when it is time to light the lamp in the house.

She sighed, stood to go inside to ready the wicks. Right away, she felt the hot seep of her monthly courses between her legs.

She leaned against the doorjamb for a moment, nearly weeping from the disappointment of it—again, *again*—then hurried through her kitchen into the bedroom to get the rags that would collect the evidence of her failure to conceive.

———————————

Polly Thompson opened the ribbons to the cloth bag tied to her waist. She leaned over, started pinching the blue-green berries off the low junipers and dropping them within. They were easy enough to pick—the bushes were thick with them, and her fingers were quick.

So here's the spread of it, she thought: Lydia with six; Lizzie with two—wanting more but fearing the economy of it; then Jane—my own sister Jane—having borne six, says she wants no more.

She shook the bag, peered down inside to gauge the measure of berries there, calculated. She moved down the wall to a fuller bush and started in again, sticking her fingers against the sharp needles, dropping berries, tumbling them into the bag together.

And as for me?

She looked up, glanced back across the wall to Sarah Ann, wandering a little now with her basket of bedstraw, droning.

Well, then: I've four of Joel's by Martha—including that one, troubled soul that she is—and two of Joel's myself. God's will or not, like my sister, I would be done with it.

A short while later, when it was full enough, she closed the bag, tied it carefully, turned back and stepped over the wall, started back across the meadow to Sarah Ann.

I have remedies, she thought, and preventions. I have infusions of yarrow and winterberry, syrups of trillium and pessaries of juniper, seeds of Queen Anne to slipper a womb; but I've not a single thing that will work for Mary Stilphen—poor Mary, carrying her shame of not carrying a child.

I have no remedy for that.

# Chapter Nine

We all must die; and if we *really* believe that we shall live here-
after, under the care of the same all-merciful God, who has
protected us here, why should we dread to die?

Lydia Maria Francis Child
*The Mother's Book*

JULY CAME in wet, gray with rain and heavy skies, but by mid-month it
had cleared nicely; the second crop of English grass rose in the fields, and
the oats and rye grew high enough to show a ripple when the breeze came
up out of the river valley.

When the month turned over, the temperature rose. The first few
days of August were thick with humidity; heat lightning flickered and
flashed in the night.

Elizabeth Call had opened the front door and propped the shed door
open with the laundry stick; the breeze slipped into the kitchen and out
through the back, cooling things just enough, Charles hoped, to be bear-
able for her.

She was carrying their third child, due in a month, and although she
did not complain of it, the heat was sapping her, he knew.

They'd had an easy dinner—bread with honey washed down with
this morning's milk, fresh greens from the garden—and now, during the
worst of the heat, they rested before afternoon chores: Elizabeth in the
back bedroom having a lie-down, young Charlie napping beside her;

Mary here with him in the kitchen.

Tired, he thought, leaning his head back against the top rail of the rocker; Lizzie and I are both so tired lately, but she's got a reason for it and I do not, and there's no time for that kind of thought, anyway.

"Pa?"

He lifted his head to his daughter; she came near.

"What's yer trouble?" he asked, reaching his hand to her, touching her shoulder before she turned away.

"Ma says she needs me to do my share of mending," she grumbled, plunking herself down on the end of the bench, leaning her elbows on the kitchen table.

"That makes proper sense to me," he said.

"But I wanted to walk up to Blodgett's," she said, "and see Eliza's new chickens—she's got some new Plymouth Rocks!"

"Ah," he said. "I certainly can understand wanting to see those chickens." He felt a tightness in his throat, coughed, took his last sip of tea. "But yer ma says yer mending needs doing first?"

She nodded, looked at him.

"Well," he said, "suppose we meet up halfway on this."

She raised her arms from the table, put her chin into her hands.

"I propose that you do some mending first—not all of it, understand, just some of it—and then when Charlie's through his rest, we can leave yer ma to her lie-down, and we'll walk up together to see those Rocks at Blodgett's."

He waited while she thought it over.

Seven going on twenty-five, he thought, watching her balance the pros and cons of this compromise.

"All right," she said.

"All right, it is," he answered. "We've got ourselves an agreement." He stood, took his cup from the table and placed it into the pan; Lizzie liked her table cleared.

"Get yer basket, Mary," he said, "and come along with me—we've both got mending to do."

"Ye're doing mending, too?"

"I am," he said. "I've got harness to mend, and I'd just as soon do my mending in yer company—work goes more quick in good company."

They sat together outside on the bench by the backhouse door, put their workbaskets in between and went to work, both with needle and thread—or twine, in his case. He pulled it across a chunk of beeswax, then threaded both his needles, one to each end.

"Well, imagine!" he said, drawing her in. "We're both mending a kind of strap: ye're mending yer apron straps, I'm mending that check rein that Jocko broke last week."

"I've forgot what that is," she said. "The check rein."

"That's the one that keeps Jocko's head up," he said. "Keeps him so he can't tip his head to ground and graze when I need him to stay up, pay attention."

They worked quietly for a bit. Charles alternated his needles and awl while Mary worked steadily on her apron strap. Her stitches were, he noticed, neater, more even than last spring.

Shade dappled the shed wall. Two gray squirrels darted along the tree line, one after the other, ran the length of a branch to the very end and then leapt into the next tree; the branches dipped with their sudden weight, the leaves shook, rustled in the summer light.

"What are they doing when they run at each other like that?" she asked, pulling her needle through the apron, pulling the thread tight. "Fighting?"

He smiled, tipped his head down over his work. "No, I don't think so," he said. "I think they're just playing."

She dropped her hands into her lap and turned to him, astonished. "Playing?" she questioned. "You mean playing a game?"

"I think so," he said, pushing his awl through the leather, working his way up the side of the rein. "Like fox and chase, maybe, or simple tag."

"Like children?"

"Yes," he said, slipping the needles through, looping the twine and pulling it firm. "Just like children."

"But they're not children," she reasoned. "*People* have children; squirrels are just squirrels."

"Well," he said, leaning back against the shed wall, "in a squirrel's life, they're children."

She paused, looked at him for a moment, then lifted her eyes to the tree line, looking for them.

"All creatures have children," he said, watching her face. "We just don't call 'em children—we call 'em calves or puppies or kittens or foals."

She found the grays, watched them scamper up another tree; they scurried around and around the trunk, their nails clicking against the bark.

"Those are squirrel children," he said, "and they have parents."

"Just like I'm yer child?" she asked, her voice softening in comprehension. "Yer's and Ma's?"

"Yes," he said, "just like that."

It had never occurred to her, he thought, and his throat filled, tightened; he felt a sudden ache, a pulling across his neck. It blossomed, burst into a shot of pain that pierced his shoulder blade and ran straight through into his chest, up his arm, and into his jawbone. His teeth ached; the light through the trees became sharp, brilliant.

Charles Call turned to his daughter. "Mary," he said, "go inside now and tell yer ma that I need her."

He stood, as if to walk away from her, then pitched forward, fell out of the shade of the maples and into the bright sunlight of his own dooryard, dead in a tangle of harness and dirt.

***

**Inventory of Estate of Charles Call, late of Pittston**

*Real Estate*

| | |
|---|---|
| *Homestead containing about 70 acres with the buildings thereon* | *1000.00* |
| *One other Lot containing 25 acres* | *128.00* |
| *One pew in the Methodist Meeting House* | *30.00* |
| | *1155.00* |

*Personal Estate*

| | | | |
|---|---|---|---|
| 1 pr. Horses | 40.00 | articles of beding | 1.50 |
| 6 Cows $10 each | 60.00 | articles of crockery | |
| 14 Sheep 2 Dol. Each | 28.00 | and glass | 2.00 |
| 1 Swine | 3.00 | articles of tin | .50 |
| 1 plow | 5.00 | 1 pr Brass candel stick | .33 |
| 1 pr wheels & cart | 3.00 | 5 silver tea spoons | 1.50 |
| 1 old chaise & harness | 15.00 | 3 waiters | .50 |
| 1 sleigh & harness | 8.00 | 12 milkpans | 1.00 |
| 1 buffalow skin | 3.00 | 2 kettles of Iron | .67 |
| 2 pitch forks | .50 | 1 pot, 1 pr flats | .58 |
| 1 grindstone | .50 | 1 shovel & tongs & dogs | .50 |
| 1 harrow | 2.00 | 1 doz kives & forks | .75 |
| 5 tons hay | 60.00 | 1 baker & tin kitchen | 1.75 |
| 2 chains 1 yok | 1.60 | | |

| | | | |
|---|---|---|---|
| 1 bureuo | 5.00 | Deceased wearing apparel | 6.00 |
| 1 wooden clock | 7.00 | | 17.58 |
| 1 Lookingglass | 1.00 | | |
| 7 Chairs | 3.00 | 1 scow, riging for same | 25.00 |
| 2 old tables | .50 | | |
| 1 table | 3.00 | 1155.00 | |
| 1 brassed bed & beding | 7.50 | 272.85 | |
| 1 brassed bed & beding | 5.00 | 17.58 | |
| | | 25.00 | |
| 1 bedsead | .75 | 1470.35 Total Estate | |
| 5 bed quilts & coverlets | 3.50 | | |
| 4 blankets | 1.50 | | |
| 4 pr sheets | 3.00 | | |
| Table Linen | 2.00 | | |
| 1 ax | .50 | | |
| | 272.85 | | |

Joel Thompson
Alfred Stilphen
Eliphalet Crocker

appraisers

---

"I'd clean forgot about that pew at the Methodist," Elizabeth Call told Lydia Crocker. "Clean forgot."

"You ever go?" Lydia asked. "With Charles, I mean?"

Elizabeth shook her head, leaned over and took a wailing Susan from the cradle at her feet, settled back in the rocker.

"Never?"

"The pew was part of my dower," Elizabeth said. She opened her waist, set the baby to her breast. "My father bought pews for all his daughters—he was righteous enough in public to make yer head swirl; his private behavior, though, was far less so."

Lydia snorted.

"I went regular as a child, but when I married Charles, he left me to my own decision; said I was free to go if I wished, but that he wanted no part of it."

"And did you go?"

"I had good intentions." Elizabeth turned her head, looked out the front window across the dooryard to the birches, stark white against the swirl of red and orange leaves.

"Are any of us still believers?" Lydia asked. She reached for the teapot, poured more into their cups, then slid Elizabeth's saucer closer to the edge of the table, well within her reach.

"Mary Stilphen, for certain—she goes down to Dresden," Elizabeth said. "And I daresay Jane Blodgett still goes over to Union at King's Mills." She took a sip of tea. "And if Jane's a churcher, it would reason that Polly Thompson is as well—sisters usually run consistent."

"Not those two," Lydia said. "Polly's like me—doesn't care for all that thunder and lightning and singing about bloody fountains—she and Joel don't go much, except to be social, keep their place."

"Yer Eliphalet?" Elizabeth asked. "What is his stance?"

Lydia leaned back in her chair. "He fought at Plattsburgh," she said. "Killed a man." She took a sip of tea, swallowed. "He told me once that he can't believe in a God that would encourage mankind to such slaughter."

The baby stirred. Elizabeth lifted her over her shoulder, patted her firmly between her shoulder blades; soon a soft burp, a sigh; back to the breast, still eager.

"Hungry girl!" Lydia exclaimed.

"She's a little piglet, this one." Elizabeth smiled. "I can barely keep up to her."

"Would you think to go back—to the Methodist, I mean—now that Charles is gone?"

Elizabeth thought about that for a moment; looked down at the strong, steady suckling of her newborn daughter, up again at Lydia.

"Didn't go when he was alive," she said. "I see no reason to go now that he's dead."

---

Eliphalet Crocker went out Thursday after first chores, before breakfast. He loaded his rifle in the shed and wrapped a cloth around the firing works to keep the damp away, then tucked it under his arm and stepped off the stoop onto the soft ground. He went up past the shed and the smokehouse, over the near wall into his first pasture, the grass brown and limp in the drizzle, the wet clinging to his boots, his pant legs.

He went over the next wall, started into the woods along his and Nate Blodgett's line, then stopped, leaned up against a maple to take a listen—heard droplets fall through the branches, soft and muted under the quilt of the mist.

So still, he thought, so beautiful.

He pushed away, headed north again through a small stand of pines, his boots quiet against the golden-brown needles on the ground, the sweet scent of dirt and decay rising up whenever he stepped.

When he reached the big oak, he paused, listened for a long time—heard nothing save the sound of his own breath moving in and out of his mouth, his chest—then turned, grabbed the first branch, and started up into the tree. It was a slow process, what with the rifle and the slip and slide of the wet bark, but he managed twenty feet or so, then settled himself along a thick branch, his back up against the trunk. He waited until he'd caught back his breath, then unwrapped the rifle, rested the barrel across a branch and draped the cloth back over the works to keep everything dry while he waited.

He looked around once, ran his eyes along the stone wall and the deer trail beside it, then shifted his weight along the branch until he found a comfortable balance.

He cleared his head, lowered his eyes, and settled in.

He sensed her—nothing much, just a shift inside his chest—and opened his eyes.

A fine doe, full and clean; she moved along the trail, her head turned away, her attention on the woods on the far side of the wall.

He pulled the cloth away, lifted the rifle.

Forgive me, he thought, and fired.

He gutted her right there, then hoisted her over his shoulders, her feet dangling down over his chest. He grasped her delicate legs—one fore, one hind—and held her there, then picked up his rifle in his other hand and walked out of the woods, walked her home.

He called to her from the dooryard. "Lydia!" he called. "Lyd?"

She appeared in the shed door.

"Got her up by the trail, up near Nate's line," he said. He turned once around to show her the full measure of the doe across his shoulders.

"She's got a good size to her," she said.

"She does," he agreed. "There's enough for us, for Lizzie and her brood."

"What about Thompson?" she asked. "They're low, I think."

"No, they're all set; Joel got one Tuesday—shared with Blodgett. But I could run some down to Stilphen—swap for some mutton, maybe."

"All right," she said.

"I'll hang her for a while," he said. "I'll cut her later; I'm too hungry to do it now—my stomach will eat itself up if I don't get something in there."

"Porridge is hot," she said, and stepped back inside.

*Town of Pittston*
*East Parish*
*October 24, 1835*

*Notice of Births in the Town of Pittston, Registered & Recorded*
*by me, Hiram Stevens, Clerk*
    *Susan, born to Charles Call & Wife, September 30, 1835*


*Notice of Deaths in the Town of Pittston, Registered & Recorded*
*by me, Hiram Stevens, Clerk*
    *Charles Call Departed this Life on the fifth day of August,*
*1835 in the thirty-seventh year of his age*

# Chapter Ten

*Pittston Town Meeting*
*East Parish*
*April 17, 1836*

*Article 15: To see if the Town shall approve a schoolhouse to serve*
*the Eastern River District to be situated on a corner lot of land*
*purchased for $73 from Eliphalet Crocker for that purpose said*
*land opposite his homestead on the western side of the road where*
*that road intersects with Caston Road.*

MID-APRIL, and the strong spring light pushed hard through the red tips of the maples in the woodlots; spring growth showed green through the brown leaves around the tree trunks. In another week, the oaks and birches would bud out; in a fortnight, the entire woods would be thick with the soft white scattering of trillium and wood sorrel throughout the dips and hollows.

The warblers were back; cardinals and phoebes sang in the sunlight.

They came up the road by wagon from their farm on the Dresden town line, Alfred and Mary Stilphen together on the board seat, Elvira tucked neatly in a slingwrap nestled within the crook and curve of her mother's elbow. In the back, tucked into the loose hay in the wagon bed, a basket of onions, beets, and parsnips, a small jug of cider.

Not much, Mary thought, but enough for the common pot when the others add their share: root vegetables, for certain, perhaps some venison or fish.

When the horses clattered onto the plank bridge over Otter Creek, she reached out, touched Alfred's near arm.

"Stop a moment," she said, "would thee?"

He turned to her, perplexed.

"Fiddleheads," she said, smiling.

He slowed the blacks, pulled them up; the wagon shifted a bit from the momentum, then stopped.

Mary handed him the baby, then climbed down to the roadway and made her way back to the start of the bridge, slid through the leaves partway down the banking toward the creek.

The horses, unsure, shuffled on the road. Alfred hissed softly between his teeth to calm them, to calm the baby, too, who'd started to stir at her mother's leaving.

Mary settled her feet and leaned over, swept aside some twigs and leaves with her fingers.

"The fiddles are up!" she called, standing straight again. "Not ready—not yet—but up!"

She gathered her skirts in one hand and scrambled back up to the road, approached the wagon and waited until he steadied the horses, then set her foot on the spoke, lifted herself up over the wheel, and settled back beside him on the seat.

"There's a plenty lot of 'em," she said, taking Elvira back into her lap. "And if thee promises to vote for the new school, I'll come back in a few days; we'll have a mess for supper."

Alfred smiled, then chuckled, leaned into her a little. "That's a hard bargain," he said, just as if he hadn't planned to vote for the school anyway, "but it's done."

They started along again, the wagon swaying in the roadway, Mary and Alfred swaying in the seat, Elvira falling to sleep again, lulled by the motion and the sound of their voices as they talked about sheep and the eleven spring lambs—three of them blackface—and the new sheds he wanted to build below the barn.

They came out of the woods and into the broad swing through Call's lower fields, noted the glittering of light on the parallel curve of the Eastern River.

"I find it hard, still," he said, "to think of Charles as gone."

"I know," she said, resting her hand on his knee for a moment. The horses clipped on up the road, birds called out across the fields.

"Lizzie's firm in staying," she said. "She thinks she can manage as long as she's got some help with the heavier work."

"We can arrange that."

"Are the others willing?"

"Yes," he said. "Blodgett and Thompson will put up her hay; she can sell most of her cows—maybe keep one for herself—and work the sheep on her own."

Mary Stilphen nodded. "We can help her with those sheep," she said, "the two of us."

"Liph Crocker says Samuel will do her plowing in the spring—he's working his own team."

"Is he!" she exclaimed. "How old is he now?"

"Fifteen," Alfred said, slacking the left reins; the blacks turned as one into Lizzie Call's dooryard, stopped near the shed door, adjusted their stance, shook their heads.

Alfred put his fingers to his mouth and whistled. Elizabeth, with Susan on her hip, and young Charlie came from the house, Mary from the coop, her skirt apron lifted to carry.

"Ma!" she called. "I got seven eggs!"

"Bring 'em along," Elizabeth replied. "We'll boil 'em up at Thompson's!"

Mary Stilphen turned on the wagon seat and slid herself down into the wagon bed to sit close by Elizabeth Call. When they'd settled into the hay—the younger children firmly in their laps, the older ones seated at the back, feet dangling off the end over the road—Alfred flicked the reins lightly.

"*Git,*" he urged.

The horses huffed a little at the start, turned out of the yard, and started up the long slope of the valley ridge roadway toward Crocker's.

"What did you bring?" Mary Stilphen asked Lizzie Call, leaning against the sideboard.

"Winter cabbage," she replied, "and some carrots for the stew." She turned Susan in her lap, opened her waist, put her to nurse. "And those eggs laid just this morning."

How easily that baby feeds! Mary Stilphen thought, watching Susan's cheeks pull, her hands reaching out for the breast. How stronger than my Elvira!

She shifted her gaze from the baby to Lizzie Call.

"She's a sturdy one," she said quietly, nodding down at Susan. Lizzie turned her head in reply, reached over to Mary's lap to touch Elvira's soft cheek with the crook of her finger; the skin across the baby's forehead was translucent, tight and white across her brow.

"I worry," Mary added softly, "that she does not thrive."

Elizabeth Call heard the smallest fear in Mary's voice, listened for a moment to the creaking of the wagon bed, the turning of the wheels along the road. Then she reached over, patted Mary lightly on the arm two or three times, kept her fingers there for a few moments before resettling against the wagon back.

Mary stayed silent; she turned her head and looked down the slope of Crocker's south field to the river.

Alfred Stilphen gave slight tension to the horses and they slowed at the foot of Eliphalet Crocker's drive; he rested his boot against the brake, cupped his hands at his mouth.

"Come along, all Crockers!" he shouted out toward the house. "Come along, come along, or we'll be late to Thompson's!"

———————————

Polly Thompson leaned over and spooned the last batch of seared venison chunks from the spider into the kettle of simmering broth hanging over the fire, then set the spider aside on the hearth to cool. She pushed the ashes and embers back into the fireplace, swept the hearth for good measure, then stood upright.

There! she thought. There's a good start to the stew; that and the cornbread in the side oven should fulfill my part of the meal; the others will bring enough to stretch it for all.

She knuckled her fists into the small of her back to ease the slight ache there, stretched from side to side as she moved from the fireplace to the open doorway, looked out.

Spring, she thought, at last it is spring!

She heard voices, the jangle of harness, the creak of wheels and axles, and then Alfred Stilphen's haywagon lurched and lumbered up over the rise and neared the drive, sending the dogs barking and the chickens squawking and scattering across the dooryard to safety in the barn and the coop.

She stood for a moment on her doorstep and marveled at the wagonful of neighbors sweeping into her yard, all of them packed into the back of the wagon, smiling, calling out—*hallo! hallo!*—as it came up into the dooryard; the older children dropping from the back, her own children spilling out of the shed and barn to greet their friends, girls flitting and chattering like birds, boys dividing already into sides to start a game of fox and chase.

When did we come to be so many! Polly Thompson wondered, counting the children on her fingers, adding by surname: one Stilphen, three Calls, six Crockers, five Blodgetts. Added to the six of ours, that's twenty children altogether, more than half of them old enough to be in school and the others crowding on the step, waiting to get inside the door.

Joel stepped up beside her on the stoop; Polly turned to him.

"You should take them all to town meeting," she said quietly, tipping her head to the children, "for if ever there be proof of need for a school on this road, that wagonload shows it full!"

He was quiet for just a moment and then, sensing both the logic and absurdity of the thought, threw back his head and laughed outright.

───────

Sarah Ann Thompson waited beneath the chicken coop.

She lay flat on her back and looked up at the floor; she could see movement in the spaces between the boards as the chickens dropped from their nesting boxes and skipped over her head to the ramps that led down into their yard.

She droned softly to that shifting of shadow and light.

She had just enough room under there to roll over, and when she heard the wagon come up the drive, heard the shouts and laughter, she turned, took a loose rock from the foundation wall, then pulled herself forward until her face was inches from the small gap that gave her full view of the yard, all the way from the main house to up past the shed, and all the way up to the far side of the barn door.

The wagon was overflowing—children spilled out over the back and thudded to the ground, boys shouting and running, girls laughing, swirling their skirts and skipping.

Time to count, she thought, her hand tight around the rock, time to name and count: there's Pa, by the wagon; there's Polly on the step, and Benjamin and Abigail and John and Junior and Laura; all here, all here.

And me, she added, and me, Sarah Ann; all here, all here.

She relaxed, put the stone back into the foundation, back-bellied out from under the far side of the henhouse. She slipped over the wall and into the woodlot, along her path through the maples—out of sight now, out of sight—and into the sunlight again; she turned south and started down the road toward all those empty houses.

———

The spring sun was slanting over the barn roof when the men returned in midafternoon. The cart tilted and bumped into the dooryard, pulled up beside the fence.

Polly moved across the yard to greet them, to be first to get the news.

The horse, nervous at her approach, stepped and snorted; Joel reined him tightly until he'd settled.

"Well?" Polly asked, hands on her hips.

"We've got ourselves a school," he said.

———

She climbed back over the wall, scurried across to the chicken coop, and slid in underneath. She inched her way across the width of it, picked her stone out of the foundation, and put her eye to her peephole.

They were all eating, all gathered around the shed and kitchen doors—the women sitting in the sun on the shed steps and the back stoop, stew bowls in their laps; the men near the shed wall, her father and Mr. Stilphen squatting low, their backs against the clapboards.

Most of the girls were in the patch of grass near the front corner of the house, their skirts spread over their knees; the boys were in two groups—the older ones near the barn door, the others in the back of the wagon, leaning against the sideboards.

She looked across the yard, found them, named, counted: Pa and Polly, Benjamin and Abigail and John and Junior and Laura; all here, all here.

She put the rock back in place, then pulled her way across the dirt to the near corner of the foundation, where she palmed some loose dirt away, felt for the top of her leather bag, and lifted it from the hole. She wrapped her hand about it tightly so it would not jingle, set it on the ground in front of her, and loosened the thong, slipped her hand inside.

Haircomb, coin, button, she thought, feeling each one; shoe buckle, nail, marble.

She added the thimble she'd found at Crocker's, then named and counted again: haircomb, coin, button, shoe buckle, nail, marble, thimble.

She retied the bag, placed it back in the hole, then pushed the dirt over it and patted it down. She slid back over to the foundation, removed the rock, and looked out over the dooryard again.

---

The town of Pittston paid Eliphalet Crocker seventy-three dollars for the lot of land for the new school, and he cashed his note at the post office on Tuesday. He folded the bills neatly into his pocketbook, secured it with the leather strap, then buried the whole thing deep in his coat, went back outside to where Lydia and the children waited in the wagon.

The April wind gusted, lifted his hair off the collar of his jacket, blew down the back of his neck. There was still a chill to it, but it wouldn't be long, he thought, not long until the fields started to rise and the rush of spring plowing and planting set in; not long until his cattle spent their nights in a new shed.

"All set," he said, climbing up over the wheel and settling on the seat beside his wife. He picked up the reins, flicked them over Ned's broad back, and the wagon pulled forward along the road through town.

"Are we rich?" Lydia asked, grinning at him, linking her arm through his. The children giggled in the wagon bed behind them.

"For about a quarter hour," he said. "Maybe longer if ye don't spend all yer part at Young's."

Lydia had a list of dry goods she needed to pick—muslin for shirts for the boys, all of whom were busy growing out of their own; a bright calico for Elizabeth, who, at fourteen, wanted her first full dress; a plainer solid for Mary, still content with a skirt—and a short list of grocery items: flour, sugar, molasses, and tea.

He slowed, stopped in front of Jonathan Young's store. Lydia and the younger children got off, and Samuel moved up to sit beside his father on the seat.

"Buy for yerself, too, Lyd," he said. "Buy something for yerself this time; I'll come back to settle with Jonathan after we do our business at Dudley's."

———

"Need to separate the house stock from working stock," Eliphalet said, unfolding his paper, showing Aaron Dudley his plan for the new shed. "Easier to keep the business end of it straight now that I'm hiring out some."

Aaron smoothed the paper on the countertop, took a look.

"I need space for three pair oxen," Liph said.

"Three?" Aaron said. "Thought you had just the two pair."

"We do, but that second pair's rightly Samuel's, not mine." He tapped his toe against the base of the counter. "So I just bought a pair of brindle-faced off George Williamson; I'll get 'em in June."

"How much?"

"Thirty-six," Liph said. "Good price for a working set of four-year-olds."

He turned his head, looked for Samuel, who'd drifted off to talk with Aaron's daughter, Caroline. The two of them stood together near the doorway, looking outside to the yard where the pit sawyers shook sawdust from their heads, their clothes, and drank full dippers of water from the bucket near the storage shed.

As Eliphalet watched, Caroline turned, tipped her head up to Samuel, said something, and Samuel, all edgy and lanky, grinned like a fool, stuffed his hands in his pockets, shuffled his feet on the floor like a colt.

Well, he's sweet on her! Eliphalet thought, amazed.

"Anyway," he said, turning back to Aaron. "Here's what I want—a south-facing closed-frame shed; forty feet long, sixteen feet to center peak with some hay storage along the north side and four ten-foot double box stalls across the south."

Aaron dipped his pen, began the list: sills and posts, rafters, joists.

"Boards and battens," Liph said. "And shingles for the roof."

"We'll get yer roof shingles from Lincoln Perry in Gardiner," Aaron said.

"I can get 'em from Thompson," Liph said.

"Too slow, too dear," Aaron said, shaking his head. "Perry's got a machine—water-powered off the Cobbosseecontee; cuts shingles the whole day long—makes more in a day than a man can do in a week."

"Well, still," Eliphalet said, "I'd like to get 'em from Thompson."

"All right," Aaron said, scratching his nib on the paper. He multiplied and added in the side margins, then transferred numbers to the column; drew a heavy line on the bottom, ready to total.

"Double the planking on the weather side," Liph said. "My grandfather had a double-sided shed; did first layer horizontal, second vertical with battens; replaced the battens and the outer layer every ten years or so."

He stopped, scratched his chin; Aaron looked up.

"It's lasted fifty years," Liph finished.

Aaron tallied the cost.

"Terms?"

"Half now, other half when you haul it off," Aaron Dudley said.

Eliphalet paid in cash, folded the receipt and the promise due, tucked them into his pocketbook.

"I'll come in for it just before first haying," he said. "Roads are still too soft now for that heavy load."

They shook hands.

Fifty years, Eliphalet thought; Samuel will be older than I am now by the time it needs replacing, and I'll be in the ground.

---

Eliphalet and Samuel Crocker walked up to Thompson's the next morning in a light spring rain, staying out of the mud and standing water in the cart tracks by keeping to the higher center of the road. They slowed occasionally to look out over the fields, where bits of green showed through the brown stubble; a group of crows picked through it carefully, their black heads moving left to right, tipping side to side.

"That would be strange," Samuel said, all of a sudden.

"What's that?"

"To have yer eyes on the sides of yer head, not the front." He stopped for a moment. "Like a crow."

He covered one eye and then the other while turning his head back and forth to look at his father.

"You look a little daft," Eliphalet said, grinning, and they moved on, their boots squishing on the soft ground.

Polly Thompson brewed a new pot for them, then took Sarah Ann and the younger children out to gather eggs, feed the chickens, clean out the nesting boxes and set new hay, sweep the alleyway in the barn—any number of small chores—to give the men time to talk, to let them be.

They sat in the kitchen, Joel and John and Benjamin Thompson at the table, Eliphalet and Samuel Crocker, as guests in the house, over near the fireplace, nearer the warmth.

"Can you give me a couple days?" Eliphalet began.

"We can arrange that," Joel said. "When?"

"Soon as it's dry enough to dig," he said, "two weeks, maybe."

Joel stirred his tea. "New shed?" he asked, then lifted the cup and took a sip.

"Foundation, leastwise," Eliphalet said. He tipped his chair back against the wall near the fireplace. "Need a base trench dug and filled before I can frame it up."

"How wide? Deep?"

"Two wide, three deep."

"I dug three on my English barn," Joel said, "and it still heaves some every winter, even if I bank it solid." He looked up at Eliphalet. "Maybe you should make it four feet."

Eliphalet shrugged. "That's considerable digging," he said, and then, after a breath, "makes me feel old and tired just to think of it."

"Me, as well," Joel said. "Maybe you should hire it out."

They all thought about this for a moment. The fire snapped, a few logs shifted and settled; steam rose from the bottoms of Eliphalet's damp trouser legs.

"We can do it," Samuel said quietly, looking down at the floor. "Ben and John and me."

Nobody said a word, but the Thompson boys began to nod; they cleared their throats and straightened up in their chairs, interested now that they'd heard there might be real earnings here.

"You can hire it out to us," Samuel said again, stronger this time. He looked at the Thompson brothers. "We can dig it, and fill it, too—I can use my own team on the stoneboat for hauling rock."

"You got rock?" Benjamin asked Samuel. "A solid supply?"

"There's an almighty pile of it not far from where Pa wants that shed—I picked most of it last year from that upper field."

John pushed away from the table, stood. "If you mark it," he said to Eliphalet, "we could dig and fill it to yer measure."

"We could start right off," Samuel added. "Ground's pretty high up where ye're thinkin'—not a lot of water—so we could probably start right off."

They were excited now, eager for the job, for the work.

"Well," Eliphalet said slowly, looking at the boys, "I don't see why not." He turned to Joel. "That seem all right to you?"

Joel nodded. "I guess it does," he said.

Eliphalet walked over to the table, set his cup and saucer on the corner. "I'd pay fifty cents a day for a man, a dollar a day for a team." He rubbed his chin, looked at his son. "That do?"

"Yes, sir," Samuel said, and stuck out his hand.

Liph took it.

Later, when they were certain the boys were out of sight and earshot, Eliphalet and Joel dared lift their heads and smile at each other.

"I wasn't certain," Liph said, "that they'd jump for it."

"It was that 'old and tired' talk that clinched it," Joel said. "I nearly laughed outright when you said it."

"Well, you showed admirable restraint," Liph said, "and I'm grateful for that."

# Chapter Eleven

Cut the hare into pieces; season it with salt, pepper, and nutmeg, and jug it with the butter. It must do above an hour,
covered close in a pot of boiling water. Make some force-
meat…lay it round the inside of a raised crust; put the hare in
when cool, and add the gravy that came from it…

Charlotte Campbell Bury
*The Lady's Own Cookery Book*

SARAH ANN THOMPSON checked her trapline in the early morning,
directly after her bowl of bread and milk and cinnamon.

She slipped out of the house and through the full length of the shed,
did what she needed to do in the privy—her "business," Polly called it—
then stepped out into the dooryard, wrapped in one of Benjamin's out-
grown coats, her hair wound about itself and tucked inside the back collar.

Her bare feet were cold in her boots.

She walked up past the barn, droning now, turned between the
wagon shed and the corn crib, went through the gate, and started up
the ridge, up into that stretch where the hemlock and spruce grew on
the edges of her father's high fields. Lots of undergrowth in there, good
shelter for the winter-white snowshoe hares that roamed at night, fed on
birch and maple saplings in the hardwood lot, and traveled through the
thickets to the orchard to gnaw the bark from her father's apple trees.

That always made him hopping mad, she thought, made him holler
and swear some, and him not the kind of man to swear much at all.

She knew the hares were about; she'd seen the occasional cluster of
droppings in the trail. Once, she'd found some pellets still steaming,

and she picked a few up, cupped them in the curve of her palm, felt the warmth there.

She held them to her nose, even touched her tongue to one; it felt like a secret—what she'd done—and she never told anyone of it.

"*Nnnnnnn*," she droned, "*nnnnnn.*"

It was still cold in the woods. There were small patches of icy snow on the north sides of the trees, but the spring sunlight had been just enough these last few days to loosen the smell of the spruce, and the air was sweet with it.

The trail ran off to the west, up to the vernal bog where the hares found water each morning before hunkering down for the day in the dips and hollows, invisible against the white snow. She followed it from aside, staying a few feet away to keep her scent off the path itself, looking for the notches that Ben had hatcheted in the trees to mark the locations of the snares he'd taught her to set along the line. The snares had loops just wide enough for a hare's head and were anchored to bent saplings that rose like whips at the release of the trip line and lifted the hare as much as five feet into the air. There it might squeal once or twice, then thrash with its feet against the air until there was no breath left to it.

She'd never seen it happen—never seen how quickly hares moved from beating heart to warm stillness—even though she'd spent long hours hiding nearby, watching, waiting cold and stiff in early light for some sorry hare to sprint along the path to the bog and run headlong into the loop, to lift into the air; to die.

The first four snares were undisturbed, but in the fifth she found a hare hanging, motionless; a good-sized snowshoe with feet nearly as long as the length of her hand. She loosened the noose from its neck, let the body fall to the ground, then pulled the sapling back down and scooched in the thick needles to repeg it. She reset the snare, her fingers quick to open the noose, spread it back over the twig frame that held it there.

Threaded the trip line, set it to the peg.

She turned back to the hare, ran her fingers lightly over its face, stroked down along its still body—soft, so soft under her hand—then lifted it by its hind legs, stood and started home, walking at first, but then, thinking of how Polly's warm rabbit pie might feel in her mouth, breaking into a steady lope, holding her skirts up, her snowshoe hare banging against her thigh whenever she took a step; droning all the while.

Polly heard the shed door latch lift, felt a quick rush of cool air as Sarah Ann opened the kitchen door and sidled in; she turned from her flour board and smiled.

"Run yer line?" she asked.

Sarah Ann's hand came out from behind her skirts; she flopped the hare across the top of the table with a thud, looked at Polly and nodded.

"Well, then," Polly said, dusting her hands on her apron. "That's a fine hare ye're giving to me—and I am thankful for yer contribution to the family table." She grasped the animal's ears, dragged it off the table. "But let's put it in the shed until after breakfast; we can ask yer Pa to gut and skin it when he gets back from Blodgett's—I'll cook a stew later."

She was starting across the kitchen when she heard Joel shouting her name from the dooryard. In the next moment he was inside, breathing hard from his run up the road.

She saw the look on his face. "What?" she asked.

"Elvira Stilphen," he said, gasping, leaning on the table, trying to catch back his breath. "Jane Blodgett just told me."

"The baby's sick again?" she asked. "Do I need to go to Mary?"

"No," he said, "yes." He pulled in some air, coughed.

"Which is it?" she asked. "No or yes?"

"No, Elvira's not sick," he said, breathed again.

"Then what?"

"Dead."

Polly Thompson looked down at the snowshoe hanging from her hand, feet dangling in the sunlight, its eyes wide open, glazed.

She took the horse, rode slowly, carefully along the muddy road, past Jane Blodgett's and on down the south slope, through the cold shadows of the pine woods and then out into the sunlight again. The spring sun was just warm on her face, and there was faint green showing on the tips of all the trees; small patches of snow hugged the rocks on the north side of Eliphalet Crocker's wall.

She rode into their yard, up the drive past the main house to the shed door, open to catch this April light.

"Lydia!" she called out. "Lyd?"

She heard the kitchen door open, heard Lydia come across the shed floor to the entryway.

"Have you heard?"

Lydia nodded, drew her shawl about her shoulders. "Going down?" she asked.

"I am," Polly said. "Can you come?"

"Of course," she said, then covered her face for a moment, the muscles in the backs of her hands tight.

Polly's horse sidestepped in the dooryard; she let him turn once, twice, then held him firm.

"Lydia?" Polly urged.

She lowered her hands. "I need to fetch my oils and a wrap," she said, and went back inside.

They rode two astride to the Stilphens', their skirts bunched up a little above their knees, their shawls drawn close about their shoulders. Polly gave the horse free rein, and he picked his way carefully along the ruts; the women swayed on his back and rump, Lydia holding Polly's waist for balance.

"I've left the housekeeping to Elizabeth and Mary," Lydia said. "They're old enough now to fix a supper, take care of the fires."

"And I've got Abigail for that."

"Sarah Ann?" Lydia asked.

"Sarah Ann will do whatever Abby asks her to do."

"Good, then."

They passed by Call's upper field, looked down the slope to the house, smoke rising from Lizzie's kitchen chimney, and beyond to the river. The road to the boathouse was shining with snowmelt; the Eastern curled alongside the fields below the riverbarn, bright in the spring sunlight.

"I feel guilty," Lydia said.

"Guilty?" Polly asked. "For what?"

The horse's hooves sucked in the mud; he crossed the center of the road to the other side, found more solid ground.

"For having a husband and children that are still alive," Lydia said.

When they pulled into the yard, Alfred was sitting on the shed steps. He stood, walked across the dooryard to greet them, to hold the horse still while they slid to the ground, rearranged their skirts.

"I'm glad to see the both of you," he said. He looked back at the house, then at Polly. "Mary's distraught."

She touched his forearm. "Take me to her," she said, "and Lydia will tend to Elvira."

Lydia Crocker took a breath, unwrapped Elvira Stilphen, pulled the folds of the woolen blanket apart, and took a look; the baby's mouth was slack, her eyes deep in their sockets, open and dull.

Her skin was so white against her bones!

Lydia ran her fingers lightly over the lids to close the eyes—nothing there now, nothing—and gently placed a strip of linen beneath the stiffening jaw, lifted it closed, and tied the ends atop the baby's head.

In the kitchen, she poured warm water from the kettle into a basin, carried it back to the parlor, and closed the door. She washed the last of the pain and struggle from Elvira Stilphen; she wiped the chest and back, cleaned between the thighs and buttocks with a small flannel, wiped the arms and legs, fingers, feet.

A hymn, she thought, Mary would want me to sing a hymn, to sing something—a lullaby, maybe:

> Hush, my babe, lie still and slumber;
> Lambs and angels guard thy rest…

She poured warm oil into her palms, smoothed it over Elvira Stilphen, spread it over her skin; the scent of it rose from beneath her hands, the room filled with the sweetness of it.

She wrapped the baby tightly in the sheeting, opened the door, and called to Alfred to come for his daughter.

---

Polly told her on their way back up the road.

"She's carrying again," she said.

The horse stumbled over a rock in the road; Lydia tightened her grip around Polly's waist, held her breath for just a moment, just until he found his balance again. "Mary?"

"Yes," Polly said. "She told me while you were tending to Elvira—this one due, she thinks, in August."

"Well," Lydia said, "well, that's fine."

---

In the spring of 1838, Eliphalet Crocker saw the first trace of open water on the twenty-first of March, a small strip right down the center of the Eastern. It broadened each day as the current broke pieces of ice away from the mass along the shorelines; on the first of April, the very last of it shifted and fell away, moved down past Call's boathouse on the outgoing tide.

Almost time to plow, he thought.

He walked up to his high fields every morning to feel the soil, to lean over and take a handful, to squeeze, release, and hope for it to break apart in his palm.

And each morning, when it was not yet ready, he came back down, cleaned his boots, and went through the shed and on into the kitchen for some of Lydia's fresh biscuits and a cup of strong tea.

"Not yet," he said to Lydia each morning, "not yet."

---

The branches of the trees along the wall were still bare, but there were hints of green at the tips; the stones in the walls were cool to the touch despite the spring sunlight.

He walked Noah and Ham up to the field and settled them into the long yoke, the extra length putting enough space between them so that Ham could walk deep in the most recent furrow while Noah stayed up on the unplowed ground, the bow spread between them at an angle.

He was still on his first quarter—had made only three or four passes up his near and center lines—and was still rough and rusty, but the oxen were pulling steadily and the soil was riding smoothly up and off the curve of the moldboard. His muscles were loosening, the sun was warm; he heard a vireo in one of the trees along the stone wall.

They made the turn at the far end—Noah taking short steps on the inside of the turn, Ham keeping a longer stride to stay even on the outside—and then, without warning, Ham's head came up, pulled back. His eyes grew wide and he staggered, then bellowed—a long roar of pain and confusion.

Eliphalet watched him fall—first to his knees, then over onto his side—the yoke pulling Noah off balance as well; he, too, went down, thrashed against Ham's heaving side.

Eliphalet tipped the plow, came forward and struggled to pull the pin; finally it came loose, releasing Noah from the yoke. The ox found his footing, heaved himself up and turned, white-eyed and terrified. Eliphalet slapped at his rump and he started away, started down the slope to the barn, slobbering and groaning in his distress.

Eliphalet sat down on the ground beside Ham, lifted the great head—eyes still wide open, blood dribbling from nostrils, mouth—and rested it in his lap. He smoothed the huge forehead and face, whispered and wept, eased Ham on his way.

Lydia was at the well filling buckets when she heard the commotion, heard the thudding of Noah's hooves and the eerie sound of his crying. She turned in time to see him lurch into the barnyard and lumber through the open doorway into the safety of his stall.

Oh, Lord, she thought, fear rising sharp and swift in her throat.

She left the buckets right there beside the well, turned, lifted her skirts on either side and began to run, up past the pigpen and around the back end of the barn, up the slope.

When she reached the top of the rise, she looked to the left, then right; she saw her husband at the far end of the row, mid-turn, sitting in the furrow with his dead ox, his head down across Ham's head, his face buried in the shag of his neck.

"My dear," she whispered, standing in the spring sunshine, "my dear, my dear…"

Then turned and went back to the house, turned and went back to care for the one left behind.

———————

*Pittston Town Meeting*
*East Parish*
*December 18, 1839*

*Surveyor of Highways     Eliphalet Crocker*
*School Agent*
*        District 10        Joel Thompson*
*Tax Collector             Nathaniel Blodgett*

*Notice of Births in the Town of Pittston, Registered & Recorded by me, John Dow, Clerk*
*        Benjamin Franklin Crocker, born to Eliphalet & Wife Lydia Crocker, March 8, 1837*

*Now here comes Alfred Stilphen, Eastern River District, to make a record of the children born to him & Wife Mary Call Stilphen,*
*        Elvira born October 26, 1835*
*                Departed this Life April 16, 1837*
*        Isabelle born August 14, 1837*
*                Departed this Life April 16, 1838*
*        Alfred L. born December 3, 1839*
*                Registered by me, John Dow, Clerk*

# PART III

# 1841–1850

# Chapter Twelve

It is evident that the greatest safeguard against improper
attachments consists in the character…

Lydia Maria Child
*The American Frugal Housewife*

NATHANIEL BLODGETT did first chores at dawn, was out early feeding and watering the horses, scattering fresh straw in the pens, straightening up the barn.

He needed time away from the house to think, to work it all out; had
to get it right, or Jane would break her all-holy wrath over him.

He'd go all the way down to Stilphen's first, he reasoned. He'd buy
the sheath from Alfred and pocket it before he stopped on the way
back up the road for Lydia Crocker and her children. If anyone noticed
him passing by at first and coming back a short while later, he'd mention some question he'd had for Alfred—something about sheep—and
nobody'd question that, for Alfred knew more about sheep than anyone
in the Eastern River Valley, Christ, yes, and he had the flock to prove it!

Nate tossed some grain before the cow, then settled the stool at her
right hindside, clenched the bucket between his knees, wiped at her teats
with a handful of clean hay.

Lizzie Call wouldn't have him, he knew, without that sheath—she
might not have him anyway—but she wanted no bastard children, and
that meant a trip down to Alfred Stilphen's for a new sheath. He'd slaugh-
tered a sheep a fortnight ago, Nate knew, so must have a new supply
ready by now; he needed only a week to clean out the gut, he said, rinse

it with sulphur and lye, cut it in lengths and knot the one end in each. After that, knead each one soft with lard, roll it, wrap it tight in a small piece of linen.

The milk steamed in the bucket. Nathaniel thought about Lizzie Call, felt a tightening in his lower belly—needed that sheath, needed to keep himself clean, as well, for fear of carrying a pox home to Jane, and then just talk about all-holy wrath!

He covered the milk bucket with a cloth and set it in the corner, then turned the cow out to the near pasture, slid the rails into the posts, retrieved the bucket, and headed back to the house.

So, he thought as he walked across the dooryard, go to Stilphen first, then drive right past Lizzie's—not even look up her drive, just go right past—to Crocker's, pick up Lydia and carry her and the children back up to the house where she and Jane could spend the day together.

Hide the sheath in the barn, get it later on his way to the woodlot.

———

Rolls, thick with butter, drizzled with honey.

"You said you'd go down to get Lydia and the children, carry them back here this morning," Jane prompted, pouring him a cup of strong pekoe. "Remember?"

He tried to feign surprise; tried to suggest he'd forgotten about carrying Lydia back here for the day.

"She's helping me set the edge to that new quilt today." She picked a piece of straw from his hair, patted his shoulder. "And the children can all play in the dooryard."

"I did forget that," he said. He took a bite of roll, chewed, swallowed; it nearly stuck in his throat with the lie.

He took a final drink of tea, stood up from the table.

"I'll be off, then," he said, and smiled at her, went out to the barn to harness the horse, hitch the wagon.

He dropped the reins in the drive—no need to anchor the horse, he knew; it would stay put—looked over to the house and saw Mary Stilphen framed in the shed doorway, but going in or coming out he could not tell.

"Alfred still at table?" he called.

She turned round at the sound of him, smiled, shook her head.

"Down to the sheds," she replied, then reached down and shook the dust and dirt from the hem of her skirt.

Going in, he thought, then waved at her and headed across the dooryard past the gable end of the barn to the long line of sheep sheds that ran along the top of the high meadow.

The sheep were outside in the pens below, working on the last of the short grass there, but off to the west, just beyond the fence, there was a half-foot of new growth shining in the morning light, and a few blackface looked longingly at it through the slats.

"Lo! Alfred!"

Nathaniel opened the half-door and stepped inside the near shed. The boxes on either side of the center alley were freshly bedded; the alleyway itself swept clean.

He went back outside, moved down to the second shed, entered the side door and peered down the alleyway.

"Stilphen!" he called.

"Here, I'm here!" Alfred hollered, moving up the center aisle, rake over his shoulder.

They stood together in the shed doorway, looked out across the pens and into the meadows beyond.

"They look some pitiful," Nate said, nodding at the blackface, still mooning over the good grass in the other yard.

Alfred laughed. "I know," he said. "I'm lookin' to shift 'em this afternoon—if I move 'em over there this morning, they'll eat too much, get scours from that good grass."

They stood quietly for a moment, watching the sheep move in and out of the shadows. Nate scuffed his boot on the ground, then looked out over the fields, down the run toward the Eastern.

"I need a new sheath," he said.

Alfred looked up, surprised. "So soon? Hain't had that last one more than a month!"

Nate looked away. "Well, no matter, I need a new one now."

Alfred shook his head. "I can't figure that," he said. "That other one should last a good while more than two fortnights."

Nate was silent.

"Didn't break on you?" Alfred asked. "I'd feel some guilt if that were the case."

When Nate stayed still, Alfred turned, looked at the side of his face for a long while, then leaned one hand against the side of the shed, rubbed his chin with the other.

"Y'ain't sniffin' around Lizzie Call, are you?" he asked.

A couple of blackface bleated, nosed into a small group of mixed-breed ewes feeding in the corner of the yard, pushed them away from the good grass.

"Look," Nate said, puffing up against his irritation. "Sell me the sheath or not, but don't give me a hard talk about stayin' away from Lizzie Call."

Alfred sighed. "I'll sell to you," he said, "but only to keep you from messin' Lizzie's life—and yer own—more than it is now."

He turned, started back through the shed.

"Come on," he said to Nate, "they're in a box in the tool room."

———

The fields were lovely in the moonlight, dappled with shadow from passing clouds, bright when the face of the moon was clear. The white light danced on the edge of the road, then ran down the slopes toward the Eastern.

When Elizabeth Call neared the north boundary fence that separated her meadow from her woodlot, she stepped off the roadbed and pushed into the field. She followed the fence line, resting her left hand on the top rail for balance, holding her skirts up above the tops of the grasses with her right, keeping her hems out of the dew. Crickets hushed as she neared, then started up again as she passed by.

She counted fence posts as she made her way down the slope, and when she reached the tenth, she stepped and slipped between the rails onto the other side, put her back to the post and headed straight across the short width of wagon track, near to the edge of the woods.

"Nate?" she whispered. "Nate, are you here?"

"Here," he said, from within the woods, off to her right someplace, but not far.

She paused. "I cannot see," she said. "'Tis too dim in there."

"Stay, then," he said. "I can see you fine."

She heard a rustle, the snapping of twigs, and he came to the edge of the wood, stepped out into the soft light, was there in front of her.

"I'm late, I know," she said, reaching her hands out, circling him at the waist, "but the children stayed awake so long!"

She moved up against him, buried her face in his shoulder, his neck; she felt his heart beating in his throat, heard the rush of his breath against her ear.

"I've got a new sheath," he whispered, his voice thick, full.

She tipped her head back to look at him for a moment, then raised up on her toes and brushed her mouth across his, took his lower lip between her teeth and tugged at it gently, flicked her tongue across it lightly.

He groaned, and she moved herself up against him, hips pushing hard at his thighs, and her need to have him flared up inside her.

"I feared you wouldn't wait for me!" she whispered, then drew him down into the silvery grass.

----

Jane Blodgett killed two chickens in the morning—two of her tired old layers, not two of the new Rocks—out behind the shed, away from the coop where, she thought, the sight of two of their sisters going under the hatchet might be too much for the others to bear, might send them right off their feed, off their nesting boxes, and she couldn't have that.

She'd learned to cull out the older hens and make space for the younger, more vigorous layers; she'd even hung a small piece of looking glass inside the coop to encourage production—Mary Stilphen said it worked like magic with her hens—and increased their daily rations to bring up the egg count.

After all that, she wasn't about to lose ground now, so she beheaded them out behind the shed, far from the coop and the others, then gutted them, plucked them.

All right, she thought, carrying them across the dooryard, chicken for dinner and soup for supper, too.

---

"I don't know how ye can kill them chickens," Lucinda said. "It makes me retch to even think of doing it."

Jane grinned at her daughter. "And what's in store for yer William Howard after ye're married?"

"He'll have to do the killing," Lucinda said, "or starve."

I'll be lonesome when she's gone, Jane thought; and when she goes that'll be two of my children grown and moved on: Maryann to Portland with her husband, Lucinda to Waldoboro with hers. Eliza will follow soon enough, although she's young yet, she's got a few more years here at home; Jane Adaline's got still more.

She halved the chickens, then halved them again, layered the quarters into the spider, poured water from the bucket to cover, put the lid on top, then raked some coals, set the spider over them.

Daniel and John, at least, will stay, she thought. After all, they've got something to stay for—they get the farm, no questions asked. My girls, though, have no expectations; it's marry and move, marry as best they can and move away, like I did.

"Have enough water?" Lucinda asked.

"Just enough," Jane said, "but both buckets are empty now."

"I'll go," Lucinda said, wrapped herself in a shawl, and took the buckets through the shed and out the back door to the well.

After a while, when she thought it might be ready, Jane wrapped her hand in her apron, leaned down, and lifted the lid from the spider. She poked at the chicken with a fork; the meat fell away from the bone.

"Done," she said, and grasped the handle, pulled the hot spider off the coals onto the brick hearth to cool.

"Ma?"

Jane lifted her head, looked at her daughter.

"Remind me how to make that good chicken dish that Pa likes so—I think William might like it."

"All right."

Jane pushed the cool coals back into the fireplace and raked new ones forward for the skillet; she set it onto the coals and added some butter.

"When that butter heats enough," she said, "we'll start cooking that meat, but let's crack those bones, get them and the broth into the kettle first—that's good for soup."

Lucinda spooned the chicken quarters from the spider, set them in a pan on the table. She tugged the bones away from the meat and, when they cooled a little, cracked them against the side of the table to release the juice within, returned them to the broth. "I'll skim it off in a while," she said, "and add the roots—I thought carrots, onions, parsnips from the cellar."

"Good enough," Jane said. She wrapped her hands again, poured the broth into the soup kettle, then figured the height from the fire and set the hook into the chain, lifted the iron kettle and hung it there, swung the crane back into the fireplace.

She wiped down the table with a clean rag.

"Now, let's cut up those quarters," she said, "and I'll show ye how to do the steps."

They worked at the table, standing side by side.

"We need a mix of flour and cornmeal to roll those pieces," Jane said. "A little pepper goes good, too."

Lucinda used her hands to measure to Jane's direction—a handful of flour, one of cornmeal, a dash of salt, another of pepper—and used her fingers to mix it together in a bowl.

"Roll the pieces in that mix," Jane said, "then drop 'em into the hot butter, fry 'em up good and brown."

"Can't fit 'em all," Lucinda said, leaning down over the spider, careful to keep her skirts away from the coals; her hems were full enough of burn holes and scorch marks, and she didn't need to add more.

"That's all right; we'll do two batches—change coals every few minutes to keep that skillet hot enough—and then we'll make gravy from the drippings and add some sage and put the chicken to stew in that, cover it up for a while."

"That's all?" Lucinda asked. "That's all to making that dish?"

Jane nodded. "That's all."

"Well," Luce said, "it tastes more complicated than that."

Tending the fire, Jane thought, that's the worst of it; every quarter hour either stacking wood onto the back of the fire or pulling it to the front; raking coals for cooking—pushing spent coals back or pulling hot ones forward; heaping them for trivets and spiders or spreading them for griddles and grates; lifting pots from trivets to crane, raising or lowering kettles on the chain.

All told, she thought, I spend more time tending fires and cooking than I do any other thing in my day.

———

Lizzie Call was outside, spreading her washing over the front rail fence to dry, when she saw Nate coming down the road, scythe over his shoulder.

On his way to Alfred's, she thought.

She wiped her hands nervously on the front of her skirt, waited for him by the corner post at the beginning of the turn into the drive.

Her head ached; she'd hardly slept for three days.

His stride shortened as he neared. He put his free hand into his trouser pocket—touched himself, she knew, to show her his interest—leaned the scythe against the rail.

"Tonight?" he asked. "Meet me tonight in the woodlot?"

She took a breath. "No," she said, folding her arms across her chest. "We'll not do it again."

His jaw tightened. He pursed his lips, blew out his breath, then looked past her up the drive to the house; he scanned the dooryard, the shed, the barn, looked back at her again.

"I could die from the shame of it, Nate," she said, looking down. "I'm betraying Janey, and ye're betraying her worse."

He shrugged. "Janey's always been too righteous, in my opinion."

"Too righteous?" she flared, squaring her shoulders. "Ye're speaking of yer wife like she's of poor character when, seems to me, we're the ones wrong here."

He shrugged again.

"No more, Nate," she said. "I'll do it no more."

He turned his hands over, looked down at his palms, then picked up the scythe; he walked a few paces down the road, then turned, came back again.

She tipped her head, eyed him.

"You'll not speak of it, will you?" he asked.

"What?"

"I mean," he said, shifting his weight to his other foot, "you'll not tell any of the others—the women."

She looked at him for a long moment, then shook her head. "No, Nate," she said, leaning against the fence rail. "I'll not speak of it—that would be even worse, wouldn't it, to tell the others and betray them all?"

"That's no matter to me," he said.

She looked at him full on. "You don't understand what I'm saying, do you?" she asked.

He lifted his head, a little angry now. "Ye're saying that ye're not giving to me...but I can go elsewhere for it."

"Then go." She pushed herself away from the fence. "You don't even understand what we've done, Nate, and that means I'll have to carry the guilt all by myself."

She turned away and headed back up to her house, just turned her back and left him there, standing in the road.

*Pittston Town Meeting*
*East Parish*
*March 25, 1843*

*Notise of Births in the Town of Pittston, Registered & Recorded*
*by me, Lorenzo S. Clark, Town Clerk*
*    To Alfred & Mary Call Stilphen, a daughter Victoria, Janu-*
*ary 29, 1843*

*Notise of Deaths in the Town of Pittston, Registered & Recorded*
*by me, Lorenzo S. Clark, Town Clerk*
*    Alfred L. Stilphen, son of Alfred & Mary Call Stilphen that*
*Departed this Life March 7, 1843*

*Marriages in the Town of Pittston, Registered & Recorded by*
*me, Lorenzo S. Clark, Town Clerk*
*    Mr. William Howard of Waldoboro to Miss Lucinda*
*Blodgett, October 27, 1842*

# Chapter Thirteen

If you are afraid your oven is too hot, throw in a little flour, and shut it up for a minute. If it scorches black immediately, the heat is too furious; if it merely browns, it is right.

Lydia Maria Child
*The American Frugal Housewife*

"I'VE BEEN THINKING to get one of those iron stoves," Jane said. "Hannah Soper's got one; says it works fine."

"Hannah Soper?" Nate pulled the rocker close to the fire, sat down. "When did you see Hannah Soper?"

"Last Sunday, when Polly rode with me over to the Methodist."

"Oh," he said, "I'd forgot that." He pulled out his pipe, leaned forward and tapped the bowl against the side of the fireplace, emptied the ash into the fire.

"Anyways, she's got one."

He sat back again, dug into his pocket for his fixings. "A stove seems a bit of a fancy to me," he said. "I guess that cooking on the fire works just as good."

"It's true," she answered, "that both can cook a dinner. The stove, though, does it in half the time and with half the work."

"Half?"

"That's what Hannah says." She knelt down, lifted the lid to the Dutch oven, checked the chicken.

"Smells good," he commented.

"And it's not just the cooking, Nate," she said, standing upright again, stretching her back. "It's the heat, too; Hannah says they can sit any spot in that kitchen all winter in just wraps—no need of coats."

Nathaniel rocked in the chair some more, pushed tobacco into his pipe with his thumb, not listening, not really.

"Heats all the room," she added, "not just near the fire." She wrapped her hands, leaned over and lifted the Dutch oven, set it on the hearth, then used the poker to push away the old coals. When she'd cleared the space, she reset the iron pot there and pulled fresh coals around it, keeping the chicken stewing inside.

"Well," he said, "do what you will."

All right, she thought, I'll do that.

She figured it all out, made a plan. Kept to it.

She carried her extra butter and eggs into East Pittston, the butter in a small firkin, the eggs nestled in a wicker basket lined with straw and covered with a soft cloth. Jonathan Young paid her good money for both, and he bought steadily, marking up for the profit he himself turned in the store.

She walked, mostly, carrying her eggs in one hand, butter in the other, but at least once a week she took the cart, her wash and rinse barrels loaded and strapped in the back, the firkin on the seat beside her, the egg basket steadied between her feet, on the floor under her skirts.

She saved diligently, kept her coins in an old cracked teacup tucked behind some plates on the pantry shelf; she tried not to count it too often, for her progress, though steady, was slow.

In early spring, she put her two roosters into the coop. She ignored as best she could the infernal screeching and flapping as they mounted the hens, pecked their heads and necks raw and bloody in their fierce determination.

"Keep at it, boys!" she encouraged them, tossing cracked corn in the yard. "Ye're workin' for my stove."

When the hens got broody, she took special care to let them hatch out the chicks, then sold some of them, too, including a few of the better

Plymouth Rocks, keeping enough to maintain her flock, enough to replace the ones she culled out for low egg production.

Week by week, she dropped coins into the cup, and by the fall of 1843, Jane Blodgett finally had enough money to get herself a stove.

"Here, give me the money," he said, holding out his hand.

"Nate," she said, "I earned the money, and I'll do the buying."

"And make me look the fool?" He bristled. "I'll not go along, then; you can load it yerself in the wagon."

"Suit yerself," she said, "but you'll look more of a fool when I have to ask Joel and Eliphalet to go with me to help do the lifting."

They all went, in the end, all of them, in Crocker's wagon: Jane and Nathaniel, Eliphalet and Lydia Crocker, Polly and Joel Thompson; they all left their older children in charge of the younger ones and went to town with Jane while she bought her stove.

"No Stilphens? No Lizzie Call?" Polly asked, as she and Joel climbed into the wagon bed, settled themselves in the hay.

"Alfred was up this morning," Lydia said. "He says Victoria's croupy, so he and Mary's staying to home."

"What about Lizzie?"

"She's got herself a caller."

"That's Tom Mitchell," Joel said. "I saw him at the post office the other day, and he said he's thinking to call on her."

"That's good," Jane said. "A widow and a widower; that's as good an arrangement as any."

At Young's, she settled on a step-top stove, cast iron, with a lower hearth level in front of the firebox, a two-hole cooking level a step above that, and, finally, a square, squat oven in the rear with a side door.

"It's just a box!" Polly exclaimed, looking at it skeptically. "How can you cook a dinner in a box?"

"You cook on it, not in it," Jane explained, and showed her the lids, showed her how she could lift one from the top, expose the bottom of the pot directly to the flame or keep it closed and set the pot on the lid itself.

"But you can't use a spider on it," Polly commented, "if the pot has to sit right on the top.”

“Have ye got a pot without feet?” Lydia asked. “Mine are all spiders or trivets.”

“I’ve got just the one,” Jane said, “that Hannah Soper’s given me.” She opened the door to the oven, peered in. “And I can always save for another.” She closed the door.

“How do you roast a joint?” Polly asked.

“Here,” Jane said, patting the lowest hearth level. “Just open the door to expose the fire, and set yer tin kitchen right here, up close.”

“Just like a fireplace,” Polly said.

“Well, yes,” Jane said, “but a lot smaller.”

Nathaniel went through a sullen stretch, so she let him be for a few days; he usually backed away in time, but this time he stood his ground.

“I don’t want to lose that fireplace,” he said. “I’ll figure out how to get that stove set into the chimney—Joel thinks we can connect it to the oven flue, and you won’t need the old brick side oven—but I don’t want the main fireplace all closed up.”

She looked at him, surprised by his insistence.

“I want my open fire,” he complained, nearly pouty.

There’s something there, she thought, that I have not heard before.

“I can’t figure what’s bothering you so,” she said, resting her hand on his arm. “I’ve got this stove to ease my cookwork, and to keep us warmer in the winter—I got it to convenience the two of us—and it’s bothersome to you somehow.”

He turned to face her. “Makes me sad, that’s all,” he said softly. “Things are changing—aren’t they, Janey?—and it makes me a little sad.”

In the end, they drove the pins up out of the hinges and lifted the old iron oven door away from the brick facing.

Joel squeezed his head and shoulders into the oven and joggled the new stovepipe through to the back flue, backed out again.

“That’ll do,” he said to Nate, “don’t you think?”

They filled in the space around the pipe with some of the old brick left over from the main chimney, and used small batches of cement that Nate mixed in a wooden trough in the dooryard and rushed inside to the kitchen in a makeshift hod.

Joel slathered a brick, put it in place. "This sets up quick," he said, tapping on the top of it to settle it down, even it out.

"It's that new Portland cement," Nate said. "Got it at Young's." He handed Joel another brick.

"New?" Joel smeared cement on the butt ends and slipped it in atop the others. "Cement's cement, I should think."

"The stone's ground finer," Nate explained, "and it's got some lime added so it draws up the water faster—that's why it sets quick and why you have to do small mixings."

"Well," Joel said, "I never seen any set this fast before."

"That's why ye're layin' the brick and I'm just yer helper," Nate said. "I can't do it fast enough myself."

---

It took all five of them to figure out the stove.

They came on the first Monday in October, just after morning chores, after the older children were in school and Joel and Nathaniel had gone off to help Eliphalet twitch the last of the downed logs out of his west woodlot—they had two teams of oxen ready, and when Alfred arrived, they'd have his horses as well—and they'd all be gone most of the day.

Alfred drove Mary and the baby up the road in midmorning. Sunlight flickered through swaths of red and orange in the woods along the road, and when the wagon broke out into the open at the beginning of Call's lower field, the Eastern reflected yellow from the river birch along the shoreline.

Mary turned on the seat for a quick look at Victoria, tucked in her wicker basket in the wagon bed.

Our fourth child, she thought, to ride this wagon up this same road with us; the only child we have still alive.

She leaned down to snug the blanket tight against the fall chill, then turned back, slipped her arm through Alfred's—even though he was driving—and looked out again at the river.

They stopped for Lizzie and Lydia along the way, piling them and their workbags in the back of the wagon, and they all turned into the Blodgetts' drive just as Polly appeared from up the road, walking briskly, her knitting and mending in a basket on her arm.

Alfred reined in the horses, set his foot to the brake, and waited for the women to slide out of the back of the wagon. When Mary stepped to ground, he reached back, hoisted Victoria's basket up over the seat and handed her down.

"I'm off, then," he said, grinning at his wife. "Best luck to thee with that stove; I'll be back later."

He turned the horses in the dooryard and headed back down the road to the woodlot.

They gathered in the kitchen, loosened their shawls, draped them over chairbacks; they parted the blankets and admired Mary's embroidery work on the tiny new frock, fussed a little over Victoria.

"Oh, she's even more and more lovely, isn't she, Mary?" Polly said, leaning over the basket. "She has yer eyes, I think."

"Well, my eyes or Alfred's, she's certainly the strongest of them all," Mary said. "Makes us nearly breathless with hope."

———

Alfred Stilphen passed the woodlot on his return trip, drove down the road to the pass-by—there was enough room there to turn the team around with a minimum of back-and-forth, get headed north again.

The blacks would have an easier time of it, he thought, turning the wagon now without the weight of the loaded bed.

When he came back up to the woodlot, he pulled to the side, set the brake, and got to ground; he brought the reins forward, tied them loosely to a maple sapling.

"There now," he said, and ran his hands over their necks, patted them.

The others had already twitched some of the logs out; there were six twelve-foot oak logs, limbed and sawn clean on the ends, lined up parallel to the road. At first snow, they'd come back with pikes and peaveys, roll them up onto Liph's winter sled, hitch the oxen, and pull straight off into the snow-covered road, haul the whole load right up to Aaron Dudley's mill.

For now, though, getting them from the woodlot to the roadside was enough.

Alfred stood by the logs and watched the sunlight break against the trees in the woodlot, watched it sprinkle down through the red-and-yellow canopy to the forest floor. He heard sticks and twigs snapping and breaking far off in the underbrush, then heard Liph Crocker urging his oxen forward, his voice growing louder as he neared.

Alfred moved aside to make good room; the oxen pushed side by side through the saplings into the clearing near the roadside, their muscles bunched on their white-spotted shoulders, their feet raising dust that rose into the sunlight.

"*Whoa!*" Eliphalet called, and they stopped, shifted their feet to find balance. The yoke chain was taut between their heaving sides, their breath whistled through their gleaming nostrils.

"*Back now, back!*" Together, they stepped back a pace; the chain slackened, and Eliphalet unhooked the end, grinned up at Alfred.

"They all-fired determined to try that stove?" he asked.

"They are," Alfred replied, "the whole lot of 'em. I just hope they don't burn Nate's house down in the process."

Eliphalet coughed, spit to the side. "You worried about that?" he asked. "Think we oughta go back, just to be sure?"

"No, not truthfully," Alfred said. "Joel's made a good connection for that pipe, and Janey's got a good head on her."

"Better head than Nate," Liph agreed, and chuckled.

Together, they rolled the new log up against the others; they'd have to start stacking them now, three or four high, they thought—they had hook and line for it, could wrap the line around a tree and use the oxen to come it along.

"Ye're workin' with me," Liph said. "Nate and Joel have the other team—they'll be coming out as we go back in."

"That's fine," Alfred said.

"We got about twenty trees all together," Liph said, "and half the limbs to buck up, haul out here to yer wagon—the other half goes to Lizzie Call, and we'll leave them here for later."

"Are you stumping now, or later?" Alfred asked. He reached into his pocket for a rag, blew his nose.

"Later," Liph said. "I'll hire it out to Samuel over the winter—he can burn the last of the slash, too."

———

The women smoked themselves out of the house on their first try, filled the kitchen with it, shrieked and laughed; they pushed each other through the shed door to get out of the thick of it—Mary first, with Victoria in her basket—then took deep breaths and went back inside to open all the doors and windows; back out to take in clean air, back inside again. They fanned the smoke out of the house with their skirts, coughing and laughing through it all.

"We did something wrong with the vents," Mary said, leaning up against the fence rail, holding Victoria's basket; the others clustered in the dooryard, coughing, wiping their eyes.

"It was worth the trouble just to hear Lizzie," Polly said, giggling again. "She's flapping her skirts at that smoke and she's clucking—like she's shooing chickens out of the kitchen."

"Ye're teasin' me," Lizzie whined, trying to look resentful with her hands up on her hips, trying to keep her face straight, "but it worked, didn't it now?"

They were around her in a flash. They circled her and lifted their skirts, waved them at her, flapped their bent elbows like wings, bobbed their heads and scratched at the ground with their boots; together, they raised dust in the dooryard, clicking and clucking all the while, their laughter bright and clean in the October sunlight.

They cleaned out the firebox and tried again. This time, they opened all the dampers for intake, then built a smaller fire, fed it carefully with tinder and kindling. When they got a steady burn, they shifted the grates and began to test each damper, each vent; they learned to close them to cut the air supply to slow the rate of the burn, open them to increase the fire in the box.

Polly and Lizzie went outside to check the draw, to watch the smoke rise cleanly out of the chimney.

"Looks good," Polly said. "Looks like it's a steady plume."

"Do you think it's different? From a fireplace, I mean?"

Polly shrugged. "I can't see there's much difference in how it all works," she said, "but it's figuring out the timing and the heat that might prove difficult."

A breeze came up; the smoke drifted eastward, off toward the river. A few geese flew low over the valley ridge, heading south.

"Janey'll get it right," Lizzie said. "She's the brains in that outfit."

When they came back inside, the fire was burning steadily and Jane had a kettle on top of the stove.

"For tea!" she explained. "Tea for us all, for the first thing on my new stove."

Later, after she'd cooked her first meal on the stove, washed up her dishes, and wiped her table, after the children had climbed the stairs to bed, she and Nate sat in the kitchen and regarded the new stove with wonder.

"The heat's more than enough," Nate said. He got down on all fours and reached his hand beneath the stove. "It's warm underneath, too," he said, slightly awed. "Joel was right to lay a brick floor for it." He stood up, looked at his wife.

"Go test a corner," she said.

"What?"

"Go into the corner by the front hall door," she suggested. "See what it's like over there."

He did, walked across the kitchen to the farthest corner, stood there for a moment, moved his hands in the air. "It's warm over here, too," he said, "'specially up high near the ceiling."

Jane thought about that for a moment. "Nate?"

He turned around, looked at her.

"Do you suppose," she said, "that we could get some of that heat up the stairs?"

"If we open the door to the front hall," he said, "it might travel up the stairs." He opened it, stood in the doorway for a moment. "That's not good," he said. "Too much of a draft through here."

"Might we cut a hole in the ceiling, say, and let some of that heat rise up into the east bedroom for the girls?"

He closed the hall door and came back, sat down in his chair near the old hearth. "Well," he said, "I suppose we could." He crossed his legs at the knee, swung his foot a little. "We'd have to put a grate or something over the hole—just to keep the children from dropping into the kitchen—but we could get some heat up there in dead winter."

"Wouldn't want to lose it all to upstairs," she said.

"No," he agreed, "but we could cover the grate when we wanted to save the heat in the kitchen."

"We could at that," she said.

She set up a steady pace in the rocker, timed it to the swing of Nate's foot; they sat for a long while, lulled by the warmth and the rhythm.

Just think! she thought. No sparks or cinders jumping out to catch on clothing, no skirts afire; no more raking coals, no more trammels and cranes and chains; no more leaning over to lift and shift spiders and trivets while keeping yer hems out of the fire! And no more burns on yer forearms, no smell of singed hair when ye're too long near the flame.

I can grow hair back on my cheeks and arms, she thought; I've not had hair there since I was a child!

———————

Eliphalet Crocker, true to his word, offered the last of the work in the woodlot to his son Samuel; the two of them sat in the kitchen to plan it out, to come to terms.

"I got time for it," Samuel said, "especially if I hire Ben and John Thompson to work it with me a few days." He rose from the table, went into the front room for a moment, and came back with a sheet of paper and the ink bottle.

Eliphalet eyed the paper; his brows rose.

"What, exactly, do you want done?" Samuel asked him, sitting down again, shaking the ink.

Eliphalet, now fully surprised, lowered his teacup onto the saucer and looked at his son. "Exactly?" he asked.

Samuel shifted in his chair, rested his forearms on the table. "Mr. Dudley makes us teamsters get all the conditions in writing," he said, "and then we both sign the paper as a contract."

"A contract?" Liph was astounded.

"Then there are no misunderstandings," Samuel said. "We write down what's to be done, how much we'll get for pay, the time allotted—things like that." He uncorked the ink, dipped the pen; the nib clicked against the bottleneck.

"I'll have to sign a contract with my own son?"

"You will," Samuel said, not unkindly, "if you want to hire me to do the work."

He means it, Eliphalet thought. He means to have this a business arrangement between us, like one I'd make with any other man for hire. This is my son, separating himself from me.

He picked up the teapot, fiddled with the lid, taking some time to adjust to this new space between them.

"Well, let's see," he said. "There's some more limbs in there that need bucking to stove length for Lizzie Call; some of them might need to be split—say, any over five inches in diameter. I don't think young Charlie is up to that task quite yet—he's just turned twelve."

"Bucked up, split," Samuel said, writing on the paper.

"And the wood needs hauling down to her place," Eliphalet added, pouring them each more tea.

"Stacked, too?" Samuel asked, pausing in his writing, holding the pen over the paper.

By the Jesus, Eliphalet thought, when this is over, I'll be having some choice words with Aaron Dudley.

"Pa?" Samuel prompted. "Stacked, too?"

"No, I think Charlie can do that part on his own."

"All right." The nib scratched across the paper.

---

*Made between Samuel Crocker, Teamster, and Eliphalet Crocker, Landowner, both of Pittston, Maine, a contract for work done by said Samuel Crocker for said Eliphalet Crocker.*

*Eliphalet Crocker agrees to pay the sum of one doler per day for each man working and one more doler per day for use of oxen to Samuel Crocker for work in E. Crocker's west woodlotte as follows:*
> *Haul stacked logs cut Oct. last to Dudley's Mill*
> *Buck lims to stove lenth and split big ones*
> *Haul to Mrs. Call*
> *Pull small stumps by ox and chane*
> *Burn slash and watch over said burning*
> *Set big stumps to smoulder and watch over said smoulder*

*Samuel Crocker will note all work and labor hired daily.*

*Both parties agree that work should be finished by December 31, 1843.*

*Pay for this work for hire shall be made when work is finished according to the terms of this contract and working notes presented to E. Crocker.*

*Signed this day the 15th of December 1843*

---

Samuel and the Thompson brothers dug out around all the stumps using picks and shovels, cleared the dirt from between the roots, then set hot coals and tinder in the spaces they'd created. The fires caught, and the stumps burned steadily for the first day, then smoldered for the next three.

They kept watch on them while they worked the rest of the contract. They pulled smaller stumps with ox and chain—sometimes three or four feet of twisted root pulled up, too—Prince and King held still, held the chain taut while Samuel and John and Ben axed and sawed the stumps free. They trimmed out the last of the downed limbs and bucked them into stove lengths for Lizzie Call.

Polly Thompson packed them a dinner every day; Sarah Ann delivered it at midday, dropped a basket at the side of the road and then disappeared into the nearby woods, flitted about the edge of the clearing, droning.

The boys sat on the wagon tailgate and opened the folded cloth lining the basket, found thick slabs of bread spread with butter and jam; they rummaged beneath the bread and found apples, too, and some mincemeat pies.

"I'd take a meat pie," Benjamin said, holding out his hand, and John gave him one, took another for himself.

Samuel hitched himself back, pulled his legs up onto the wagon bed, leaned against the sideboard. "You still walking out with Liz Folsom?" he asked, nudging Ben with his boot.

Ben nodded, his mouth full of pie. He swallowed. "We're thinking to marry, but I've not mentioned it to Pa or Polly yet—no need to get them all perked up until we make firm plans."

"Well, they'll find out soon enough," Samuel said, "when you file intentions."

There was a rustling in the woods, then a low drone, a soft *nnnnh* from the underbrush.

"She's probably hungry," John said, and reached for a meat pie.

Ben slid down off the back of the wagon. "Give it here," he said. "I'll take it to her." He held the pie in his hand, moved off across the stumped lot to the tree line.

"Why's she always humming like that?" Samuel asked, and John Thompson turned his head, listened to his sister for a moment.

"We don't know," he said. "It don't make sense to any of us."

A few crows passed overhead, calling, heading out across the road to Crocker's wheat field, down toward the river; smoke from the stump fires drifted across the lot, moved gently over their backs and shoulders and up into the gray sky.

"I sometimes wonder what's in her head," Samuel said, then turned back to his food, took a bite and chewed.

"Not much, I'd guess," John said. "She's just simple, that's all."

---

Late March, and the morning light came earlier each day, broke soft and gray over the top of the valley ridge and spread slowly across Alfred Stilphen's lower fields. The Eastern, swollen with ice and spring snow-melt, spilled over on each incoming tide; flocks of geese, northbound, rested on the bankings morning and night, their black heads and necks stark against the last of the snow.

Alfred heard them stir as he headed back to the house after first chores, heard them murmuring, shifting; he turned just as they lifted up into the wind; he watched them swing, veer northward, honking, heaving, thinning out into formation as they started up the Eastern.

Almost time to run the scow, he thought.

"Large flock of geese this morning," he said, shutting the kitchen door behind him.

"I heard them," she said. "How many does thee think?"

He hung his coat on the peg, combed his hands through his hair. "Hundred, at least," he said.

He pulled back his chair, sat down, picked up his book, and waited for Mary to set his tea on the table—it was his custom to read aloud as she bustled about the kitchen, did the dishes and her morning baking. "Where are we now?" he asked, opening the book.

"At the tournament at Ashby," she said, "where Ivanhoe's revealed himself and the Sable Knight has vanished!"

"That's right," he said, turning the pages, looking for his place. "That's right; and Rowena's bestowed the chaplet on Ivanhoe, gravely wounded."

Mary poured herself some tea, sat at the table. "I'll sit for a moment," she said. "I just want to have a sense of where the story's going first."

"All right," he said. He found the page, cleared his throat.

Mary took a sip of tea, waited.

"Chapter Thirteen," Alfred began, and settled back in his chair.

I do love the sound of Alfred reading aloud, she thought, reaching for her yellowware bowl.

She measured out the flour, then mixed the butter in with her fingers, added a bit of water and a dash of salt, then mixed some more, pinching and releasing the dough until it felt right to her. She rolled half of it out on the kitchen table, then punched out two dozen crackers with a tin cutter, slid them into the oven.

There, she thought, spread with some jam or honey, fine enough to go with our tea at Polly's today, and Victoria can gnaw against one or two just plain, help with her teething.

"How long does thee need?" Alfred asked, as he closed the book and pushed his chair back from the table, stood to go out to the sheds, see to the sheep.

"I can bake two batches in an hour," she said. "One batch to take with me up to Polly's, one to stay here for us."

"That's fine," he said. "I'll check on those lambs—maybe turn 'em into the pens—finish chores and harness up." He took his spring coat from the peg, shoved his arms into the sleeves. "We carrying Lizzie?"

"We are, and Lydia, too."

"All right," he said. "I can take that scythe up to Liph for a new handle, leave it off when we stop by for Lyd."

He hitched his coat up, stuffed his mittens into his pockets, and went out the kitchen door to the woodshed, out the shed door to the outside.

Mary stood by the window and watched him cross the dooryard, watched him step carefully around leftover patches of spring snow and ice, look up occasionally to check for more geese.

She turned back to Victoria, lifted her, rubbed her nose against her soft cheeks, nuzzled her neck; the baby grinned, kicked her heels. "Good thing he'd not yet read *Ivanhoe* when thee was born," she whispered, "or thee'd be a Rowena for certain."

———

"Goodness, Polly," Lydia Crocker said, finishing off a patch over the hole in her old apron. "How many stockings have you to mend?" She knotted her threads, then raised the apron to her mouth, bit off the ends, spit them gently to the side.

"Near all I've got in the house," Polly answered, slipping the darning egg into another heel. "The boys just wear through them one after the other." She rounded the heel over the smooth wood, snugged the handle in her left hand. "They should be more like Sarah Ann." She worked her needle near the edge of the hole.

"Whatever are you talking, more like Sarah Ann?"

"She goes in her boots with bare feet," Polly said. "She never gives me a bit of darning to do."

They all laughed at that, just a little, but then grew quiet.

They always do, Polly thought; they all grow quiet whenever I speak of Sarah Ann. They are all grateful for their untroubled daughters who are, one by one—as they are destined to do—finding husbands and moving off and away to Waldoboro and Gardiner, Portland, Dresden— while I am left coping as best I can with a straggle-haired, half-witted, half-wild...

The logs shifted in the grate; Lydia reached out, brushed her fingers across the back of Polly's hand.

"Got another egg?" she asked. "I'm done with this skirt—I'll help on those darns."

"I do," Polly said, reaching into her workbag, "but it's a china one— no handle to it."

"That's fine," Lydia said, reaching out for it. "I'm used to darning with a china egg."

"Alfred's mother gave me one of stone," Mary said. "Sharpens the needle as you do yer work."

"That's clever, I'd say."

"I've got this little cushion filled with sand," Jane offered. "Both pins and needles sharpen when I stick them in; I store them there—they don't rust out, either."

"I should get one of those," Lizzie said. "Mine are in a leather case, but if I don't wipe them down, they turn." She bit her thread, stuck her needle into her sleeve for safekeeping, then held the shirt she was mending out before her, gave it a shake.

"There," she said. "Finished my mending." She folded the shirt, tucked it into her workbasket. "I might need some of Mary's crackers, though," she said, "before I start on pieces for my new quilt."

"Crackers with jam," Jane said. "We need our strength, after all."

"I'll start a pot to brewing," Polly said, standing, "and get cups."

"A new quilt, Lizzie?" Mary asked, gathering scraps and bits of thread from the table, making space for the spread of their tea.

"I thought to make a new one," she said. "I've got some of the squares sewn already. I'd like to have some from each of you, though—a combined effort for the whole piece."

"I've got some muslin with me," Jane said, "and a spare patch of calico; I daresay I could make two or three."

"And I've got some striped blue right here in my bag," Lydia said, "and ye're welcome to it, but why a quilt now that it's coming up spring?"

Lizzie paused, just a moment. "It's always good to start a marriage under a new quilt," she said, fiddling with her apron pockets, "and Tom Mitchell asked me yesterday."

———

*Pittston Town Meeting*
*East Parish*
*March 30, 1846*

*Births in the Town of Pittston, Registered & Recorded by me,*
*Jonathan Soper, Town Clerk*
   *Augustus, son of Alfred & Mary Call Stilphen, born*
*December 4, 1845*

*Marriages in the Town of Pittston, Registered & Recorded by*
*me, Jonathan Soper, Town Clerk*

*Mr. William Pottle of Whitefield & Miss Elizabeth Crocker of Pittston, April 14, 1844*

*Mr. Thomas A. Mitchell & Mrs. Elizabeth Call, both of Pittston, April 30, 1844*

*Mr. Moses Pottle of Whitefield & Miss Mary Crocker of Pittston, November 15, 1845*

# Chapter Fourteen

"...some suitable provision" for the relief of the insane, "either by aiding in the endowment of a lunatic hospital or making an appropriation in aid of those who may seek the benefit of such institutions..."

Robert P. Dunlap in
*The History of Augusta*

IT RAINED ALL DAY Thursday and well into the night, but Friday morning broke clear and clean, with a cloudless sky and a fine bright sun. In the forenoon, a light breeze moved up the slope from the river, and by dinner time, the grass in the upper meadows had dried and lifted.

"Still too wet to haul manure after that rain," Eliphalet Crocker said, settling into his chair, reaching for a biscuit, "but it least it's all shoveled; I'll get the boys to spread it tomorrow or the next—should be dry enough by then."

Lydia set the honeypot on the table, moved to fetch him a spoon from the drawer. "What's yer plans for the afternoon, then?" she asked.

He reached for his tea. "I'm going down to Alfred's—told him I'd help him fix that line of fence where his sheep keep breaking through."

"What about the boys?"

He chewed, swallowed. "Llewellyn and Ben's already down there, working for hire on Alfred's new shed; Samuel's over to Dudley's Mill— he's set to ask Caroline Dudley to the social at the Methodist."

Lydia dropped into her chair. "He's got his eye on her."

"I know it," Liph said. "Has for a long while; I told him it was about time he acted on it." He mopped up the honey from his plate with the last piece of biscuit, leaned back, set his elbows on the armrests.

Lydia finished her tea, stood, gathered their plates.

He turned his head to watch her at her work. "What's yer plans?" he asked. "Tend to the garden?"

She lowered the dishes into the pan, moved over to the window.

"Time for me to go berrying," she said, looking out over the dooryard, wiping her hands. "There'll be those wild strawberries along the wall in the upper meadow; I'll pick some—if I can beat the crows to 'em—make a berry pie for supper."

She turned away from the window, looked at Eliphalet, sipping his second cup of tea. "Or tarts," she added. "I can't decide which."

"Tarts," he said, grinning, eyeing her up and down as she walked by his chair. "I do like a good tart."

She swatted at him with the towel. "Get off with you," she said, laughing.

She walked down the drive and headed up the ridge, the spring sun warm against her back and shoulders, her basket loose on her arm. The breeze tossed her skirts against her legs as she made her way along the road; she turned her head and watched the ripple and rise of the English grass in the meadow.

This is, she thought, the first summer in twenty years I have gone berrying without one or two or all of my girls; my girls as babies and then young girls, two now grown and married—to brothers, no less— and gone.

Happens just as fast as that, it seems, just as fast as that.

She heard a crow call out, a sharp warning from a lookout in one of the trees in Blodgett's woodlot; she gazed back up the road and saw twenty more lift up out of the berry patch and head out over the upper meadow, heard them croak and caw.

She saw, too, what had startled them—a lone figure approaching, bobbing and loping down the high center of the roadbed, head down, skirts lifted just a bit.

Sarah Ann Thompson.

Lydia stood still, held her berry basket in both hands and listened to the quiet, rhythmic thud of Sarah Ann's boots in the roadway as she came closer. As the girl neared, Lydia heard the soft drone; she stepped across the wheel rut to the ditch side to give ample space and free passage.

"Afternoon, Sarah Ann," she said.

Sarah Ann skidded to a full halt. She breathed hard, fingered at her skirts.

"I'm on my way to the berry patch," Lydia said, "and you've saved me considerable trouble by scaring off those crows, provided more berries for me, too; I thank you for that."

Sarah Ann dipped her head, then leaned forward at the waist and started right off again, trotting after the forward tilt of her own head. Lydia watched the curve of her back as she made her way down the road, her neck tipped so low she looked headless.

My daughters grown and gone, Lydia thought, keeping her eye on Sarah Ann; Polly and Joel with this one never grown, never gone.

I do not know which is the worse.

Later, after she'd filled her basket nearly full of the small, ripe berries, Lydia Crocker clambered over the wall and across the ditch into the high center of the roadbed. She turned south.

The grass swished against her hems.

She heard warblers in Blodgett's woodlot, heard the crows start up again as she moved out of their territory, heard them call out to each other, gleeful at her departure. She turned her head and looked back up the road, caught sight of a few heading back into the berry patch to feed on her leavings, their bodies stark black against the blue sky.

Tarts, she decided, as she stepped up from the granite slab into the shed, tarts for Eliphalet if I've enough flour left—otherwise an open berry pie—but he prefers tarts to pies, so I'll do tarts.

The door into the kitchen was ajar; she passed through, set her basket on the kitchen table.

All right, then; slice the berries, set them with a bit of loaf sugar to pull the juices, cover with a cloth to keep the flies away.

She was lifting this morning's apron from the peg, thinking of which knife would be best for the small work of slicing those berries, when she heard movement in the back room, a shift, a shuffle across the floor. She turned around, pulled her breath in surprise.

"Goodness!" she said, her hand moving up to her throat. "You gave me such a start, Sarah Ann."

The girl stood just beyond the open door to the back room, far enough into the chamber to be in partial shadow.

"Come on out here," Lydia said gently, "and have a berry or two—I picked quite a basketful, have plenty to share."

Sarah Ann took a few steps into the kitchen, kept her arms at her sides, kept her face turned away from Lydia and her eyes fixed on the shed door, to the outside.

"Hold out yer hand, girl," Lydia said, "and I'll put some berries in yer palm; you can feast on them on yer way back home."

Sarah Ann, her face still averted, held out one flat palm.

"We'll make a little cup from yer hand," Lydia said, slowly curling the fingers, moving the thumb a bit; she then put six or seven berries into the curve of Sarah Ann's palm.

"All right?" Lydia said.

Sarah Ann nodded.

"That's good; off to home with you now."

Lydia watched from the shed door as Sarah Ann Thompson made her way slowly down the drive, holding her hand out before her, balancing the berries within the curve of her palm. At the road, though, she stood for a moment in the afternoon sunlight, then lifted her hand and pushed all the berries into her mouth at once; she stood still, chewed and swallowed, then wiped her hand first across her face, then on the front of her skirt. She lifted her hems a bit, tipped her head, and started loping homeward.

Lydia leaned against the doorway, watched until Sarah Ann was out of sight.

I'll go up to Joel and Polly later, she thought. They need to know.

———————

Joel Thompson thought about it during morning chores on Friday. He mulled it over and over as he slopped the pigs, grained the livestock, turned the horses out into the field and the oxen into the side yard. He fought with it as he forked manure out of the stalls and spread new straw for bedding.

And he thought about it while he milked the cows, starting with Flossie, then moving steadily down the line of them as they stood quietly, waiting for him to come by.

All the while, Sarah Ann trotted around the perimeter of the barn. He could hear her droning; when she passed by the doorway to the cattle yard, he had a flash of color—a blink of blue skirt—as she loped past then disappeared around the southwest corner of the barn, making yet another round.

He moved from Flossie to Bessie.

Thirty-four years old, he thought. Sarah Ann is thirty-four years old and hasn't spoken a word; she runs counterclock around the barn whenever I am within it; she trots through the woods cradling dead rabbits that she sometimes remembers to bring back to the kitchen before they turn; she spends time under our coop, clucking and cooing at our chickens, droning.

He moved again—from Bessie to Birdie—and sat on the stool, leaned his head against her side, pulled steadily at her teats. The hot milk hissed against the side of the pail with each tug; the thick sweetness of it rose up into his nostrils.

Birdie to Sadie.

Worse yet, he thought, she appears in the neighbors' yards and barns, seems to melt out of the woodlots into their dooryards like smoke— wispy, vapory; slips all of a sudden into their houses, into their kitchens and parlors, even their bedchambers, according to Lydia.

He knew something had to be done.

He stripped the last of the milk from Sadie's teats, then slid his palm up and down the length of her flank.

"Good girl," he said softly, to let her know he was finished.

Sadie tossed her weight from side to side in the stall, eager now for the outside, so he turned her out into the yard with the others.

He called out to her as she passed by the open door.

"Sarah Ann?"

She stopped, turned to face him; her blue skirt, grimy at the hem, swayed, skimmed the ground. She suddenly looked so much like her mother—like Martha when she was young, whole, lovely—that his breath caught inside his chest.

He sucked air in between his teeth, remembered to smile at her, to keep his voice gentle. "Would thee take the cows up to the high meadow for me?" he asked. "Take their calves, too?"

She nodded, bunched the cows together and prodded them across the side yard, the calves following their mothers, obedient and trustful.

He stood in the doorway and watched the morning light halo around Sarah Ann's hair, soften the sharp shadows across her shoulders.

Polly heard him scrape his boots at the back step then whack his feet against the granite for good measure, heard him cross the shed floor. When he opened the kitchen door, the light from the window splashed across his face and hair.

He's coming on gray, she thought; I can see it in the turn of the light.

He handed her the milk bucket and sat heavily at the table. "Something has to be done, Polly," he said.

She knew him well enough to wait a bit, let him sort out what he wanted to say, so she took the pail and turned to the table, poured the warm milk carefully through the loose weave of the straining cloth into the pitcher; bits of chaff and dirt settled into the muslin.

She opened the trap and went down the steps into the chill of the cellar, switched today's pitcher for yesterday's—yesterday's milking separated now to milk on the bottom, thick cream on the top—and climbed back up into the kitchen.

"Something," he said. "I don't know what, but something."

Polly dipped the cream from the top of the pitcher into the churn, then sat in the rocker and thumped the lid down on the barrel, reached for the dasher.

"About Sarah Ann," he said quietly.

"Sometimes," Polly confessed, "I sense she tries to keep me from you—afraid I'll take you away, somehow." She worked the dasher up and down; the cream splashed inside the churn; she imagined it turning over and over itself within.

"Take me away?" he questioned. "Ye're not planning to take me away." He tapped the tips of his fingers together, then lifted his head, looked at Polly. "Shouldn't she know that by now?"

Polly shrugged. "All she knows," she said, "is loss." She stopped churning and shifted in the rocker, drew the barrel closer to her knees, started up again. "First she lost her ma—and we know she's not ever got over that."

Joel nodded.

"And Abby's gone to Gardiner, in service and home only once a fortnight."

"That's another loss to her, that's right," he admitted.

"And Benjamin's married and moved off—he's only four miles away, but he might be a thousand miles away for all the difference it makes to her." She kept the rhythm with the dasher. "And John's gone to New-castle to work the shipyards."

"All that's true enough," he said, fiddling with his teacup, moving it in small circles on the tabletop.

"That's her whole family," Polly added. "Except for you, and I think she fears losing you as well."

They were quiet for a moment. Outside, the breeze lifted the leaves on the maples, billowed the washing Polly'd draped over the side fence rail to dry; Joel thought he heard Blodgett's dog barking across the road, somewhere down near the river.

"But she's still got Junior and Laura," he said. "They're her family, too."

The cream *whish-whished* inside the churn.

Polly shook her head. "No," she said. "That's not quite right."

He tipped his head, looked at her.

"Junior and Laura are yers and mine, not yers and her ma's—they're not hers in the same way."

She was right, and he knew it.

He leaned forward in his chair, watched the sunlight fall through the window onto the kitchen floorboards; the shadows of leaves from the maple in the side yard flickered across his trousers, his boots.

"What do we do, Pol?" he asked. "Should we send her away?"

"What, send her to the poor farm?" she answered. "I can't see that they can do for her any better there than us keeping her to home."

"What about the hospital, then?" he asked. "Up to Augusta."

"The Insane Hospital?"

"Yes."

She let go the dasher, pushed some loose hair back from her face, then dropped her hands to her lap, twisted them together, and turned her face to him.

"No," she said, her voice no more than a whisper. "I've heard dreadful words about that place."

He raised his eyes, looked at her.

"From Harriet Davenport," she said.

"Charles Davenport's wife?" he asked. "From King's Mills?"

Polly nodded. "They were thinking to put Judith there, so went to see the place, talk with the overseers there."

"And…?" he prompted.

"And Harriet said it was frightful—full of screechers and jibberers," she said, her voice rising. "She said there was madness there—true madness—tortured souls who rip their clothes to tatters and smear the walls with their own…"

She looked around the room, fumbled for the right word.

"…shit!" she said.

He pulled his head back sharply, as if he'd been slapped; he stared at her for a long moment.

"Forgive me," she said. She reached for the dasher and started up again; the sound thickened, dulled inside the churn.

"They'll lock her up, Joel," she said softly. "They'll lock her up, and that would be more loss than she—or we—could stand."

---

When Alfred Stilphen came in from evening chores, she was in the kitchen rocker, dozing, her shawl wrapped about her shoulders; the balled fringe swaying back and forth as she rocked.

Like little bells, he thought, tiny church bells, ringing changes.

"Mary?" He pulled his chair away from the table, sat down and leaned forward, rested his hand on her knee.

She opened her eyes, looked at him.

"Is thee all right?" he asked. He cupped his palm around her knee-cap, squeezed gently.

"I am," she said. "I'm quite all right, indeed; just a little tired this evening, that's all."

"I'm glad for just that," he said, and let go her knee, leaned back in his chair. "Children abed?"

She nodded. "I've kept supper for thee in the warming oven," she said, and started to rise.

He put his hand out. "I'll get it myself," he said. "Stay right there."

He ate his meat and potatoes at the table. Between mouthfuls he told her of the ewes he'd confined in the sheds, all showing signs of lambing soon.

"Six blackface," he said. "They're due; I may sleep out there tonight."

"What about the merino?" she asked. "Are they ready, too?"

He shook his head. "Not yet; another week or so, I think." He scraped the bottom of the bowl, lifted the spoon. "I'm thinking to hire Jimmy Goud for the rest of lambing season—Tom Mitchell told me he's lookin' for work, and I could use the help."

"They're on hard times," she said, "the Gouds."

"His sister's looking, too; I thought thee might like some help keeping house."

"Sarah Goud?" Mary crossed her legs, started rocking again. "She's but sixteen."

"Old enough to work, I'd guess." He stood. "Want some tea while I read? We've got a book to start."

"Yes, that would be good," she said. "What's the book?"

"The one by Currer Bell," he said. "The one some think might be a woman—not a man."

"*Jane Eyre?*" Mary asked.

"Yes, that's it," he said. "She could live in."

"What?"

"Sarah Goud—she could live in," he said, scooping tea from the bright blue tin into the pot. "In the little room behind the stairs." He lifted the kettle from the stove, poured the water, covered the pot to steep while he collected cups and saucers.

Help in the house, Mary thought. Never in all my life could I think to have hired help to keep my own house, not ever; I am less tired by the mere thought of it!

"Can we afford wages for help?" she asked. "Have we the money for that?"

He set the cups on the table, turned to her. "We have," he said. "We've got the money, we both need the help—now that our respective flocks are growing—and I can't think of a reason not to hire the Gouds."

―――――――

Joel and Junior Thompson each had a bucket of warm oat mash with which to tempt the pigs out of their pen. They leaned down, put the pails at snout level and started backwards; the pigs caught the scent and followed happily, grunting, twitching their tails.

"Don't feed yet," said Joel. "Wait until we get to the orchard."

They led the pigs around the back of the barn and into the edge of the orchard, over to a pile of falls—Pippins, mostly, with a few Greenings as well—and held the buckets for them there, allowed them to feed.

When they were through, Joel nudged some falls over to them with his foot; a few sniffs, a couple of trials, and they were off, snuffling around the trees, munching up the damaged fruit.

Sweet meat, he thought; those apples make sweet meat for us.

"Pa, I need a word," Junior said.

"All right," Joel said. He watched the pigs for a moment, smiled, then turned to his son. "What's on yer mind?"

Junior stood there, holding his empty mash bucket; he bumped it gently against his thigh once or twice, looked off through the trees to the road, then back to his father.

"What's yer trouble?" Joel said, a bit impatiently; there was work to do, after all.

"I've been with Janie Crocker," Junior said.

The pigs snorted in the grass, crunched the old fruit; Joel watched apple juice drip from their mouths, shine on their chins, then turned back to his son.

"Been with?" he said. "Meaning what, exactly?"

His son shrugged, looked away.

Joel lifted his head, took a breath. "Ye're saying there's been some foolin' with Janie Crocker?" he said, disbelief pushing his voice a shade high.

Junior nodded.

Joel stared at his son. "Janie Crocker's just turned fourteen years old," he said, slowly. "And ye're a grown man."

Another nod.

"She's a neighbor's child!" Joel said, pushing the words between his clenched teeth. "Ye're rutting at a good neighbor's child."

"She says she's carrying," Junior said, and squared his shoulders.

Joel Thompson lifted his arm, spun on his heel and backhanded his son across the jaw, then threw the mash bucket against the back side of the barn. It held—cracked, but held—and bounced back into the grass.

The pigs, startled, squealed, then trotted a few yards away, their snouts smeared, mouths dripping with sweet falls.

*Pittston Town Meeting*
*East Parish*
*November 29, 1849*

*To see if the Town Selectmen will order the purchase of two hearses, one for the East Parish one for the West Parish and find suitable storage place for each…*

*Marriages in the Town of Pittston, Registered & Recorded by me, Alphonso H. Clark,, Town Clerk*
    *Mr. Samuel Crocker & Miss Caroline Dudley, both of Pittston, May 30, 1847*
    *Miss Mary Call of Pittston and Mr. David W. Houghton of Watertown, Massachusetts, December 19, 1847*
    *Mr. Benjamin Thompson & Miss Elizabeth Folsom, both of Pittston, June 22, 1848*
    *Mr. John Thompson of Pittston & Miss Lucinda Peaslee of Newcastle, July 20, 1848*

*Births in the Town of Pittston, Registered & Recorded by me, Alphonso H. Clark, Town Clerk*
    *George E., son of Samuel Crocker & Wife Caroline, March 15, 1848*
    *Cyrus, son of Jane A. Crocker & Joel Thompson, Jr., July 7, 1849*
    *Alfred Livingston Stilphen, son of Alfred Stilphen & Wife Mary, November 25, 1849*

---

1850 Census
Town of Pittston, Kennebec County, Maine

| | |
|---|---|
| Thompson, Joel | 58 |
| Mary | 47 |
| Sarah Ann | 37 |
| Abigail | 27 |
| Joel | 22 |
| Laura | 18 |

50 acres improved, 15 unimproved; $400 cash value of farm
1 horse, 4 milch cows, 2 working oxen, 6 other cattle
10 sheep, $250 value of live stock
30 bushels corn, 50 oats, 10 Irish potatoes
275 lbs butter, 30 lbs wool, 25 tons hay

| Blodgett, Nathaniel | 56 |
|---|---|
| Jane | 54 |
| Daniel | 25 |
| Eliza | 23 |
| John | 17 |

30 acres improved, 40 unimproved; $400 cash value of farm
1 horse, 2 milch cows, 2 working oxen, 2 other cattle
11 sheep, $140 value of live stock
15 bushels corn, 12 oats, 4 pease & beans
150 lbs butter, 25 lbs cheese, 30 lbs wool, 18 tons hay

| Crocker, Eliphalet | 60 |
|---|---|
| Lydia | 58 |
| Isaac | 23 |
| Leander | 20 |
| Llewellyn | 16 |
| Benjamin | 13 |
| Crocker, Jane A. | 15 |
| Thompson, Cyrus | 1 |

| Crocker, Samuel | 27 |
|---|---|
| Caroline | 26 |
| George | 2 |

50 acres improved, 25 unimproved, $700 cash value of farm
1 horse, 2 milch cows, 6 working oxen, 2 other cattle
2 swine, $155 value of live stock
45 bushels corn, 50 oats, 5 pease & beans
40 lbs butter, 20 tons hay

| Mitchell, Thomas | 55 |
|---|---|
| Elizabeth | 48 |
| Thomas A | 16 |
| Mercy N. | 14 |
| Call, Charles M | 18 |
| Call, Susan K. | 14 |

40 acres improved, 40 unimproved, $700 cash value of farm
1 horse, 3 milch cows, 6 other cattle
10 sheep, 1 swine, $115 value of live stock
30 bushels corn, 15 oats, 5 pease & beans
200 lbs butter, 32 lbs wool, 20 tons hay

| Stilphen, Alfred | 47 |
|---|---|
| Mary | 40 |
| Victoria A. | 7 |
| Augustus M | 4 |
| Alfred L | 1 |
| Goud, Sarah | 16 |

55 acres improved, 75 unimproved, $1000 cash value of farm
2 horses, 6 milch cows, 2 working oxen, 6 other cattle
20 sheep, 1 swine, $280 value of live stock
75 bushels corn, 99 oats, 50 potatoes, 16 barley, 7 buckwheat
350 lbs butter, 55 lbs wool, 55 tons hay

# PART IV

# 1851–1860

# Chapter Fifteen

WINTER.—Cold winter has come at last, admonishing all to prepare for the merciless attacks of Jack Frost.

*Cold Water Fountain*
Gardiner, Maine
December 20, 1851

THE COLD was brutal. Temperatures stayed well below zero for a full week. The trees in the woodlots squealed in the stiff winds; at night, their brittle branches groaned, then snapped, crashed through the underbrush to the ground below.

And then, when the winds died down and the temperature finally eased, a broad band of gray pushed in from the northeast, moving slowly over the valley ridge from King's Mills. It started to snow at suppertime; it snowed all that night, through the next day, and into the night again.

It snowed for three days.

The farmers along the Eastern wrapped their heads and faces in wool scarves; they tied lengths of rope from their sheds to their barns, gripped the ropes to guide them across their dooryards for morning and evening chores.

Children shorter than the height of the snowdrifts were not allowed outside for fear of being lost in the swirl.

In the dark morning, Alfred Stilphen lay in bed and listened to the snap and crack of the river ice splitting with the rise of the incoming tide. It sounded to him like rifle fire—sharp, singular shots that spread across the width of the Eastern River Valley, echoed over and over between the ridges.

He shivered, then turned on his side, spooned up to Mary's warm backside and waited for first light, his arm draped across her hip, his palm curved against her belly.

Another son would please me, he thought.

———

In mid-March, when the temperatures began to rise and snow-melt dripped steadily from the eaves, Alfred stood on his shed steps and looked down his sloping fields to the Eastern. Each day, he watched the strip of open water widen as pieces of ice broke away from the larger floes, moved downriver; finally, on the second day of April, the very last of it slid from the bankings and drifted away on the outgoing tide.

He turned, walked across the shed and opened the kitchen door.

"Mary?" he called.

Sarah Goud turned from the dry sink, porridge bowls in her hands. "She's in the back," she told him. "I'll fetch her for you."

Mary came from the back bedroom—must have been dressing the children, he thought—and smiled at him.

"Ice is out!" he said to her.

She clapped her hands together. "None too soon," she said, "for I'm short on patience."

"Me, too," he agreed. "Anyway, I'm off to Call's, but I'll be back by dinner."

"All right," Mary said. "That's good timing; could thee lift the rugs then?"

He groaned, and she grinned at him. "I know, I know," she said, "but they need beating, and Sarah and I don't have the strength."

"I'll put them over the front fence rail," he said, "and let her have at 'em."

He thought about taking one of the horses, but the notion of walking felt right; he needed to stretch his legs, and it was only a half mile.

He walked for a bit between his own upper meadows, then slipped into the shade for the short stretch of woods on either side of Otter

Creek. It was chilly; there were patches of snow still on the northern sides of the larger trees, and Mary's fiddleheads not yet poking up on that south-facing pitch just across the plank bridge.

Not at all ready now, he thought, but soon enough.

And then he was out of the woods and into the spread of Call's fields. The wind came brisk off the Eastern, pushed up the slope and whipped at his hair. He wished he'd thought to wear a scarf and mittens; he turned his collar up and shoved his hands into his pockets, but by the time he got to the house, he was chilled through.

He went up the drive, paused to scrape his boots on the back step, then went in through the shed, knocked at the kitchen door.

He heard a chair scuff across the floorboards, then Lizzie appeared.

"Morning, Alfred," she said. "If ye're lookin' for Tom, he's out in the barn."

"No," he said. "It's yer Charlie I came to see."

"It's Charlie ye're after?" She seemed surprised. "Well, we're at table still," she said, "but ye're welcome to come in for a biscuit and some coffee—you like coffee, don't you?"

"I've never tasted it," he admitted, "but I'd not mind a try if there's some to spare."

She opened the door wide, and he went in.


"When are you planning to make the first run to Dresden?" Alfred asked, looking across the table at Charlie Call. "It's pretty near time, and the scow's still in the boathouse, isn't it?"

"Me?" Charlie asked. "You've run it every year since Pa died—you and Mr. Thompson, or Mr. Crocker."

"I'm just suggesting," Alfred added.

"Suggesting?" Charlie asked, baffled. He folded his arms on top of the table, looked across at Alfred.

Alfred smiled at him. "It's yer scow," he explained. "Yer father left it for you; I'm suggesting that ye're old enough now to take over."

Charlie sat for a moment, silenced by the thought; the fire shifted in the grates, settled.

Alfred waited.

Charlie cleared his throat, cleared it again. Then he stood up and went to the stove, wrapped his hand in a cloth and reached for the steaming coffeepot.

"More coffee?" he asked, suddenly host now to his father's old friend, Alfred Stilphen. "You're welcome to more, if you like it."

Alfred nodded. "I do like it," he said, "but I think I like it better with the cream in it than plain—it tastes a little harsh to me when it's plain."

Charlie poured more into their cups; he set the pot back on the stove, came back to the table.

"About the scow," he said, pushing the little cream pitcher closer to Alfred's elbow. "I'm a bit fidgety about it—do you think I can do it?"

"Sure you can," Alfred said. He poured cream into his coffee, examined it closely for color, added more and stirred. "I was thinking that you might need a hired hand for yer first few runs, and I've come up to ask for the job."

"He talks like a book," Charlie said.

Lizzie laughed.

"Don't laugh, Ma!" Charlie said. "I mean it—I don't understand him at all sometimes."

"I'm not laughing at you," she said, patting his arm. "We all feel that way, but we're used to it after all these years." She went around the end of the table, sat down. "It's just that he reads all those books—out loud, no less, to Mary and the children—it's no wonder he talks like one."

"Well, he does, for sure."

She smiled at her son. "What was his point, anyway?"

"He thinks I should run the scow" Charlie said. "Says it's mine—from Pa—and that I should take it over."

"I think he's right," she said, and rose from her chair.

———

Two days later, they opened the boathouse doors to the sunlight.

Samuel Crocker came down at low tide. He spent a good thirty minutes rigging rope and chain—checking the angles, the tension—then hitched Prince and King and hauled the scow straight out of the boathouse. The oxen dragged it down to the banking, their feet sucking in and out of the soft mud; Samuel shortened the chain and drove them far enough into the river to leave the scow on the edge of the waterline, released the chain, and turned them back, led them up the banking to dry land.

"That'll do it just fine," he said, and pocketed the coin that Charlie Call handed him.

When the tide changed at noontime, the scow started to shift on the rising water; it was afloat by midafternoon, moored to the pilings at Call's wharf by darkfall.

"We've got some ready work to do," Alfred said. "Check for gaps in the seams below decks, go over the cordage for fraying, test poles—things like that."

They found a few gaps on the inside hull; Alfred showed Charlie how to push fresh caulking between the boards with his fingers, then hammer it in tight with a wooden mallet.

"That'll set?" Charlie asked. "It'll set even as it's in the water?"

"It will," Alfred said. "Thompson and I caulked the outside last fall when we hauled it into the boathouse—it's just extra protection for us to plug the inside for good measure."

They uncoiled the lines, looked for fraying and kinking in the ropes, then recoiled; finally tested the poles.

"Don't want a pole to snap when we're running that fast section," Alfred said. "We'll be overboard for certain."

"You think these are all right?" Charlie asked, hefting a pole in each hand.

"I'd say they are, but try 'em against the bottom for sure."

Charlie put them over the side of the scow, pushed hard against the bottom. "Good and firm," he said.

"All right."

They stood for a moment, feeling the scow shift beneath their feet, feeling the breeze against their cheeks and chins. The water lapped against the hull, gently, gently.

"When should I make the first run?" Charlie asked.

"Well," Alfred said, "everybody needs a few days' notice, and the tides need to be right." He turned to Charlie. "When's the next early-morning low water?"

"Don't know," Charlie said.

Alfred coughed, spit to the side of the boathouse ramp. "Figure it," he said. "It was dead low this morning at about six o'clock…"

Charlie watched the water, counted days on his fingers, finally turned to Alfred. "…so it'll be low at that time in a fortnight or so."

"That's about right," Alfred said. "Go upriver when the tide's moving in, and downriver on the outgoing."

Charlie turned to Alfred. "I say let's spread the word that we'll run upriver to load on, say, the sixteenth; we'll come back on the outgoing, tie up overnight at pilings here, head down to Dresden; back up the next day."

"That'll work fine," Alfred said, "and I'd be glad to work the stern on the downriver run; upriver should be yers to handle."

---

Charlie Call and Alfred Stilphen made four runs to Dresden that spring.

They loaded the scow on the first trip: six of Nathaniel Blodgett's winter barrels and four small firkins stowed within each; two loads of Joel Thompson's shingles, as well as a barrel of his winter apples and five jugs of syrup; two of Eliphalet Crocker's hams and a few live shoats; a dozen jugs of Tom Mitchell's wheat ale.

"None of my sheep," Alfred said. "I'm keeping them all, growing the flock."

They brought back two kegs of turned nails, ten bolts of both solid and patterned broadcloth, sacks of coffee beans and a packing crate full of tins of English tea, wheels of various weights of chain, a box of new scythe blades.

They sold it all to Jonathan Young.

Best of all, they brought back the knowledge that, after the long winter, Portland desperately needed hay for the hungry horses at hostelries and hack companies throughout the city; better still, they didn't need to run all the way to Bath to meet the Portland boat—Dresden merchants were buying for resale, would transport all the way, cutting out the middlemen.

In the next week, they made another three trips, piling the scow high with hay wintered over in the riverbarns on the Eastern. Charlie Call hired Junior Thompson and John Blodgett to stack and stamp the loads; they lashed an old canvas sail atop the tumble of hay, roped it down and tied it to the railing.

They ran once at night to accommodate the tides. Alfred knew the river well enough to navigate by moonlight, and the trip was uneventful, other than a bump or two from water logs. Charlie Call found himself enchanted by the sparkle of light on the water, the soft, shadowed shoreline whispering past in the dark.

"It's beautiful," he said softly to Alfred as they slipped through a turn. "Peaceful, like a dream."

Alfred smiled. "Ye're right," he said, "it is."

They made good money on the hay runs. They paid Joel Thompson and Nathaniel Blodgett the cost of their hay and a slice of the profit; they split the rest between them.

"I need a haypress," Charlie Call said. "Bales would be easier to load, easier to stack; I could get more hay on each load—and there's good profit in running hay."

Alfred nodded. "I seen one of them over to King's Mills," he said. "Had horses to power the screw." He folded his money, tucked it into his trouser pocket. "I bet you could buy one cheap enough."

"Hell," Charlie Call snorted. "I bet I can build one myself."

Alfred tipped his head back and laughed, then dropped his arm around Charlie Call's shoulder.

"Ye're definitely yer father's son," he said, and walked off the wharf, headed down the road to home.

Mary never cared to shear in April; she liked to wait until mid-May at the earliest, when the longer days carried enough heat to keep the newly shorn sheep warm through the cool spring nights.

"It's too early for them," she said, wrapping her shawl about her shoulders, "too chill."

"Thompson shears in April," Alfred said, "but he has to keep 'em in his shed for a month after, and they sometimes get springsick, all closed up together like that, without fleece."

Mary nodded.

"We could do the blackface in April," he suggested. "They stay warmer than the merino."

"True enough," she said. "But then we'd have to shear twice each spring, and that's more work than worth."

They waited another three weeks.

Alfred spent his spare time in the pens, cleaning up the sheep, brushing out bits of fern and chaff from their bellies and chests, picking out twigs and burdocks. The dealers in Dresden would pay two cents per pound more for clean fleece, so it was worth the effort.

"Better to sell a clean fleece than a dirty one," Mary said.

"I'm heading out to the sheds," Alfred said, rising from the table. "I'll sharpen the blades and sweep the alleyway; come on out when thee's ready."

"All right," she said. "I won't be long."

He went through the outkitchen to the shed, found the shears, took them back to the steps and sat in the sun, put a stone to them, working steadily until he could shave the back of his thumbnail along the edge of each blade.

Sharp enough, he thought, to shave a tick!

Mary left Sarah Goud to do the washing up after breakfast. She slipped into her bedroom, shut the door behind her, and undressed; she folded her clothes neatly, stacked them on the dresser.

From the bottom drawer, she pulled a pair of trousers—a pair of Alfred's that she'd shortened and hemmed—stepped into them, pulled them up over her hips. She tucked her chemise into the waistband and fastened the button; added an overshirt of Alfred's, rolled up the sleeves.

Have to shorten those sleeves, she thought, shorten them and make new cuffs; it would save me considerable trouble of rolling them all the time.

She grabbed some hairpins, stuck them in her mouth and headed back into the kitchen, winding her hair.

Sarah Goud turned from the table where she was washing up the breakfast dishes in a broad bucket; she raised her hands out of the water and looked Mary up and down.

"Good gracious!" she said, her eyes wide.

Mary set one hairpin, took the others from her mouth, dropped them on the table. "Never seen a woman in trousers?"

Sarah shook her head. "Never have." She lowered her hands back into the bucket, back to her work. "I'd not know you out of the house—if I just saw you in the road, or in town."

"Well, that's not likely," Mary said, "so you needn't worry yerself on it." She reached for another hairpin.

Sarah smiled. "No, I think not."

Mary finished with her hair; she patted the sides of her head, then looked at Sarah.

"It's a hard enough job," Mary said, "shearing is, without having skirts in yer way—I can shear faster and cleaner than he can, but not in long dress."

She sat down in a kitchen chair, pushed her feet into her brogans. "Can you keep a sharp eye on the children while I'm in the sheds?" She leaned over, pulled at her laces.

"I can," Sarah said.

Mary sat up in her chair, tapped the toes of her shoes together. "By the by," she said, "I'm to have another in late August."

Sarah smiled. "Thought you might be," she said. She lifted the wash bucket, headed for the back door. "I heard yer retchin' last winter." She braced the open door against her hip and threw the water outside. "Ye're a champion retcher, I must say."

Mary laughed.

"Is it all right for you to be doing hard work—since ye're carrying, that is?"

Mary stood up. "Never felt better in my life," she said, smiling. She walked to the outkitchen door, opened it; before she went through, she turned back and wagged her finger at Sarah Goud.

"Not a word," she said to Sarah, "not a word of this to anyone."

Sarah nodded.

"Alfred would be hounded by the others," Mary said, "if they knew I was doing a man's work, and I won't have it."

"No, ma'am," Sarah said. "Not a word."

———————

He swept the shearing stall, put the shears in the corner for safekeeping, then went through the gate into the pens, murmuring softly, touching them, picking bits of hay and twigs from their shoulders and backs. They bumped against him, bleated, bumped again; he leaned over and held out his palms, fed them dried beets from the barrel.

Mary came up the alleyway, turned into the shearing pen. "All set," she said.

Alfred took the greasepot through the exit gate and closed it behind him, looked back over the partition wall and nodded to his wife.

"All right," he said. "Let's get to it."

Mary reached for the first sheep and took it to ground, then hauled it backwards onto the shearing platform, tipped it upright onto its rump— singing softly all the while. The ewe, surprised and befuddled, gave in, went limp with the uncertainty of it all, slumped up against her knees.

Mary leaned over and sheared four courses across the belly, working lower with each pass, her left hand stretching the fleece away from the body, her right working the shears, over and over, careful not to nick the folds of pink skin; slow and gentle around the teats, down between the thighs—gently, gently—and up the outside of the legs.

She straightened for a moment, hitched the animal up higher against the front of her, then leaned back down and started in again at the belly, but upwards this time, up over the chest; she tucked the ewe's head under her arm and trapped it there, stretched the neck out long, and ran courses up the throat, up the outsides of the shoulders, up around the ears.

Mary hefted the ewe again, then clipped under the forelegs and down along the sides, down across the haunches; she tipped it to its side onto the shed floor—two courses to the left of the backbone, flipped it over and ran two to the right—then ran the final track from the rump straight up and out of the tangle and mat.

The fleece dropped off, all of a piece, dark on the topside, stark white on the under; Mary pushed it aside.

She righted the sheep, bare and clean; slid it through the side gate into the holding pen to Alfred, who welcomed it into his hands, clasped it gently between his knees and ran his palms over its head and ears, down the neck, throat, shoulders and chest, searching for nips and cuts, for traces of blood; dipped his fingers into the greasepot and smoothed the salve over the tender skin, making that sound inside his throat, singsong, easy, easy…

He heard a sharp bleat as Mary dropped the next one and pulled it to the shearing platform, heard her murmur and sing as she reached back for her shears. The blades whispered in the heat of the sheep shed, the light grew soft in the doorway.

Later, they stood in the yard, rested their arms on the top board of the fence, and looked out over the upper fields. The grass was greening nicely, and, down below, the Eastern glittered in the sunlight.

"Forty-eight pounds," Alfred said. "That's nearly twenty dollars."

"That's taxes," she said, "and new shoes for us all."

They watched their sheep move across the hillside, stark white against the new growth, leaping and prancing, joyous in their near nakedness.

"It's clear to me," Alfred said, "that the shedding of winter clothes is good practice—it brings such simple delight."

"A sense of recklessness, it seems," Mary said, smiling. "A certain frivolity."

Two ewes passed by, bleating, their skins twitching and jumping in the cool air. They kicked back, hopped, spun around; they butted heads, sidestepped, trotted away to join the flock.

"I could use a little of that recklessness," he said. "I'd like to suggest that we, too, shed our clothes and have ourselves a little romp out there in the field."

"Lecher," she muttered, then turned her head and grinned up at him; her hair slipped loose, and he caught his breath.

She gathered it in her fingers and tucked it back again, reset the pin at the back of her head.

"I've a better plan," she said.

He lifted his eyebrows, looked at her.

"A good wash would serve us both," she said. "And later on, after the children are abed, we'll have ourselves a romp, all right."

———

After she finished her breakfast, Sarah Ann handed her bowl to Polly, then went out through the shed to the privy. She sat on the seat and looked out the little window while she did her business; she counted all the crows she could see in the orchard—seventeen altogether.

When she was through, she went back to the shed, pulled her boots out from underneath the bench, and put them on, then stood and stamped her feet twice each to snug her heels against the soles.

She opened the shed door and stepped outside into the clean, early sunlight, took a few deep breaths, and crossed the yard to the barn. She paused just inside the door, leaned against the side of the grain bin and listened; she heard the sweep of her father's broom against the alleyway floor as he tidied up before morning milking.

She went back outside, got herself all ready, and started to lope around the barn, settled quickly into a comfortable pace, worked a soft drone, counted each complete round: one…two…three times, four…five…

When the sun had risen up over the shed roof and she came around the west corner of the barn and started along the long south side, she saw her father standing in the doorway and knew it was time for her to do her summer job.

"Sarah Ann?" he said, starting with her name in a question, as if she might be somebody else this time around. "Sarah Ann," he said again, "would thee pasture the cows for me?"

She nodded. She always nodded, for that was part of it—part of her job—then took Flossie's rope and turned away, led the cows up behind the barn, keeping pace with the dinging of Flossie's bell. The others followed in a line up the path, past the north end of the orchard and through the stone wall into the cow run, up from there into the near pasture.

The gate was open; she named and counted them one by one as they passed through the gap and into the pasture—Flossie and Bessie and Sadie and Birdie and the new cow, too—Molly, the new cow.

One, two, three, four, five.

She drew the rails across, turned her back to the pasture, and started off, loped back down the cow run, her breath fogging out ahead of her. But instead of turning back to the barn, she veered off onto the path through the orchard and onto the road to town.

She turned right at the fork and thumped over the plank bridge, then started left around the big curve. When she made the turn and reached the straightaway, she lifted her eyes from the roadway and saw him there, saw the man with the soft hands, saw him waiting for her in the tall grass by the side of the road near the empty, tumbled house.

When she neared, he smiled at her gently and her heart lifted inside her throat. He took her hand and led her slowly through the high grass in the dooryard, through the broken shed door into the kitchen, and onto the mattress on the floor in the corner, where they lay together under a blanket, close and warm.

Her beautiful man, her very own, her secret.

———

Every morning, when the sun rose up over the eastern ridge of the river valley, Polly Thompson's kitchen filled with light; even in the chill of midwinter, the undefined gray of dawn broke into yellows or soft pinks and spread color along the walls and the floor.

Porridge steamed in the pan, the tea brewed in the pot; Polly Thompson sat at her end of the table in the sunlight, waited for her family to rise for first breakfast and early chores.

Polly couldn't place the sound at first, couldn't figure it—a steady wail, a high keening from the upstairs back room.

Sarah Ann, she thought, and hurried across the kitchen to the door to the back hallway. She lifted her skirts and started up the narrow stairway, tripping on the risers, barking her shins against the edges of the treads.

"Ma!" she heard Laura call out. "Come quick!"

The keening stopped; Polly came over the top of the stairs, turned and pushed through the door to the little back bedroom.

Sarah Ann stood in the center of the room, her night pot up to her face; she retched, swayed and droned, retched again.

Laura appeared in the doorway. "This is the third time this week," she said softly.

Polly looked at her, astonished. "The third?"

Laura nodded. "I didn't think to tell ye."

It can't be, Polly thought, but it was, and she knew it; she turned back to Sarah Ann. "Ye're carrying!"

Sarah Ann sat down on the edge of her bed. She lifted the night pot, coughed, spat into the bowl, lowered it again to her lap, wiped her mouth on her sleeve.

Polly leaned over her. "Who did this to you?" she demanded. "Who did this?"

After Polly stripped her down—after she peeled off the soiled shawls and waist and the two skirts and even the chemise and dumped them into a washbucket to soak—Sarah Ann stood naked in the big wooden tub in the warm kitchen while Polly helped her wash herself clean with softsoap and a piece of cloth.

"You won't tell me who did this?" Polly asked, drying Sarah Ann with a length of toweling, then wrapping it around her shoulders. "You won't tell?"

Sarah Ann shook her head, and the water flicked from the ends of her hair onto her face, sprinkled across her nose and her cheeks like spring rain.

———————

*Pittston Town Meeting*
*East Parish*
*October 22, 1852*

*Insofar as inhabitants of Pittston and persons travelling with teams are annoyed by cows and sheep running at large, no swine or cows or sheep shall be allowed to run at large on the roads of East Pittston from the meeting house to the sawmill at the upper end of the Eastern River district...*

*Marriages in the Town of Pittston, Registered & Recorded by me, Alphonso H. Clark, Town Clerk*
*Miss Eliza Blodgett of Pittston to Mr. John Buckman of Plymouth, Massachusetts, October 3, 1851.*

*Births in the Town of Pittston, Registered & Recorded by me, Alphonso H. Clark, Town Clerk*
*Walter Scott Stilphen, to Alfred and Mary Call Stilphen, August 20, 1851*
*Charles Henry Crocker, to Samuel and Caroline Dudley Crocker, August 12, 1852*
*George P. Thompson, to Sarah Ann Thompson, October 15, 1852. Father unknown.*

*Town of Pittston*
*Taxes 1851*

| | |
|---|---|
| *Joel Thompson* | *8.74* |
| *Nathaniel Blodgett* | *11.77* |
| *Eliphalet Crocker* | *10.17* |
| *Thomas Mitchell* | *12.73* |
| *Alfred Stilphen* | *18.62* |

# Chapter Sixteen

HOLLOWAY'S PILLS
Delicate Females
All irregularities and ailments incident to the delicate and
sensitive organs of the sex are removed or prevented by a few
doses…

*Northern Home Journal*
Gardiner, Maine
1853

JANE BLODGETT left the bowl of batter on the table and dashed
through the shed out to the privy; she hiked her skirts, turned and sat on
the board. She released just a small stream, not even enough to fill a common spoon, but the pain of passing her water left her breathless.

She took a handful of straw from the box, blotted herself, and tossed
it down the hole, stood, headed back to the house and her baking.

In the late forenoon, she leaned against the shed doorway and
watched the sky as clouds slid in from King's Mills; they bunched and
turned over the valley, reflected soft and white on the Eastern River.

Her back ached; there was a sharp pain between her hips, deep in her
belly, just above her low bone.

She sighed, then lifted her yoke and water pails and made her way
across the drive to the well. She pulled on the sweep rope to lower and fill
the bucket, and when it was full, she let go her hold; the counterweight
raised the sweep, drew the full bucket up and out of the well. She poured

the water into her pails, balancing the load left and right, then bent her knees, slipped her shoulders beneath the yoke, lifted.

As she straightened her legs, the urge came upon her again, so great she knew she could not hold it in. She dropped the yoke—tipping both buckets—and squatted right there beside the well, trying in haste to move her skirts away, but her hands were busy with the yoke, the pails; water and urine spilled onto her hems, her bare feet.

Time to visit my sister, she thought. Time to go to Polly.

Polly Thompson worked her laundry outside, her wash and rinse tubs set up on a low bench beneath the spread of the oak tree in the side yard. Sunlight dropped through the leaves and sparkled in the washwater; shadows flittered over her washboard.

She pulled one of George's diaper cloths out of the tub and wrung out the water, the muscles roping in the backs of her hands. She shook it loose, dropped it into the rinse tub and reached back into the washtub for another.

A squirrel chittered sharply high in the tree—a warning—and she looked up, put her hand over her brows to shield the glare, peered down the road. The water from her hand ran down her forearm, wetting her sleeve at her elbow; she lowered her arm, wiped herself dry on her apron, then looked again, saw Jane near the meadow above the woodlot, coming up the road.

Good, she thought, pleased. I'll finish my washing, we'll have a cup of tea.

She shook out a cloth and dropped it into the basket; she'd ask Sarah Ann to do the hanging on the line.

"Did you see the flowers in the meadow?" Polly asked, reaching for Jane's hand. "There's wild aster starting now."

Jane shook her head. "No," she said, squeezing Polly's fingers gently, then letting go. She moved her palm across her belly, looked away, then back at Polly. "No flowers."

Polly saw something in her face, her eyes—a tightness. "Then what?" she asked. "What's wrong?"

Jane lowered her gaze. "I've been unwell," she said, "for some time now; unable to hold my water."

The wind picked up, and a swirl of dust rose from the drive, traveled across the dooryard to the chicken coop; Jane saw Sarah Ann moving about inside the yard, throwing corn for the chickens from a scoop she carried in her hand.

"It's happened before," Jane went on, "but this is different."

"How so?"

Jane took a breath. "I have burning pain when I void, and this morning I found blood in my pot."

Polly paused, looked away down the road for a moment, then back at her sister. "I'm afflicted, too, off and on again, if that's any consolation to you," she said. "But not with blood—nothing like that."

"Good," said Jane, relieved. Then quickly, "Not good that ye're having some difficulty, but good that I am not alone."

Polly smiled, rested her hand on Jane's arm. "It's all right," she said, "I knew that's what you meant."

The door to the coop slammed, and Sarah Ann started across the yard, droning, holding a basket heavy with eggs.

"I feel so unclean," Jane said, and started to weep.

They sat in the shed doorway on the granite step, their skirts touching; sunlight washed over them, warmed their shoulders, their knees. Across the drive, Sarah Ann draped her son's clean diapers over the line to dry, arranging them carefully.

"It used to bother me," Jane said, "when me and Nate was at each other too much." She turned her head so Polly couldn't see her shame, looked up the drive to the barn doors, deep in shadow. "But he's at me less now that we're older."

Polly smiled. "There's one small blessing to aging, then, isn't there?"

Jane grinned, leaned her shoulder against Polly's. "There is," she said, "but now I can't find a cause for my troubles—if it's not from being with Nate, I'm at a loss."

Over in the coop, a few chickens squabbled over the corn; they flapped and squawked, scratched up the dust; settled again.

"Ma suspected it's about going through the change—and washing after doing yer business," Polly said. "I'm unsure why, but she was fierce about it."

"She had it, too?" Jane asked, turning to Polly. "Our ma?"

Polly nodded. "She had it—we all have it, it seems, some more than others." Polly leaned down, brushed some dirt off the tops of her shoes with her hand. "Ma started having more trouble after the change; she could tame it some by washing a lot, but the older she became, the more she had trouble."

"Well," Jane said, "I'm having it constant." She folded her hands, nestled them into her lap. "Makes me feel shameful, it does."

As if to prove the point, she stood suddenly, turned on the step and went inside, hurried across the shed to the back door and started out along the path to the outhouse.

Polly waited, sat still in the sunshine, watched Sarah Ann rearrange the diapers over and over again, using her index finger to calculate precise gaps between them, setting and resetting the pins.

They'll never dry unless she quits picking at them, she thought, but she thinks they need to be hanging just right, just so—poor thing!

Jane came back through, sat on the step again.

"Are you leaking?" Polly asked.

Jane lowered her head. "All the time," she said. "I'm thinking to start using my rags again; I'm no longer having my courses—and there's another blessing to be counted—but I can use them to catch my drips."

Polly patted her hand.

"Worst of all," Jane said, "is that I'm beginning to smell rank—even Nathaniel notices."

"From the leaks?" Polly asked. "Yer skirts?"

Jane nodded. "Skirts and smalls."

"How many changes have you?"

Jane thought for a moment. "Three skirts," she said. "The blue broadcloth, the green cotton, and this black." She looked down into her lap, brushed her hands across her thighs. "Four sets of smalls, but I sometimes go without in hot weather."

"Well," Polly said, "I've got a spare brown skirt I can part with. You won't have to launder so often."

"I'd be grateful," Jane said, "but more grateful for a cure of some kind."

Polly shrugged. "It's beyond that," she said. "There's nothing to do for it but to ease the discomfort some. I've a tea—birchbark, dandelion root, and juniper berry—that will ease the pain some, help flush it out."

"All right," Jane said, and then, after a moment, "It's my lot, then, isn't it?"

"It is," Polly said. "In yer case, perhaps it's punishment for being such a loose woman."

Jane turned to her, surprised. "Loose?" she asked. "You consider me a loose woman? Yer own sister?"

Polly smiled, moved in close. "For wearing no small clothes," she whispered. "Sounds like loose living to me."

Jane lifted her head. The golden sunlight fell across her face, her eyes; she put her hand over her mouth, leaned into her sister and started to laugh.

---

Lizzie Call Mitchell was out of the big house and into the ell at first light. She joggled the dampers in the cookstove, opened the lids and the firebox, and raked for some hot coals, added small pieces from the chip basket, then leaned in and pursed her lips, blew gently.

When the fire caught, she dropped the lids, went through to the out-kitchen to lay tinder and shaved kindling in the boiler, then went back to the cookstove to add wood. She used a shovel to take a coal from there back into the outkitchen, where she slipped it under the boiler tinder—it smoked a little, and Lizzie fanned it with her bellows, carefully, encouraged it to full flame.

She went back and forth, then, from one fire to the other, adding kindling, then full lengths, shutting vents and dampers in the cookstove in the ell, shifting the set kettles into the boiler in the outkitchen.

She wrapped her shawl around her shoulders, grabbed her buckets and went out the shed door, made four trips to the well. She filled the set kettles on her first three trips; filled both to three-quarters full—for her hot water wash and rinse, for her cleaning—then filled the buckets once more, took them to the kitchen.

Added wood to the stoves, adjusted the dampers.

Put some of the water in the porridge pan, threw in a few fistfuls of oats, stirred and covered; put some in the big pot for stew and set both on the woodstove. She poured the rest of the water into the dishpan in the dry sink; put the empty tote buckets by the shed door to fill again after breakfast.

Fed the stoves again.

She scooped coffee beans from the jar—time to roast some more, she thought, getting low—and poured them into the grinder, braced it against her hip and worked the handle. When it turned easily, she knew it was ready; she opened the drawer and dumped the grounds into the coffee pot, added water, set it on the back lid to boil.

Checked both fires.

She readied the table with spoons and bowls, cups for coffee, the honey jar and a knife. Went back to the shed for two armloads of wood—one for the boiler, one for the cookstove—dumped them into the woodboxes.

Sat for a moment—just a moment—in her chair at the table.

Above her head, the children—boys in the east bedroom, girls in the west, chattered as they dressed, paced back and forth across their bedroom floors; Tom himself came in through the shed, back from the barn and his first chores.

There, she thought, as her family clattered into the kitchen, there, the day's starting.

———————

Caroline Crocker and her mother-in-law cleaned up their shared kitchen together, then went outside, stood near the front step in the morning sunshine. The grass was up to their shins; they lifted their skirts, moved them back and forth to keep the bugs out of their folds.

"What would you say to flowers along that fence?" Caroline asked, pointing with her finger, moving it the full length across the yard. "All the way up and down?"

Lydia nodded. "I'd say that might look nice."

"All the women in town have flower beds now," Caroline said. "I thought we might plant some ourselves—keep up with the times."

"What kinds of flowers?" Lydia asked, hoping Caroline might talk about flowers she knew: bluettes, violets, daylilies with fat orange heads.

"Daylilies, to start," Caroline said at once. "I know you like them, and they'd be fine along those white pickets."

Lydia smiled. "And?"

"Well, Abby Averill's got some crocus bulbs she says she'll give me—I could mix them in; she's also got lots of iris."

"What do they look like, the iris?" Lydia asked. "Crocus I know, but I'm not sure about the iris."

"Purple," Caroline said, "with tall, broad leaves that fan out a little." She thought for a minute. "There's a patch of them beside the door of that little white house down to Dresden," she said, "just beyond the Middle Bridge."

"Oh, I know that place," Lydia said. "I like that color—looks pretty in the spring."

Caroline turned to her. "If we plant now, we'll get some daylilies this year," she said, "but the others won't bloom until next spring—seems unfair, it does, but that's how bulbs and corms work; they need some time to settle in together."

"Like us," Lydia said. "A little bit like us."

They were quiet for a moment.

"So, you wouldn't mind if I planted along the picket?" Caroline asked, turning, lifting her skirts to step up onto the stoop, head back inside the house to tend to her children.

"Wouldn't mind a peep," Lydia said. "And it's yer house as much as mine now; no reason you shouldn't plant what you like, where you like."

———

When she was certain that Mrs. Stilphen was busy in the back room dressing the children, Sarah Goud wiped her hands on her apron and moved over near the chair by the window, to the little table where Mr. Stilphen kept his book.

She picked it up, opened it at the marker—a strip of newspaper from that week's *Northern Home Journal* he had tucked inside to keep his place—and looked at the pages.

The words made no sense to her.

That somebody could look at that mess of lines and curves and jiggles and actually say out loud what was written there—well, she thought, that was, for certain, some kind of magic.

And when he read to them all after breakfast, his voice shifting—rising and falling with the excitement and the tension, changing whenever different characters spoke—Sarah found herself distracted from her work, gazing out the kitchen windows at the Eastern, seeing instead the Mississippi, seeing Tom on the riverboat, seeing Eliza running, running for freedom with her child...

Mr. Stilphen would turn the page or clear his throat, and she'd come back to herself with a little twitch, continue with whatever it was she was doing, just as if she'd never paid any mind to what he was reading.

Sometimes, there would be an engraving, and Mr. Stilphen would rise from his chair and walk over to where she was working to show her the page; she felt a ripple of fear when she saw that man with the slouch hat pulled down over his eyes, the man with the whip—that Simon Legree—the man who bought Tom, took him away.

Bought him, like a chicken or a sheep.

Or a horse, she thought; he bought Tom like a man might buy himself a horse.

Later, as she was washing up the porridge bowls, she watched out the window as Mr. Stilphen and Charlie Call stood in the dooryard, talking: Mr. Stilphen with his arms folded across his chest and his head tipped forward, the way he did when he was intent to listen; Charlie, standing at ease in his linen shirt and brown trousers, his hair tossing in the light breeze.

She watched as he smiled at something Mr. Stilphen said, put his hands into his pockets; his trousers pulled across his hips, and her eyes lingered there.

Oh, but I'd like to know him, she thought, then felt the heat spread low in her belly, felt it rise up, flush over her chest and throat.

# Chapter Seventeen

Don't forget the eclipse that is to come off week from to-morrow—we don't have one every day. Take a bit of glass, hold it over the smoke of a lamp until it is pretty well coated, and then you can watch with impunity.

*Northern Home Journal*
Gardiner, Maine
May 18, 1854

ALFRED STILPHEN went out the back door of the shed and past Mary's laundry yard, across the stretch of grass to the stone wall. He climbed over the rocks and waded into the jumble of the house dump, used the toe of his boot to push aside some of the larger pieces—an old commode set, a worn iron pot, some broken bricks from the old chimney—then leaned down to pick through the refuse for pieces of glass.

He found a few shards of a chimney lamp Sarah Goud had broken; he found, too, three pieces of a kitchen window pane, one that Mary herself had backed a broom handle into last fall while sweeping crumbs and such from the floor.

Window glass is better, he thought; it's flatter and thicker.

He found a stone and knocked it against the biggest piece to make a few more smaller ones, then gathered them all in a stack on his left palm, covered them with the other, and carried them back to the house.

"Ho, Sarah!" he called from the shed.

She was at the worktable, trimming lamp wicks and wiping the chimneys clean with old newspaper, when he moved through the door into the kitchen.

"You're not finished with the lamps yet, I hope," he said, putting his hip against the door and closing it behind him.

"I'm about to be," she said, "but no, not yet."

"Would you mind holding up on that, then," he asked, "so I can use one of last night's to smoke up these pieces?"

She stopped her work and looked at him, puzzled.

"For the eclipse," he explained. "So we can watch the eclipse."

He waited.

"Of course," she said, backing away from the table. "But what do the lamps have to do with it?"

"If we smoke up the window glass," he said, "we can watch the eclipse through it; it will keep the brightness from harming our eyes."

He lighted a lamp, turned the wick a little higher, then held the pieces over the chimney, watched the soot form, dark and greasy on the glass.

He held a piece up, looked through it. "I can't even see the barest light from the windows," he said. "That's what we want." He put it down, picked up another.

"I don't understand it—the eclipse, I mean." She looked down, then back up at him. "What happens, that is."

He stepped back a little from the table. "It's when the moon moves between the earth and the sun," he said. "It makes a big shadow on the earth, and we'll be in that shadow."

She picked up the two clean chimneys and took them to the cupboard, set them on the second shelf; came back to the table, trying to work it through.

She shook her head. "I can't see it."

He folded his arms across his chest, thought for a long moment. He went over to Mary's rocker and rummaged in her sewing bag, came back with her darning egg and a thimble.

"All right," he said. "Let's try it this way."

He moved the burning lamp to the center of the worktable. "This is the sun," he said, "smack in the middle of things."

She nodded.

"And this," he said, picking up Mary's darning egg, "is the earth—it's smaller; it goes around the sun." He moved the egg around the lamp to show her.

"Just goes around and around?" she asked.

He nodded. "It takes three hundred sixty-five days for that earth to take one turn around the sun."

Sarah's eyes widened a little. "That's one year," she said, making the connection. "A whole year of time just to go around once?"

He nodded again; he was still moving the egg around.

"And what, then, about the moon?" Sarah asked.

"Right here," he said, picking up the thimble. "It's even smaller, and it goes around the earth—about once a month."

He moved them around a few times—held the earth in his left hand, moved the moon around it with his right; he swept the whole business around the lamp in a funny, tilted arc, careful not to singe his sleeves whenever he passed over the top of the chimney.

"And every now and then," he said, "they all line up just right; the moon comes between the sun and the earth." He angled them into position, close to the burning lamp. "And when that happens," he said, "the moon's shadow travels across the earth."

He moved his hand, and the little shadow of the thimble moved over Mary's porcelain darning egg.

"Oh!" she breathed.

"That's an eclipse," he said.

She turned to him, her face full, eager, her eyes wide with wonder; she looked back at the egg and thimble in his hands.

"Do it again," she said.

———

Mary Stilphen packed a basket—thick slabs of bread wrapped in a clean cloth, some good cheese—and tucked a jug of sweet cider under the seat. She sat there beside Alfred, hooked her arm into his while he drove.

Sarah rode behind in the wagon bed with the children; she held Scott in her lap and kept a strong eye on the others, coaxing them away from the back of the wagon whenever they moved too near.

"Should've brought some old rope," she said, "so to tie them to the corner posts—keep them from falling out."

Not a bad idea, Mary thought; not a bad idea at all.

They met at Call's, all of them.

They anchored their horses in the shade along the drive and walked up into the near field, spread their blankets and quilts in the upper quadrant, up near the tree line. The adults lazed on the ground or sat along the stone wall; the smallest children played in the short grass up near the trees.

They sat together on the wall, Alfred Stilphen and Polly Thompson. He was comfortable enough in his shirt and jacket; she, though, had a shawl—her newer one, the one with the green fringe along both tails—spread across her shoulders and over her upper arms.

The sunlight was warm on their faces; the cool breeze running up from the Eastern lifted the grass in the field, carried the faint hint of river water and mud.

"Smells good," Polly said. "Smells like spring, don't it?"

He nodded, his lips moving. She knew he was counting; she watched his eyes move from family to family, taking tally.

"How many?" she asked, when she was certain he was through.

"Thirty of us altogether," Alfred said, "in three generations."

"And that's not counting the ones who've married and gone off," Polly said. She brushed her skirt, shifted her weight on the wall beside him, hoping for a more comfortable spot, shifted again, found it.

"That's true," he said, "but in spite of that, we still have ample proof that we've done our Biblical best around here."

It took her a moment, but she figured it: Genesis, she thought: *be fruitful and multiply.*

When it happened—when it really happened—Sarah Goud looked through the smoky glass and saw the circle of the sun, saw the shadow start across the face of it. The hairs on her arms pricked and stood, the back of her neck tingled.

"Oh, Lord, Lord, Charlie," she said in a whisper, "would you just look at that!"

Charlie Call, his left eye squeezed shut, his right eye up to his own piece of smoked glass, sat close by; there was heat where their shoulders touched, and the grass was warm and damp beneath them.

"It's like coming on dusk," he answered, his voice soft as the shadow inched across the bright of the sun.

A small group of crows flapped out of the field, cawing; they circled once, then headed to the woodlot; sparrows and robins joined them, headed to nest. Down in the lower meadows by the river, the cows, confused by the early dimness, lumbered to their feet; they turned, started up the hillside, headed for the barn. Their soft lowing moved up the slope as they neared, their heavy udders dripped in anticipation.

"They think it's night!" Charlie whispered. "They think it's time for chores, time to be milked."

———

Sarah Ann Thompson came out of the barn; she took one look at the black shadow across the sun and lifted her hands to her mouth, started to keen. She rocked on her heels a few times in the barn doorway, then lowered her arms, lifted her skirts, and trotted hard across the drive to the chicken coop. She scrambled around the corner of the henhouse to the back side, got onto her belly and crawled through the gap in the foundation, hauled herself as far under the coop as she could go.

She turned onto her side, pulled up her knees and lay there; she listened to the chickens scurry in from the darkening outside, their bony feet scratching on the floor above her head; she saw the dust of their droppings sift between the floorboards.

———

Still the shadow moved across the sun, steady, certain. The glimmer of light grew slimmer, finally became a crescent—a bare fingernail of brightness—and then there was nothing but a thin circle of light around the blackened sun.

It's nearly gone, Sarah Goud thought, a lick of fear in her throat. The sun's nearly gone, and whatever would happen to us all if it should never come back?

She leaned closer, pushed her shoulder tight against Charles Call's upper arm and felt him there.

He lowered his glass and looked at her. "Will you marry me?" he asked, ever so quietly.

"Yes," she said, and smiled at him in the dim light.

They moved closer together, sat there on the slope of the upper field, surrounded by their families and neighbors; watched the shadow slip off the side of the sun; watched the world brighten again, all clean, all new.

———

Joel Thompson banged his heels together to knock the barn off his boots, then stepped up into the coolness of the shed, across the floor to the outkitchen door. He heard young George, wailing in the kitchen, heard the undercurrent of Polly's comforting murmur.

He opened the door, and the baby stopped his crying for a moment, distracted by the sound of the latch.

"I'm off to Crocker's," Joel said, leaning in. "We're all meeting there, to set up for the week."

Polly looked up. "Going down with Nate?" she asked, jouncing George gently on her lap.

Joel nodded.

"Take the cart," she said. "He's not up for that walk any longer."

The baby took a breath, twisted up his face and started in again; Polly lifted him to her shoulder, gave him small pats.

"Where's his mother?" Joel asked.

Polly shrugged. Sarah Ann's not here, she thought; wherever she is, she's not here, but I am.

"What's his complaint?"

"New tooth, I think." She brought the baby down to her lap again. "I'll put the rum to him," she said. "That'll quiet him down."

"Can't believe it's mid-month already," Joel said, holding the horse still in the dooryard while Nate pulled himself up over the wheel, settled next to him on the seat. "Can't believe it's time to cut oats."

He flicked the reins lightly; the horse started up, walked a slow circle in the dooryard and out to the road, where Joel turned him left, relaxed the reins, and gave him his head; he knew the way.

"Seems to go faster as we get older, don't it?" Nate said. "It's like somebody's moving the clock hands too fast."

"That, and things get harder to do," Joel said.

They bumped along in the cart, down past Nate's south field on the left, all bright with goldenrod along the near side of the road with clusters of wild aster, pale purple in early bloom, nestled back against the stone wall. They rolled into the shade of the woodlot, then out again, past the narrow wagon track that ran along Nate's property line down to the Eastern; past Mitchell's rail fence and his first stand of field corn, tall and green, moving gently in the breeze that came up from the river.

"It's peculiar," said Joel.

Nate turned his head. "What's that?"

"Time," Joel said. He coughed, spit over the wheel. "I mean, time goes faster, but I seem to go slower."

Nate shifted in the seat, worked his cuff button. "Me, too," he said. He started rolling his sleeve, turning it back carefully, evening out the folds. "John and Daniel are doing all the cutting now."

"I can still cut grass if I go slow," Joel said, "but I don't have the muscle to do oats or wheat anymore." He turned his head, looked at Nate. "It's the extra weight of a cradle; my back gives in."

Nate started on his other sleeve. "Yer back and my hip," he said.

"Bothers you that much—yer hip?"

Nate nodded. "Janey keeps giving me a liniment for it—I think it's one yer own Polly brewed up—but it don't seem to do much, except to make me smell bad."

"You never said it was hurting that much."

Nate shrugged. "Saying it don't change it," he said, "so why say it?"

---

"So, who's in for gangs this year?" Eliphalet asked.

He looked around, tapped his fingers lightly on the table. "I got me and all four boys."

"Me and Thomas," said Tom Mitchell. "And Charlie Call."

"I got Daniel and John," Nate said. "And me, for the little I'm worth."

"I got only Junior still to home, so it's me and him."

"Just me," said Alfred, "but give me a few years and I'll have a whole crew of my own."

"We can make shook gangs out of the girls," Thomas Mitchell said. He rocked back in his chair, hooked his feet over the rungs. "Mercy and Susan from my place; Laura and Abby Thompson."

"Not Abby," Joel said. "She's got work in Gardiner."

"Sarah Goud, then," Alfred said, "if Mary can spare her."

---

They stood in the shade of the tree line and stretched their muscles, talked quietly; leaned against the side of the wagon and honed their scythes. The stones sang along the blades.

Alfred Stilphen, Isaac Crocker, Charlie Call.

They started in as soon as the morning breeze rose up from the Eastern and threw the dew off the oats. They set themselves in a line, then staggered four paces apart—no sense taking the risk of a cut tendon by running too close together.

Alfred called cadence as they moved across his own fields.

"Swing!" he called; he counted the off beats quietly, "Two, three, four," and, again, loudly now, "Swing!"

They fell in together, caught the rhythm, and moved as one across the stand of oats; the blades flashed in the early sunlight, the brown stalks dropped with a rattle, swished into the cradles, tipped out in neat swaths at the end of the swing.

Behind them, two shook crews: Laura Thompson and Sarah Goud, Susan Call and Mercy Mitchell, their hair tied back, skirts rolled a bit at their waists to raise their hems, to give them free footing; sleeves folded up to their elbows in the morning heat, gathering swaths, binding them with a couple of stalks into shooks, standing the shooks in groups of ten or so.

And, finally, the wagon: Nate Blodgett driving Alfred's blacks, pausing at each stand, resting his foot against the brake and holding them calm while Lew and Ben Crocker loaded the shooks into the wagon bed, piled them against the sides. They hauled each full load to Alfred's threshing barn, slid and tossed the shooks off the back of the wagon into the side bay, turned and came back for more.

———————

Sarah Goud kept her eye on him.

She worked her line. She leaned forward to gather the oats, her hands pricking against the stubble of the aftermath; she bundled and tied the stalks, stacked her shooks together with Laura Thompson's.

And she watched him the whole while, watched his hips dip at the start of his swing, the muscles pull across his shoulders and down his long back as he turned through the arc and up into the high end of the sweep; she watched his hair fall whenever he tipped his head.

She heard his intake of breath on his backswing.

"Get your eyes off Charlie," Laura teased, poking at Sarah's side with her forefinger, "and pay better attention to making good shooks."

She leaned over, started to gather another bundle. "You'll have him all to yourself soon enough."

They took a break when Mary appeared with her barrow. She rolled and bounced it from the house across the fields, brought them a jug of switchel to slake their thirst, a bucket of cold water and lengths of flannel to wipe over their faces and forearms.

She set up next to the stone wall, poured full mugs, and handed them around, watched as they all lifted them to their mouths, tasting the bite of the vinegar first, sharp against their thirst, then the sweet molasses on the backs of their throats, soothing the scratchiness there.

Alfred lowered his mug, held it out to her for more; she smiled at him, tipped the jug.

"Good batch," he said.

The girls climbed over the wall and disappeared into the woodlot to relieve themselves behind a growth of shrubby maples. While they were gone, the men stepped behind the wagon, unbuttoned their trousers; they watched the crows fly to ground from the tree line, pick through the aftermath for dropped oats.

The girls came back, sat on the cool stones and tossed out their hair, combed the heat from it with their fingers, rewound and repinned. Sarah Goud lifted her chin whenever Charlie Call looked her way, looked boldly as he wiped a wet flannel inside his collar.

Too soon, the creak of the wagon came back across the field from the threshing barn. They all sighed and stood, took their last sips of switchel, put their cups back in the bed of the barrow with the jug and the bucket.

"Next break is dinner," Mary said, lifting the handles of the barrow, starting back to the house. "I'll ring the bell."

They shouldered their scythes, moved to the end of the row and got themselves aligned again, shuffled their feet, got balanced.

"All right, then," Alfred called. "Ready?"

They nodded, waited for the call.

"Swing!" he sang, and they started in again.

The crows, startled, lifted from the field, rose up and turned, headed down the slope to the Eastern.

*Pittston Town Meeting*
*East Parish*
*June 11, 1856*


*Marriages in the Town of Pittston, Registered & Recorded by
me, Alphonso H. Clark, Town Clerk*
    *Miss Sarah Goud of Pittston to Mr. Charles Call of
Pittston, August 29, 1854*
    *Miss Abigail Thompson of Pittston to Mr. William Adams
of Lynn, Massachusetts, January 17, 1855*
    *Mr. Joel Thompson, Jr. of Pittston & Miss Nancy Blackwell
of Sandwich, Massachusetts, June 7, 1856*

*Births in the Town of Pittston, Registered & Recorded by me,
Alphonso H. Clark, Town Clerk*
    *Amanda Crocker, to Samuel and Caroline Crocker, April 7,
1854*
    *Frederic Granville Stilphen, to Alfred and Mary Call Stil-
phen, May 8, 1854*
    *Ida Belle Call, to Charles and Sarah Goud Call, November
2, 1855*

# Chapter Eighteen

*EUREKA FAMILY SOAP,*
*Manufactured by the*
*New England Eureka Soap Company,*
*BOSTON, MASS.*

*Warrented to wash in Hot, Cold, Hard, Soft or Salt Water*

*This new and valuable article, manufactured by a process never before used in this country, has won the approbation of all house-keepers…*

Northern Home Journal
Gardiner, Maine
1856

AFTER HER BREAKFAST dishes were done up, Sarah Goud Call carried her wash and rinse pans to the outkitchen. She split the soapy water between two of her soaktubs, then poured half the rinse water into each as well.

She sorted tomorrow's laundry, tossed trousers, shirts, and two waists into one tub, kitchen rags, wash flannels, and toweling into the other.

She made a quick trip to the well, then filled a third tub and shoved the filthy diapers in; she pushed them under the water to cut the smell, covered them, left them to soak in the shed.

———

Tom came in from the barn; gave Lizzie a smile. "You're all set to go up to sewing," he said. "Harnessed, ready to go."

"I'm grateful," she said, reaching already for the pot on the stove. "Coffee?"

"If there's leftover," he said, and pulled his chair back from the table, sat down.

She put a saucer and cup before him. "I'm not going for long," she said.

"Are you going to tell them?" Tom asked, stirring his coffee.

"Yes," she said. She was quiet for a moment, then looked at him. "Thirty years," she said. "I have lived here on the Eastern for thirty years."

"Is it hard to know ye're leaving?"

She turned away, went back to her worktable. "Harder than I thought it might be," she admitted, "but it's all right." She split and buttered a biscuit for him.

"No regrets?" he asked. "About marrying me?"

She brought the biscuit over, set it before him on a clean napkin; she leaned down, kissed him, then drew his head to her breasts, held him there.

"No, my dear," she said. "Not a single one."

———

They all met at Lydia's. They arranged themselves around the kitchen table, opened their sewing bags, and took out their pins, their needles, their thimbles and darning eggs; they clustered their spools of thread in the center for all to share.

Lydia hemmed napkins; Mary Stilphen went to work on darning socks, picking odd colored threads from the spools on the table.

"Spice things up," she said, working a red patch on a black sock of Alfred's. "Give him a little jolt."

Jane and Polly had two bedsheets of Polly's to turn; they worked them together on a long board set between two kitchen chairs.

"How does that go?" Mary asked. "I never learned that."

"Sheets always wear out in the center," Polly said, "so cut them in half the long way, flip the sides to the middle and sew 'em back together again."

"Use the board to lay out the two sides, pin them in place," Jane said. "Then it's just a tight stitch all the way up—Polly and me sew a similar stitch, so we can work them together and still keep the center seam smooth and even."

"We've been talking it over," Lizzie said, "Tom and me."

There was something in her tone, something different. The others hushed, stopped their sewing in mid-stitch, looked over at Lizzie; Lydia stopped her sewing, but kept her head down.

"I have news to share," Lizzie went on, "and figured it's time to tell the rest of you—just so it's all in the open."

She faltered a bit, felt her throat tighten, so she turned her head and looked out Lydia's kitchen window for a moment, looked south down the road, down the slope of the field to the stone wall.

"When Tom married me," she said, turning back to look at them all, one by one, around the table, "he knew the farm was always for Charlie—from his father."

They were still, barely breathing; Mary Stilphen's hand came up to her throat, Jane Blodgett looked at Polly, then back to Lizzie.

"Now that Charlie and Sarah are married, starting a family already," Lizzie said, "Tom thinks it's time for us to get out of their way, and I agree with that." She took another breath. "So we'll be moving down to Massachusetts in the fall—Tom and me and the other children—leaving the farm to Charlie and Sarah to run as their own."

Lydia Crocker leaned back in her chair, slumped her shoulders.

"We all started here…" Lizzie began; she looked down, away from Lydia, fumbled her fingers in her lap.

She lifted her head and tried again.

"We all started here on the Eastern," she said, "all of us together; it breaks my heart, being the first one to leave."

She put her hands over her face and burst into tears.

The June sun lifted slowly up over the ridge, brushed the tops of the maples and beeches with light; mist rose from the Eastern, drifted through the reeds along the opposite shore.

Slack tide; the water was still.

Alfred Stilphen watched a lone heron lank its way through the low water, head down, one beady eye fixed on the shadows beneath the surface; it lifted each leg carefully, stepped slowly in the shallows.

Don't worry yerself, old man, Alfred thought; there's enough fish here for both of us.

He unrolled his netting in the damp grass along the river, pulled it out long on the top of the banking, taking care to keep it straight, untangled. He shucked off his boots and stockings, then poked the fingers of his right hand through the mesh at the near end and started down off solid ground into the mud, through the mud into the low water, dragging the length of net behind him.

By the time he reached center stream, the water was up to his thighs; by noon it would be over his head.

He tied the top end of the net to the tip of the center pole, then leaned over, stretched both arms into the water and tied the bottom. He made his way back to shore, stopping at each set pole to lift the net from the water and tie it at the top, slip the stone weights into the pockets Mary had worked along the bottom edge. The weights fell against the tide, kept the net stretched down to the riverbed.

The finished line of netting angled back to the shoreline, suggested an upstream channel that diverted the bluebacks from their spawning run upriver; sent them instead into the curve in the shoreline where Alfred would wait for them in the spring sunlight, wait patiently with his scoop net, lift them out of the Eastern and tip them onto the grassy shore.

Mary wouldn't work the fish.

"No," she said. "I'll lend a hand for most everything else on this farm, but I won't rack fish."

"But thee has such quick hands," he countered. "And those fish give our sheep better fleece, give good shine to the wool."

She turned to him, set her hands to her hips. "They'll give good shine no matter who cleans and racks 'em—and it doesn't have to be me."

He shoved his hands into his pockets, looked at her.

"No," she said again, shaking her head. "I won't do it—the smell's enough to knock me senseless."

———

He had a long, low smoke shed down near the river, with cutting tables on the sides and a center trench for the fires, rack lines above for hanging the fish.

In the end, he tended the nets himself, fed the fires while Jimmy Goud and young Lew Crocker worked the shed. They arrived each morning an hour after the tide turned in, cleaned and racked his morning haul—cut off the heads, slit the body nearly to the tail, gutted and boned, then separated the halves and draped the fish over the rack line. The oil dripped from the bluebacks down into the fires, sizzled onto the coals; the smoke rose up to the peaked roof, wrapped about the fish as they dried, kept the flies away.

"Why don't he block up the whole river?" Lew asked, running his knife up the underside of a herring. "He'd get all he needed in a shorter time if he ran that netting from shore to shore—he's only half across." He hooked his finger inside the fish, gutted it in a single pull.

"We used to do that," Jimmy Goud said, "but the law says you can't do it now." He stopped work for a moment, looked out to where Alfred stood on the banking, dipping his net into the Eastern. "If you block up the whole river, the fish can't get up to spawn, and if they don't spawn, we don't get any fish at all."

"I'd do it anyway," Lew said, "if it made this work go faster."

The tables turned slippery with guts and oil; the men shoved the heads and leavings to the ends of the planks, pushed the entire mess over the edge to the ground. Alfred shoveled loads of it—covered with buzzing, frantic flies—onto a barrow and wheeled it all back to the river and dumped it in, flies and all.

When the fish were ready—fully dried, somewhat smoky—they fed them into the grinder, then packed the chewed herring into thirty of Nate Blodgett's sturdy barrels, set and hammered the lids. They rolled the kegs up the ramp into the wagon, hauled them up to the sheep sheds, and lined them along the back walls, ten barrels to a shed.

Thirty barrels, Alfred thought, heading for the house on the last day; that's one barrel of feed a week from September to April.

———————

Mary met him at the shed door. "Take off those clothes," she said, "so I can set coals to them."

He started in on his buttons.

"And scrub every inch of skin before coming inside my house—hair, too." She tipped her head to the bucket and basin by the set tubs; steam came up from under the lids. "Water's waiting."

"That bad?" he asked, lowering his trousers; they were stiff with oil and smear.

She grinned, handed him a bar of Eureka, a cloth. "Thee's enough to choke a whale," she said, turned on her heel and left him to it.

———————

Jane Blodgett was out the shed door at first light, yoke across her shoulders, the empty buckets swinging with each step, tugging at her balance, this way and that.

I've done this at least eight times every single day of my life here, she thought; maybe more when the children were babies and busy soiling their clothing as fast I could dress them.

She pulled on the sweep rope to lower the bucket—put her full strength to it against the weights on the far end—waited for the bucket to fill, then let go the rope; the counterweight sank to the ground, lifting the pole on its fulcrum, and the bucket rose up out of the well, water spilling out over the sides.

She leaned forward, grabbed the rim and pulled it to her, poured the water into one of her yoke pails, and lowered it back into the well for another fill.

At least eight times a day, she thought; a hundred feet from the house, a hundred feet back again—that's two hundred feet each trip; sixteen hundred feet every day...

When her pails were full, Jane squatted under the yoke, squared her hips, then lifted up, the long muscles in her thighs bunching with the effort, tightening under her skirts and apron. The buckets rose a foot into the air, swayed; she shifted her hands along the length of the yoke, searching to balance the load, and when it quieted on her shoulders, she started back across the yard to the house.

...sixteen hundred feet every day is more than two miles every week, she figured....

She wished the well were closer, but at least it was on even ground with the house, not slightly below like Lydia Crocker's—Lydia had to carry full buckets on a long uphill slope to her house—and I've even got a well sweep, Jane thought, which helps considerable, makes lifting full buckets from the well less of an effort. But still, it seems harder now that I'm older; my hands and arms are sore all the time from fighting the counterweight of the sweep, from lifting those full buckets.

...and that means, she thought, I walk more than a hundred miles a year—just to fetch my house water.

———

It rained on Wednesday, a steady rain with lots of bluster. The branches and leaves on the maples in the yard dipped and lifted, and the wind threw rainwater against the kitchen windows, peppered it against the clapboards and the front door.

"Hip's worse when the weather's damp and rainy," Nate said, dragging his chair over to the stove, easing himself down. "Aches and stabs something fierce."

"Want some of that liniment?" Jane asked, standing up from her work at the table where she was cutting up a rabbit for stew. She wiped her bloody hands on her apron. "I can heat it up some."

He shrugged, looked away, looked out the window and thought of all the things he could no longer do.

On Thursday morning, the sun broke clean and bright up over the ridge. The early light angled over the shed roof and fell into the dooryard; the wet trees shimmered and dripped, and small puddles glinted in the low spots in the drive.

Daniel Blodgett loaded his mother's wash and rinse barrels, rolled them up into the cart bed, and tied them to the corner posts. Jane filled them with water, added soap to the wash barrel, then put in the clothes— trousers and shirts, her skirts and aprons, her cleaning and drip rags.

She fisted the lids down herself, turned to Daniel.

"Could you load me two more for yer Aunt Polly?" she asked.

"All right," he said. "I can just fit two more in the cart—no more than that, or you'll have to take the wagon."

She went down the drive and turned into the road, her egg basket braced between her feet against the bump and lurch of the cart. The water sloshed inside her barrels; the horse's hooves sucked out of the mud in the ruts as he picked his way carefully up the rise. Timothy along the roadway sagged with wet; everything smelled of water and dirt.

By the time she got near Polly's, the stones in the walls were steaming, the vapor wisping off the rocks, drifting into the meadows. Below her, in the valley, the Eastern glittered in the sunlight.

She pulled into the drive, stopped near the shed door, cupped one hand to her mouth. "Hallo!" she called out. "Ho, Polly!"

She waited, held the horse on a tight rein to keep the cart steady, and Polly appeared in the doorway.

"I'm to town, to Young's," Jane said. "I've got two barrels for you; gather yer washing and come with?"

"How long?" Polly asked.

Jane shrugged. "We'll be back by dinner."

"Laura don't mind watching George?" Jane asked as Polly climbed up into the cart. She snapped the reins lightly, urging the horse forward.

Polly shook her head. "Now that Abby's gone, Laura spends most of her time caring for that baby." She arranged her skirts, pulled her shawl across her shoulders. "Keeps her busy, I think; keeps her from feeling left behind."

"She won't be left behind; she'll marry," Jane said. "She's pretty to look at, clever enough, can keep a good house."

"I know, but she worries."

Jane laughed. "Didn't we all worry about that?" She leaned into her sister, bumped against her in a tease. "We all did—remember?—all six of us girls—and we all married."

"True enough," Polly said.

They stopped at the post office.

"I've got a letter to Eliza to post," Jane said, "and I want a copy of the *Journal*—Nate will read it all," Jane said. "And it keeps him off his troubles."

She handed the reins to Polly, climbed down over the wheel to the ground. "I'll be right back," she said. "Then we can go down to Young's."

Polly Thompson waited, sat on the seat in the sunshine outside the post office, held the reins in her hand; she moved her fingers over the soft, smooth leather, thinking about Laura, her last at home.

She'll marry soon enough, she thought, she'll marry and leave; I'll be tearing my hair without her, that's for certain, what with young George and Sarah Ann.

Polly paid the clerk for her bluing, her pen nibs, and one bottle of ink; she tucked them into her bag.

"Remember when we had to make our own ink?" she asked, turning away from the counter—expecting to see Jane standing there, waiting to leave—but Jane was over by the back door with Jonathan Young, talking, gesturing.

"What's up?" Polly asked, coming closer.

"A pump," Jane said, "a water pump!"

"For what?"

"For the well." Jane showed her the handle, grasped it, moved it up and down. "It takes the water up out of the well," she explained, "so there's no need to lower buckets, haul 'em up again."

She turned to Jonathan Young. "Does it really work?"

He nodded. "Works good in three seasons," he said. "It freezes up in winter—you might have to still haul buckets in winter—but it works fine the rest of the time."

"Tell me how," Jane said, her eyes on the pump, on the curved spout at the top.

He reached for the pump and lifted it away from the wall. "You sink this bottom end into your well," he said, "and secure it."

"But how does it work?" she asked. "How does it take up the water?"

"It's complicated," he said.

Jane Blodgett rested her hands on her hips, arched an eyebrow and stared at him.

He looked away for a moment, looked back at her again. "You know how you can suck water up through a hollow reed?"

She nodded.

"It works because you're sucking the air out first, and the water rises to fill the space."

"That makes sense to me," she said.

He turned to the pump. "Well, here, the tall box is the hollow reed, the pump handle provides the force to lift the water up; when it reaches the top, it takes the easy way out—just falls out of the spout into yer buckets."

"Just like that?" Jane asked, her eyes round.

"Just like that," he said, snapping his fingers. "Just like one-two-three."

Jane looked at the wooden handle, ran her fingers along the long, square pump box. She thought of the well sweep—the pole, the counter-weight, the bucket; she thought of the ache in her arms and shoulders, the burn of the rope in her hands—and turned to Jonathan Young.

"How much?" she asked.

It took them a while to figure out how to get the pump into the well, how to secure it.

In the end, they built a well cover with an opening for the box pump, slipped it through and dropped it down into the water, then fastened it to the cover itself.

"Ma's got to stand on the cover to work the handle," Daniel said. "What if she falls through?"

"If it holds us together, it'll surely hold Ma," John said.

They worked the handle, pumped it hard, but nothing happened.

"Doesn't work," said John, quick to bristle. "I knew it, just another slick promise."

"Wait, now; hold yer temper," said Daniel. He turned to Jane. "Did Mr. Young say to prime it?"

"What?" she asked.

"Prime it," he said. "Pour some water down it, get it started, build a force first; a force that keeps moving is better than one off and on."

John snorted. "Ye're sounding pretty smart," he said, "as if you know something about it."

"I do," Daniel said. "It's simple hydraulics."

"Hush—the both of ye," Jane said, "and go get one of the full kitchen buckets, bring it back here."

"It's Ma's pump," Daniel said. "Let her pump it first."

John came down off the well cover and Jane stepped up, squared her feet, and grasped the handle. Daniel poured a bucketful down the spout; Jane began to work the lever. It felt too easy at first, but then she felt a shift, felt the handle resist some; she looked up at Daniel.

"Keep pumping," he said.

The pressure started to build, and then she felt the water rise, heard it moving inside the pump; it spilled out the spout onto the well cover, clean and cold.

"Get a bucket!" she called out, grinning. "Get every bucket we've got!"

# Chapter Twenty

THE VALUE OF NEGROES.—A singular but accurate way of estimating the price of field hands may be found in the price of cotton. For every cent a pound for cotton, a field hand will bring $100; for instance, the present price of cotton is ten to twelve cents, and the price of a [N]egro man is from a thousand to twelve hundred dollars.

*Gardiner Home Journal*
December 30, 1858

JOEL THOMPSON sat at the table, a copy of the *Journal* spread out before him. He heard Polly's chatter, something about how George was doing his letters already—and him only six!—and how he could write his own first name.

"Not very well, mind you," she said, "but in print letters."

He nodded at her, not listening, not really.

A thousand dollars for a slave, he thought; a thousand dollars to twelve hundred dollars for a slave—a person.

"…and Caroline Crocker told me that Charles Henry can write his first and last name—"

"A thousand dollars, Polly," he said angrily, standing up, pushing his chair back.

She stopped working her biscuit dough, rested her hands on the rim of her yellowware bowl and looked at him.

He slapped the paper with the flat of his hand. "Says here that a Negro field hand—a slave—is worth a thousand dollars." He looked down at the paper. "Sometimes more than that."

"To buy?" she asked. "It costs that much to buy a slave?"

He didn't answer; he looked away.

"That seems a lot of money," she said.

"It's not that," he said, "although that's bad enough."

"Then what?" she asked; waited.

He took a breath. "I'm a free white man," he said, "and my entire farm—everything I own—isn't worth a thousand dollars." He shook his head. "After all these years and all my hard work, I'm not even worth the price of one Negro field hand."

She started over to him, but he shook his head, kept her away; he took his coat from the peg and went out the door, off to the barn to do midmorning chores.

———

Sarah Ann Thompson crouched beside the rabbit path; she reset her last snare, then kicked some powdery snow over her boot prints and backed away.

It was cold.

She lifted her hands to her mouth, breathed into her cupped palms, rubbed them together a few times to make some heat, then breathed on the backs, across her red knuckles, rubbed again. She lifted her skirts and wiped her runny nose on the inside edge of the hem—where Polly wouldn't see it, where she wouldn't see the smear and tell her to use a rag instead—then dropped the skirt to the ground again.

She leaned over, touched the two rabbits; they were both stiffening in the December cold, but their fur was still soft. She patted and stroked them gently.

Hungry, she thought; time to go.

She picked them up by their long hind legs and turned, started a low drone for them deep in her throat, and headed back along the path.

She passed the bog—all frozen over now—and then she was out of the woods and over the stone wall that marked the uppermost pasture.

It was worse out in the open, colder without the break of the stand of fir and pine. She tipped her head forward to keep the wind out of her eyes and trotted across the frozen snow, her nose running again, her lips chapped and sore.

Hungry, she thought, hungry, hungry.

———————

Polly put a little lard into the skillet, then set it atop her cookstove to heat. When it started to sizzle and spit, she fed chunks of rabbit to it, seared the meat to seal the juices inside, keep it moist.

She turned back to her cutting board and peeled an onion, chopped it; she scraped it off into the skillet and fried it up a little, then put the meat, the onion, and the skillet leavings into the pot, added some salt pork and some water, slid the pot to the back of the stove to stew.

Couple of hours, she thought, I'll add potatoes then, maybe cut up a squash and some carrots, add them, too.

She heard the latch lift; George pushed through, started across the floor with his chip basket.

"Door," she reminded him, and he turned back, pushed it closed; the drop bar settled with a soft click.

"I got a lot of chips," he said, holding the basket out for her to see. "It's cold out there but I got 'em all off the shed floor."

"Well done," she said, smiling.

He puffed out—just a little, she thought, just enough pride there, but not too much—and set his chip basket near the woodbox, came back to her at the table.

"Rabbit?" he asked, trying to work out of his coat.

"Yes," she said, looking down at him. "Yer ma got us some rabbit this morning." She leaned down, helped him with his buttons. "Hang that up on yer hook, now."

He came back and leaned up against her.

"I went once with her," he said, "but when I saw the rabbit was dead, I cried—I couldn't help it."

She put her hand on him then, pulled him tighter against her hip and roughed his hair a little.

"That's all right," she said, and let him go.

---

Joel ducked his head and passed through the short doorway on the back end of Eliphalet Crocker's barn, moved into his pig shed.

"How many?" he asked as he neared the pen.

"Ten so far," Liph said, standing within it, shaking out new straw. "She was slow to start, but she dropped 'em all this forenoon." He finished spreading the bedding, then leaned back against the rail, stretched. "I think she's done now."

Joel stepped up closer, looked down at the piglets, their snouts pushed up tight against their mother's belly, cheeks pulling, suckling already.

"She's no Chester White," he said, eyeing the sow. "She's lean like one, but her color's off a bit."

"Ye're right about the color," Eliphalet said. "She's the Yorkshire—some pinker than a Chester." He leaned down, scratched the sow behind her ears, gave her a pat; she opened her eye, grunted. "I like Yorkies better than Chesters," he added. "They're better tempered."

They stood for a while, watching the piglets. One lost the teat and started to root and snuffle frantically. Eliphalet leaned over, picked it up, and made space between two others, set it right again.

"The sow looks a little flushed," Joel said, "up by her jowls."

"Well, I guess I'd be a little flushed, too," Liph said, "if I was poppin' out all those little grunters."

---

He had to get out for a while.

He stood from the table after supper, left them in the kitchen: Samuel finishing up his dinner; Caroline—huge and lumbering near the end of her fourth pregnancy—cleaning up their three children, wiping their faces and sticky fingers with a wet cloth; Lydia, back into her apron, starting the washing up; Lew off to a social at the Methodist Church in Dresden; Ben and Isaac to a card party at the Marson house; Lee off someplace, somewhere—to Laura Stilphen's, maybe.

They'll marry soon enough, he thought. Lee and Laura Stilphen will marry and Alfred and I will become cousins—well, not true cousins, but something like that; uncles-in-law, cousins by marriage. Removed once or twice. Something.

He took up one of the lamps and headed back out to the pen; he moved his way through the shadowy workroom, the woodshed, down past the open privy door, and on into the barn, went along the alleyway past the ox stalls where Victor and Albert stood motionless in the dimness, then through the side door to the pen.

He raised the lamp and looked down.

They were there, all ten of them, sleeping soundly, tucked up against each other, safe and warm within the space between the sow's front and back legs.

He leaned over the rail to smooth Roxy's head and cheek; her bristles prickled against the smoothness of his palm.

"Well done," he whispered; she raised her head into the curve of his hand.

When he came back into the kitchen, Samuel and his family were in the parlor, and the kitchen was theirs again.

Lydia was finishing the dishes; she lifted a bowl out of her rinse water, tipped it upside down with the others on the clean towel, wiped her hands on her apron.

"They're gone," she said, "in their own half of the house for the night."

"I know," he said. "But still, it's some packed in here with all of us together." He put the lamp down on the worktable and adjusted the wick; the light pushed away into the corners, reflected brightly in the window glass.

"Well?" she asked. "How are they?" She picked up a hand towel and dried the last of her dishes; the plates chinked softly as she stacked them. "Those piglets, I mean."

"All there," he said, "and in good health, far as I can see."

"Oh," she said, "that's fine."

He sat down in his rocker, watched her as she carried the plates to the cupboard, set them on the shelf, came back again.

"So, we've got ten," he said, "and maybe ten more when Lilly drops hers—we might have twenty by the end of the week."

Lydia leaned up against the worktable, grinned at him. "We might have twenty-one," she said, "by the looks of our daughter-in-law."

It stayed warm during the night. In the morning, just after dawn, the Eastern was gray with river smoke that smoothed out over the bankings and covered the lowland. The shrubs and bushes there, thick with budding leaves, pushed slender fingers up out of the mist into the soft, pink light of sunrise.

He watched from the kitchen window, watched the breeze clear the smoke from the water; he watched the mist rise up the slope of the bankings and slip away into the air.

He turned to Lydia. "We're meeting today about the smokehouse," he said.

"Well, ye're not meetin' up here," Lydia said, pouring the last of the tea into their cups on the table. "Caroline's too uncomfortable for all that commotion, and I'll have my hands full with the little ones."

"All right," Eliphalet said. He came back from the window, sat down with her. "Well, me and Samuel can take the wagon down to Alfred's."

"But then I can't get word up to Polly when I need her—not if the wagon's gone."

They sat together, quietly. Eliphalet ran his finger around the rim of his cup—it annoyed her a little, he knew, but the motion calmed him somehow.

"It's getting to be a muddle," Lydia said, "figuring how to get everybody where they need to be."

"Maybe it's time we got a second horse," he suggested, still pushing his finger around. "Then we could run the wagon and the cart at the same time."

"Maybe not," she said, reaching out, stopping his hand. "Let me think for a minute."

"In the end, it all settled out," Eliphalet told Mary Stilphen. "Me and Samuel went up for Joel and Polly, got Nate and John on the way back down, stopped at the house to drop Polly off to help with Cal—she's started her pains, so it won't be long—then kept on down to here."

"She's started, has she?" Mary motioned Liph to a chair, turned to Samuel. "How's yer nerves," she asked, "yer fourth time around?"

"I'm a little on the edge," he admitted.

She patted his arm. "A new baby's enough to sharpen yer nerves a little."

They dragged up chairs, settled themselves around Alfred Stilphen's kitchen table: Joel Thompson, Nathaniel and John Blodgett, Eliphalet and Samuel Crocker, Alfred himself at the head.

"No Charlie Call?" Alfred asked.

"He's not yet back from running the scow down to Bath," Samuel said. "He'll probably be in on the next tide—but he's all for it."

"All for what, then?"

"We're thinking to build a smokehouse," Eliphalet said. "Samuel and me—up across from the far corner of our barn."

"Need a new barrel?" Nate said. "I've got one I can trade off."

"No," Eliphalet said, shaking his head. "Our barrel's holding up fine, but we're thinking broader than barrels—we're thinking to build a full smokehouse, one we all can share."

Alfred set his elbow, rested his chin in his upturned hand.

"Now that the bridge is up and we can get over the Kennebec to Gardiner," Eliphalet said, "we could supply smoked meat to the town markets—if we had enough meat to make it worth our while."

He looked around; saw interest in their eyes.

"Sell for profit?" John asked, leaning forward.

"Yes, for profit," Liph said. He ticked his fingers, counted his points. "Share the cost and labor to build, share the work of wood, of slaughter and dressing, of firing; take turns hauling to Gardiner." He dropped his hands to the tabletop. "Together, we can share a bigger load, a bigger market; we can get a bigger profit in return."

"So, raise our own, slaughter and smoke collectively?"

"Right—cheaper and more efficient to do it all together."

They sat there for a moment, thinking it through. Outside, over near the fence surrounding the sheds, one of Alfred's ewes bleated desperately for her lamb.

"I could smoke mutton," Alfred said, "and could cure more than one at a time; my barrel limits me to one."

"Mutton, pork, veal—even venison, whenever one of us gets one."

"What about chickens?" Nate asked. "Could we smoke Janey's chickens, sell 'em in Gardiner?"

"We could," Eliphalet said.

"Well, then," Nate said. "I'm in; I hate them chickens."

———

They started the smokehouse in late May.

They built it eight feet square, with ten feet at center peak; an outside firepit to keep the smoke cool and prevent the spread of ash inside the house itself.

"For Chrissake's," Nate said. "What's wrong with letting the ash build, like in a barrel?"

"Those shop people in Gardiner won't want to scrape a layer of ash off every time they have a customer," Liph said. "Our meat's got to be clean—the cleaner we keep it, the more we'll sell."

They worked at it on and off through the middle of June. It was difficult to find the time, what with the usual spring work to do, but they figured a schedule, kept to it.

Alfred Stilphen and Charlie Call spent a full day hauling lumber from the mill in town, then worked off and on with the Crockers to frame it out. They ran two layers of board for siding—horizontal and vertical—finished it all off with battens on the seams.

Joel Thompson and Nathaniel Blodgett laid a brick-and-mortar floor, using Portland cement for a quick, tight set. They built, too, an underground brick-lined firepit with a double-flue chimney—one flue in through the center of the floor, the other going in half the distance up the chimney—both managed from the outside.

The Crocker brothers bought the ironware from Oliver Wyman, the blacksmith in Pittston; six rods for thirty cents and twenty hammered S-hooks for twenty more. They fitted four of the rods high up between the gable ends and ran the other two at a lower level; the hooks were moveable, and slid easily along the rods.

A solid door—no chinks or gaps—with a tight latch, and they were done.

They fired the smokehouse for the first time in late August.

Jane Blodgett dressed out ten of her chickens, gutted and plucked them and rinsed them out in a barrel. She patted them dry with a cloth, rubbed them with some salt, and then hung them on the S-hooks—five on a top rod, five on a lower.

"Both'll work," she said, "but I want to see what the difference is."

Polly Thompson brought two of Sarah Ann's rabbits, skinned and gutted; Alfred Stilphen stuck a lamb, bled it out and dressed it; Eliphalet Crocker added two shoats and an early market hog to the mix—not a full house, by any means, but a satisfactory first fire.

Alfred and Mary Stilphen rose at dawn.

Mary scratched around the kitchen, made him a plate of eggs and fried bread while he readied the horses and wagon. When everything was hitched and set, he led the horses up near the shed door, dropped the anchor in the drive, and came back in to eat his breakfast.

"Is thee gone all the day?" she asked.

"I'm not certain," he said, mopping up rich yolk with a crust; he tucked it into his mouth, chewed, swallowed. "If we can find buyers quick enough, I'll be home early."

"What about chores?"

"Jimmy Goud'll do the heavy work," he said. "Gus and Livingston said they'd turn out the sheep this morning; they can shed them this evening if I'm not back."

"All right," she said. "Jimmy and I can manage the rest."

He was on his way shortly thereafter. He started up the road, the spring wagon rattling in the dry ruts; he rolled over the bridge at Otter Creek, came up out of the woods into Call's lower fields, and caught a glimpse of the Eastern, glimmering in the early light.

Looks the same, he thought; it's a comfort that it always looks the same, even though everything alongside it changes all the time.

He met Eliphalet and Samuel Crocker at the smokehouse.

Together they loaded the wagon: all the meat from the smokehouse, a peck of beans, and a basket of clean, early potatoes from Caroline Crocker's garden.

"Get what you can for 'em," Samuel said to his father, hefting the baskets into the bed, sliding them up closer to the front.

"All right."

Liph tugged a canvas over the top, tucked it securely under the load, and climbed up onto the board seat beside Alfred.

Jane Blodgett flagged them down as they passed the bottom of the drive.

"Got room for more?" she asked.

"Yes, indeed," Liph said. "What's there?"

"Two dozen eggs," she said, "packed in clean straw; two pecks of yellow beans."

"Hand up those eggs," Alfred said. "Safer up here with us."

She did, then carried the baskets of beans to the rear of the wagon; she lifted the tarp, slipped them in, and tucked the tarp back underneath, stepped away.

"Butter," Polly said, "fresh made yesterday—be sure to tell 'em it's salted."

She wedged the firkin between the baskets of beans, secured the tarp again.

"What's in the jug?" Eliphalet asked. "Syrup?"

She nodded. "Joel wonders if there might be a market for it over to Gardiner."

"I'd guess so," Liph said. "It goes quick in Dresden off the scow, so I'd guess it'll go quick over there, too."

The horses were fit and strong, eager to work. Alfred didn't push them; he walked them up the long hills, trotted them on the downside slopes and on the flats. They had to turn out once on the county road to allow for a load of logs—the drover tipped his hat in gratitude as he passed by—but the road that ran alongside the Kennebec was wide enough for traffic both ways.

By the time they got to the bridge, there were six or seven wagons lined up to pay the toll.

"Oh, Lord," Liph said. "I forgot about the toll."

"I got fifteen cents," Alfred said. "That should get us across."

They sold everything.

Sarah Ann's rabbits, Jane's chickens and all the pork—both the whole hog and the two shoats—went to the butcher at Bridge & Morrell's; Eliphalet counted the coins as they drove down the rest of Water Street.

"We're rich," he said. "We could eat out, have a sit-down meal in the fancy dining room at the Johnson House."

"Well, I guess," Alfred said. He was quiet for a moment, then chuckled; he turned the corner and went down to the end of Mechanic Street, handed the reins to Eliphalet.

"Ye're pretty smart for an old man," he said, and hopped down, crossed the sidewalk, and knocked on the back door of the kitchen at the Johnson House, then pushed at it, went in.

He came back outside with the cook, who stood on the board sidewalk, his apron tied about his waist, his shirtsleeves rolled up to the elbows. He had a paring knife in his hand.

"I'm starting the dinner right now," he said, "so make it quick."

Alfred threw back the tarp and showed him the goods.

"Fine potatoes," the cook said, beaming. "All of a size, and clean, too—I can't tell you how much time I waste cleaning produce."

He leaned over, fingered the beans, nodded.

"I'll take the potatoes and the beans," he said.

"We got some eggs and some butter, too," Eliphalet said; he remembered Polly's instruction. "It's salted a little—not the eggs, of course; the butter is a little salted."

He opened the firkin; the cook touched the end of his pinky finger to the butter, tasted it.

"I'll take that, too," he said. "And the eggs." He wiped his finger on his apron.

"Syrup," Alfred said. "We got syrup, too."

"I'll take it all," the cook said. He started back toward the door, turned. "Well, come on," he said, beckoning them across the sidewalk. "Carry it all in—we'll figure the numbers and get you your money."

They were home by late afternoon.

# Chapter Twenty-one

TO FARMERS and GARDENERS.
THE SUBSCRIBERS OFFER FOR SALE
60,000 BARRELS
OF THEIR NEW AND IMPROVED
POUDRETTE
Manufactured from night soil of New York city...in lots to suit
purchasers...still defies competition, as a manure for Corn and
Garden Vegetables...*free from any disagreeable odor...*

Advertisement
*Gardiner Home Journal*
Gardiner, Maine

CAROLINE CROCKER dropped her hands to her lap; the newspaper crumpled against her heavy thighs and over the tops of her knees. She looked over at Samuel.

"Can this be true?" she said, her mouth flat. "Can it?"

"What's that, Cal?"

"This," she said. She raised the paper and shook it at him; turned the page back at the fold and dropped it back into her lap, then jabbed her forefinger onto the paper. "This advertisement!"

"Let me see," he said, and rose from his chair.

"Night soil," she said, holding it out to him, "for sale!"

He took the paper from her, carried it back to the table and sat down to read; he followed along with his finger, so as not to lose his place in the jumble of words on the page.

"Are you asking about the night soil?" he said. "If it's true or not?"

"Of course that's what I'm asking."

"Well, I'd guess it's true enough," he said. "Folks in cities produce a lot of night soil; they've got to do something with it all, don't they?" He stood, brought the newspaper back over to her.

She looked up at him. "You don't find it offensive?" she said, reaching for the paper. "That those city people are barreling up their business and shipping it here by rail for us to dispose of?"

He shook his head. "We do the same thing, Cal; I shovel the soil from our privy into the compost pit, mix it into our stock manure, and spread all of it in our fields."

She humphed.

"Everybody we know does that," he said. "Our neighbors all do it."

"Well, I won't be putting city night soil on my gardens; it could be foreigners." She tapped her fingers on the newspaper again. "Or Gypsies—it could be Gypsies—and I can't bear the thought of our children eating food dressed with Gypsy night soil."

"Everybody does it, Caroline."

She leaned back against the curve of the rocker, turned her head to him. "Everybody does their business, or everybody spreads their business on their fields?"

"Both," he said.

"Well, I won't have it," she said. "I just won't."

"You don't have to," he said, trying not to smile.

"I'm not a squirmy woman," she said, "and you know that."

He nodded.

"But the thought of all those city people's night soil on my vegetables is enough to make me shiver."

"Well," he said, "I don't suppose ours is better than anybody else's."

"Well, yes, it is," she insisted. "We're a family."

———————

"I can't do it any longer, not with this hip," Nathaniel said, working fixings into his pipe; he put the pipe in his mouth, leaned on the arms of his chair, pushed himself up to his feet. "It's time for me to turn it over to the both of you."

He lifted the corner lid from the stove and, using the short tongs, stuck a sliver of wood down into the firebox; when it flamed, he withdrew it, touched it to the bowl of his pipe, drew in. The tobacco caught and he pulled on it some more; the sweet smoke rose up to the ceiling, settled between the beams.

He replaced the stove lid, then looked at his sons, sitting still as rocks, their forearms resting on the tabletop.

"I split it up," he said. "Made two parcels of it."

Through the window, he saw the leaves lifting in the wind, saw Jane struggling to gather her washing; shirts and linens flapped against her body as she moved up the line; her waist was thicker, fuller now, her hair full gray against the sharp blue sky.

I should have done better by you, he thought, watching her pull pins from the line, drop them carefully into her apron pockets; I should have done better.

"Daniel gets his share now," he said. "It's a smaller parcel—not by much, but by some." He backed away from the stove, eased down into his rocker, looked at Daniel. "Is that fair enough?"

Daniel nodded. "As fair as can be," he said.

"And Johnny," Nathaniel said, "there's a reason the bigger share goes to you: ye're getting me and yer mother in the bargain, so…"

"All right," John said.

"Ye're not to forget that we've got life interest here," he said, "and if I die first, her interest still holds."

John picked up his coffee cup, raised it to his mouth, took a sip. "So," he said, rattling his cup back into the saucer, "I'm head of household now?"

Nathaniel Blodgett turned away, looked out the window again; pushed his good leg against the floor and started to rock, just a little.

Daniel coughed, looked down.

"Papers are all done, all signed," Nathaniel said. "They're here in the document box."

They heard the squeak of the shed door as Jane returned from the laundry lines; she opened the kitchen door and came in, her basket on her hip.

"Well?" she asked, setting the clean laundry on her worktable. She looked at her sons, then turned to Nathaniel.

"Done," he said, softly. "It's done."

———————

Later, much later, Jane Blodgett turned down the lamp, cupped her hand at the top of the chimney, blew out the flame.

She slipped into bed, turned onto her side and stretched out beside him, lifted her head so he could slip his arm beneath; she rested her hand on his chest, looked past his profile and out the window at the shadow of the barn.

"Have I done right, Janey?" he whispered.

"I think so," she said. She felt his breath against her forehead; his thumb made small circles on her shoulder. "It will keep them both to home, keep the farm going smoothly."

They were quiet for a long moment.

"And provide for us in our old age," she said, patting his chest.

He shifted in the bed to ease his hip.

"I keep thinking of Joel," she said, "with nobody."

"I know—so much work to do and no manpower at home to help him do it." He coughed. "The place is looking a little poorly, and he used to be so particular."

She nodded against his shoulder. "And Polly's got Sarah Ann and George to care for," she said.

Again, they were quiet, easing into drowsiness, to sleep.

"We'll all have to do what we can," she murmured, "until George grows up."

———————

*Pittston Town Meeting*
*East Parish*
*November 15, 1860*

*Marriages in the Town of Pittston, Registered & Recorded by*
*me, Benjamin S. Jones, Town Clerk*
    *Miss Laura Thompson of Pittston & Mr. Seward McKenney*
*of Phillips, February 14, 1858*
    *Miss Margaret Shea & Mr. Llewellyn Crocker, both of*
*Pittston, April 3, 1859*
    *Miss Eulalia Marson & Mr. Benjamin F. Crocker, both of*
*Pittston, June 6, 1859*
    *Mr. Daniel Blodgett & Miss Adelaide Ware, both of*
*Pittston, November 5, 1860*

*Births in the Town of Pittston, Registered & Recorded by me,*
*Benjamin S. Jones, Town Clerk*
    *Charles L. Call, to Charles and Susan Goud Call, March 5,*
*1857*
    *Samuel Crocker, to Samuel and Caroline Dudley Crocker,*
*May 11, 1858*

---

1860 Census
Town of Pittston, Kennebec County, Maine

| | |
|---|---|
| Thompson, Joel | 68 |
| Mary | 57 |
| Sarah Ann | 47 |
| George | 7 |

35 acres improved, 30 unimproved; $800 cash value of farm
1 horse, 1 milch cow, 2 working oxen, 1 other cattle
1 swine, $130 value of live stock
2 bushels corn, 50 oats, 60 Irish potatoes
18 bushels barley, 100 lbs butter, 18 tons hay

| | |
|---|---|
| Blodgett, Nathaniel | 66 |
| Jane | 64 |
| John | 27 |
| Blodgett, Daniel | 35 |
| Adelaide | 23 |

100 acres improved, 40 unimproved; $2000 cash value of farm
1 horse, 5 milch cows, 4 working oxen, 5 other cattle
10 sheep, 1 swine, $487 value of live stock
30 bushels corn, 75 oats, 12 pease & beans
150 bushels potatoes, 56 bushels barley,
300 lbs butter, 100 lbs cheese, 35 lbs wool, 50 tons hay


| | |
|---|---|
| Crocker, Eliphalet | 60 |
| Lydia | 68 |
| Isaac | 33 |
| Leander | 30 |

130 acres improved, $1200 cash value of farm
1 horse, 2 milch cows, 2 working oxen, 2 other cattle
8 sheep, 1 swine, $159 value of live stock
25 bushels corn, 100 bushels oats, 26 lbs. wool
2 bushels pease & beans, 100 bushels potatoes
10 bushels barley, 100 lbs. butter, 38 tons hay


| | |
|---|---|
| Crocker, Samuel | 37 |
| Caroline | 36 |
| George | 12 |
| Charles Henry | 7 |
| Amanda | 6 |
| Samuel | 2 |

75 acres improved, $1200 cash value of farm
1 horse, 2 milch cows, 2 working oxen, 2 other cattle
9 sheep, $179 value of live stock
25 bushels corn, 80 oats, 35 lbs. wool
2 bushels pease & beans, 100 bushels potatoes
38 tons hay


| | |
|---|---|
| Call, Charles | 28 |
| Sarah | 26 |
| Ida Belle | 4 |
| Charles L. | 3 |

124 acres improved, 20 unimproved, $2500 cash value of farm
1 horse, 6 milch cows, 2 working oxen, 4 other cattle
10 sheep, 1 swine, $520 value of live stock
50 bushels corn, 150 bushels potatoes, 50 bushels barley
900 lbs butter, 30 lbs wool, 40 tons hay

| | |
|---|---|
| Stilphen, Alfred | 57 |
| Mary | 50 |
| Victoria A | 17 |
| Augustus M | 14 |
| Alfred L | 11 |
| Walter Scott | 9 |
| Fred G. | 6 |

150 acres improved, 80 unimproved, $3500 cash value of farm
2 horses, 8 milch cows, 4 working oxen, 6 other cattle
20 sheep, 1 swine, $454 value of live stock
70 bushels corn, 60 oats, 100 potatoes, 45 barley, 7 buckwheat
500 lbs butter, 55 lbs wool, 70 tons hay

# PART FIVE

# 1861–1865

# Chapter Twenty-two

Now, therefore, I, Abraham Lincoln, President of the United
States, in virtue of the power vested in me by the Constitu-
tion and the laws, have thought fit to call forth the militia of
the several States of the Union, to the aggregate number of
seventy-five thousand…Abraham Lincoln

April 16, 1861

POLLY THOMPSON used her scissors to cut last week's newspaper into
strips, then she set those carefully out on the table; she smeared them with
rosin and sweet oil, using her fingertips to spread the mixture evenly over
the paper. She sprinkled them with sugardust from the cone sugar tin and
left them to dry, to stiffen up a little.

That'll do it, she thought; I'll hang them tomorrow in the kitchen
and pantry, catch all those spring flies, get 'em out of the house.

She heard the horse snort as Joel turned into the drive; heard the car-
riage wheels squeak on the axle, then the crunch of stones in the drive.

"Polly!" he called. "Polly, come quick!"

Lord! she thought, and dashed out through the shed and down the
stoop to the ground; she rushed across the dooryard to meet him.

"It's war," he said, and held out the new *Home Journal.* "We're moving to war!"

They met at the Crocker farm, all of them—Thompsons and
Blodgetts, Stilphens and Calls—a wagonload from both the north and
the south ends of the road.

It was too chilly to meet outside, so they piled into Eliphalet and Lydia's kitchen. The older people sat in chairs at the table; the next generation stood, leaned against doorjambs, counters, and cupboards, perched on Lydia's flour and meal crocks; the children spilled into the shed and the front hallway, sat directly on the floor and on the stairs leading up to the second floor.

"So, it's all here in the paper," Joel said; he held the folded paper in the air, waved it to get their attention.

"Read it," Samuel Crocker said. "Somebody should read it out loud so we all know what's what."

There was a murmuring of agreement, a general rustling; Joel passed the paper to Alfred Stilphen.

"All right now," Alfred called out. "Settle down, settle in." He waited until it was quiet, then lifted the paper and began to read to his neighbors.

"'Whereas the laws of the United States have been for some time past and now are opposed,'" he read, his voice full, the words and phrases clear and strong, "'and the execution thereof obstructed, in the States of South Carolina, Georgia, Alabama, Florida, Mississippi, Louisiana, and Texas, by combinations too powerful to be suppressed…'"

———

Later, after all their neighbors had left, Lydia Crocker put her kitchen back to order.

She wiped the table with a damp rag, pushed all the kitchen chairs back into place; she swept the floor, scooped the grit onto a sheet of stiff paper, then carried it to the back door, threw it out into the yard.

They'll all go, she thought, all our boys.

After supper, Lydia cleared his plate, took it to the counter.

"They'll all go, won't they?" she asked, coming back, setting his tea before him at the table.

Eliphalet lifted his cup, blew gently, then sipped; he rattled it back into the saucer.

"No," he said. "Samuel won't go—we need him here on the home farm."

She felt some relief at that, but pushed on. "The others, though," she said, "you think they'll go?"

He turned his head, looked at her, his eyes deep, tired.

She waited.

"Yes," he said finally, and reached for her hand.

———————

Spring, she thought; I like spring very best of all.

Mary Stilphen stood at her southeast kitchen window. The light was different now—the sun higher in the sky each day, and the shadows on the side of the main barn sharper against the whitewashed boards; she thought she could see the barest beginnings of leaf buds on the tips of the tree branches.

She looked across the drive, watched Alfred as he worked in the near pen, watched him shuffle his way through the crowd of blackface with his bucket of dried vegetables and lean down to offer them handfuls of beets or carrots. The sheep pushed their shoulders gently against his knees, nudged their heads—thick with fleece—at his thighs.

Almost time for lambing, she thought, and turned back to her morning chores.

She treated the new lamp wicks in the pantry. She soaked them in fresh vinegar until they were wet clean through, then lifted them out of the bowl; she pulled them through her fingers to strip the excess and draped them carefully over the top edge of a cupboard door to dry.

Brighter light, she knew, and a cleaner burn—well worth the extra work and the sharp prick of the vinegar in her nose and eyes.

She heard Sarah Call's voice in the shed, then a quick rap on the kitchen door and the squeak of the hinge as she stepped in.

"Ho, Mary?"

Mary wiped the last chimney clean, set it on the pantry shelf, and came through the doorway into the kitchen, cleaning her fingers with her apron.

"It's more chill than I thought," Sarah said, and blew on her hands;

she went to the stove and reached out for the heat, rubbed her palms together and reached out again.

"I've got hot tea," Mary offered. "Just steeped it." She brought out another cup and saucer and set it on the table; she gave Sarah her own chair nearest the stove, settled herself in Alfred's.

"What's on yer mind?" she asked.

Sarah Call took a breath, then looked up at Mary. "Well, Charlie and me's got ourselves into kind of a tangle."

Mary kept quiet. She lifted the pot, put her fingers against the lid to keep it still while she poured tea into their cups.

"We've not the money to hire out," Sarah said, "so I need yer help— if ye're willing, that is."

"All right." Mary waited.

Sarah put her spoon to her cup, stirred, then rested the spoon into her saucer and looked up.

"Will you teach me to shear?" she asked.

———

At first Charlie Call was dead set against it.

"I won't have it," he said. "I won't have you strutting around in trousers and shearing sheep like a man; ye're not—and thank goodness for that blessed difference—but I can't see my way through to allow that."

Sarah Call slumped back in her chair, closed her eyes for a moment. "Well, I'm not shearing in a skirt," she said.

"I can shear our sheep." He paced across the kitchen, spun on his heel when he neared the door, paced back. "All of 'em."

"Oh, Charlie," she said. "Listen for a moment—just listen, will you?"

He heaved a sigh, but paused, folded his arms across his chest.

"I know you can shear 'em," she said, "but, truth told, you do a poor job of it—ragged fleeces, sheep nicked and bleeding."

He looked down at his feet, said nothing.

"We're losing money on poor shearing," she said. "They'll pay more for good clean fleece; and you've always said Mary can shear better than any man on the Eastern."

"That's true," he admitted. "She can."

"So, tell me," Sarah said, "why it's all right for Mary to shear—and you admire her for that—but not all right for me to learn from her and shear our own."

"It's not about that," he said.

"Yes, it is," she said, "because nothing else makes sense."

On Thursday, Charlie Call spent the forenoon forking hay onto the scow, stacking and stamping it down, tarping it.

Sarah's brother Fred came over after evening chores, slept the night in the back room, and was up at dawn with Charlie—the two of them were on the scow when the tide changed, were on their way to Dresden by seven o'clock.

Sarah watched the scow slip around the last bend in the Eastern.

Tomorrow, she thought; I've got until the incoming tide tomorrow.

Mary and Victoria Stilphen arrived in the short wagon just past eight o'clock.

Sarah met them in the dooryard.

"We waited until they passed by," Mary said, "then left the house, carried the children up to the schoolhouse on the way—saved them the walk."

"We'll pick them up on our way back," Victoria said, "but meantime, I'll watch Ida Belle and Charles while you and Ma do the sheep."

"All right," Sarah said. She smiled at both of them, then led them across the dooryard to the house. At the stoop, she turned, looked square at Mary.

"Is Alfred angry?" she asked. "Does he think I'm wrong to do this?"

"He's amused more than anything," Mary said. "Now, go put your trousers on."

At first she felt odd, walking around in trousers.

Her legs seemed strange, separate from each other, and there was too much fabric between them when she walked.

"Ye're walking like a duck," Mary said. "Get yer feet closer together; walk normal, and it'll work better."

Mary helped her brace the ewe up against her knees and thighs.

"Curve her back into that space between yer legs, just below yer knees," she said, "and keep her head up on yer thighs."

Sarah adjusted the weight.

"Now keep yer arm down over the front of her," Mary said, "or she'll tip her head out, catch you in the chin with it when you lean over."

Sarah did; the ewe slumped against her legs.

"She's not fighting me," Sarah said, amazed.

"They give up," Mary said. "They figure ye're in control, and they get flippy-floppy—sometimes ye'll wish they held more tension in their backs."

Sarah leaned over with the shears, started in.

By the fifth sheep, she had it figured out.

She was slower than Mary, to be sure, but she had the geometry of it—she saw how the process, done right, left a clean fleece and an unmarked sheep at the end.

"All right," Mary said. "Now, don't think about it anymore—just do it, over and over again, the same way each time."

---

Sarah Goud Call took the children out after supper, walked with them across the dooryard and up to the sheep pen where the ewes milled about in the fresh straw, their shorn bodies small and clean in the evening light.

Ida Belle and Charles walked among them, delighted; they smoothed their palms across their backs and warm sides, wondered at the whiteness of them.

I did that, Sarah Call thought; I did that for me and Charlie, and did it on my own.

On Saturday afternoon, Charlie Call and Fred Goud came up the

Eastern on the incoming tide.

They tied up at the wharf, raised the sweep up out of the water, checked and coiled all their lines; they spread the canvas tarp out in the field grass beside the boathouse to dry in the sun, weighted the corners with rocks, then walked up the dirt track to the house.

When they came around the corner and started up to the sheds, Charlie saw Sarah standing near the fence, her right arm resting casually along the top board, her left hand perched on her hip; inside the pen, their sheep—all clean and shorn—were bright-eyed and prancing.

"Well, now," he said, slowing down, straightening his shoulders, turning grim.

Fred, unsure, slowed with him, glanced between Charles and his sister; he stepped away, just a little.

"'Well, now' what?" Sarah countered. "Here are yer sheep, all done for the year," she said, "and here's yer wife, back in her skirts."

# Chapter Twenty-three

ADVICE TO FARMERS. The newspapers are urging farmers to plant and sow every acre, because of the prospective demand for all that can possibly be raised the present season.

*Gardiner Home Journal*
Gardiner, Maine
May 16, 1861

"I'M CONSIDERING a haypress," Charlie Call said.

"To buy?" Joel Thompson asked, leaning up against the wall of Charlie's boathouse, looking down the slope to the river where the sunlight played tricks on the water, sparkled and jumped on the incoming tide.

"Can't afford to buy," Charles said. "I can build one, though, if I can get a clear idea of how it works."

"All right," Joel said. "Let's stop in at Tibbets & Lander when we make the market run to Gardiner this week." He pushed away from the wall. "Lander's got one in his workyard; you can see how it's put together."

"It's simple, really," John Lander said. "Come out back, take a look."

He led them through his store, past the nail kegs and tool racks, the tins of paint and linseed oil.

"Four horses, two men," he said, as he opened the back door and stepped out, took them into the workyard. "They can press five bales an hour—that's near a ton of hay every two hours."

Four dull-eyed horses plodded around a capstan, powering a wooden screw that pushed a top plate down inside a framed box of loose hay, compressed it into a tidy, rectangular bale.

Joel and Charlie stood in the dust of the workyard and watched Lander's men tie the bale, lift it from the press and stack it neatly against the warehouse wall.

"Will you look at that?" Joel marveled. He shoved his hands into his pockets. "They'd stack up good on the scow, huh?"

"A lot better than loose hay," Charlie agreed, "and we'd get a lot more hay on each run."

They stood in the sun, watched John Lander's crew press another bale, watched them fork loose hay into the box and set the plate. When they started the horses, the dust from the yard rose in thick clouds up around their legs, pushed against their bellies. The screw turned slowly, pushed the plate down into the box—tighter, tighter; the guy ropes strained under the pressure, relaxed when the men tied the bale and backed the horses off the load.

"Those bales are two hundred pounds each," Lander said. "You can reduce the pressure and make a lighter bale—a hundred pounds, say— easier for one man to handle."

They watched the men press still another bale.

It wasn't hard work, Charlie thought; not half so tiring as all the fork- ing, loading, and stamping that a ton of loose hay called for; those bales would stack slick enough on the scow, too.

"I could use two oxen," Charlie said, "for power."

Lander shrugged. "Four horses is faster."

"I hain't got four horses," Charlie said, "but I got two oxen."

They sat together up on the seat, each with a store-bought bottle of ginger beer, and talked about it on the way home.

Joel drove, kept a tight rein on the horses up the length of Water Street and across the bridge over the Kennebec, but when they turned onto the open road, headed south, he dropped the leathers, looped them around the toe of his boot.

"Think you can make one?" he asked, reaching for his beer.

"I could," Charlie said. "Shouldn't be so hard; I could see all the parts—the workings are pretty simple." He took a sip, swallowed. "The hardest part is chiseling that screw, but I could pay Seth Soper to turn one for me—he could do it faster on that lathe he's got."

They rolled along; Charlie sipped his beer, thought about the convenience of it—the ease of stacking, storing, and shipping those bales rather than forking all that loose hay, stamping it down, tarping it onto the broad deck of the *Ida Belle*.

Could build the press down by the riverbarn, he thought; press all the hay we want to ship right there, store it until the market's high; can store hay loose for our own stock in our high barns, just as always.

He took another couple of swallows, turned to Joel. "Could double the load on the scow, I should think," he said, "so could double our profit."

"Talking of profit," Joel said, "I heard hay's up to seventeen dollars a ton down to Boston."

"Seventeen?" Charlie whistled. "It's only eleven in Gardiner."

When they neared the corner of their road, Joel rested his bottle between his feet, picked up the reins again, shifted them in his hands.

"You know," he mused, as he started the team into the turn. "This war could open markets for us."

The outside wheel dipped into a crossrut, and the wagon lurched a bit; Charlie grabbed the edge of the seat to keep from sliding out, then found his balance, shifted more to center.

"Sorry," Joel said. "Wasn't paying attention."

"Me neither," said Charlie. "I'm too busy making hay."

They started up the long slow rise up the ridge. Off to the left, just over the stone wall that lined the roadway, fields of English grass rolled all the way down the slope to the Eastern, green and supple in the sunlight.

"Anyways," Joel went on, "I was thinking that the army's going to need a lot of hay—think of all the horses they've got to feed."

"Ship Eastern River hay to Boston?" Charlie asked. "For the army?"

Joel nodded. "Or to dealers down to Portland, anyways," he said. "Portland prices might split the difference—give us fourteen a ton, say— but it would still be good profit, especially with yer haypress in our favor."

Jane Blodgett tucked the letter into her apron pocket, then stepped back from Charlie Call's wagon and started back up the drive to the house.

I never know to be glad or worried whenever a letter comes from one of my girls, she thought.

She went through the shed into the kitchen, draped her shawl over the back of her rocker. She smiled at Nate, then reached into her pocket.

"Letter from Eliza," she said, handing it to him. "Charlie just dropped it off on his way back from town."

"Oh?" he said, taking it from her. "Did he think to drop off our market money, too?"

She shook her head. "He'll figure it out tonight, he says, bring it up in the forenoon tomorrow." She started over to the cupboard for cups and saucers. "Open Liza's letter," she said. "Let's hear what she's got to say."

"He should have given us our money today," Nate grumbled.

"Goodness sake, Nate," she said. "Read the letter."

She heard the rustle of paper as he slit the envelope with his knife; heard him pull the sheet out, unfold it; she went back to the pantry to get the honey pot, to cut two slices of bread and place them on a plate.

He looked up at her as she came back to the table. "She's coming home," he said. "John's enlisted; Eliza's coming home with the children for the duration."

"Well," Jane said. "We got the room."

The only one we've got old enough even to think to go is Augustus, Mary Stilphen thought, and he's just sixteen.

She herded the last of the sheep into the holding pen, lifted the heavy gate and swung it closed, latched it; she leaned on the top rail and looked into the pen, ticked her forefinger atop the fence board as she counted them—eighteen ewes, twelve lambs—all here, thank goodness, all accounted for.

She turned, headed back across the dooryard to the house, lifting her skirts out of the dirt to keep her hems clean.

I'd as soon pen Gus in with the sheep, she thought; keep him safe.

---

It was good to have her home again, Jane thought.

She and Eliza stepped out of the shed, headed across the dooryard to work the coop; the morning sunlight warmed their heads and shoulders as they crossed the drive.

"How many birds you got now, Ma?" Eliza asked. "Altogether, I mean?"

"I don't know, exactly," Jane said, "but I've got more than thirty layin'." She opened the door to the yard and they stepped in, closed and latched the door behind them.

The birds closed in, their beady eyes fixed on Jane; they made small clucks and coos in their throats, lifted their quick feet up and down, up and down.

Jane flapped her skirts to scatter them, then leaned over, picked up one of the low water pans, tossed the contents through the fencing to the outside. "Only animal I know," she said, "to dirty its own drinking water."

Liza nodded. "They're kind of dim, I'd say." She bent down, picked up another pan. "I'll get these pans cleaned up and refilled—you can get to yer raking."

Jane started in the corner, raked the entire chicken yard. She made a small pile of manure and feathers, collected it onto an old shingle, then carried it off to the compost pen behind the barn.

By the time she came back, Eliza was in the coop collecting eggs.

"Basket's hanging from the south post," Jane called.

"Found it!"

She leaned over, picked up her feed bucket.

"Chickens, chickens, chick-chick-chick!" she called, tossing fistfuls of cornmeal and buckwheat.

Got to keep 'em clean, she thought; got to give 'em clean water, good feed; they need gravel, a box of stove ashes to roll and flap in to keep the bugs off—do all that, and they'll give good eggs in return; a simple arrangement, I'd say.

"Twenty-three!" Liza called from the coop. "Good-sized ones, too, Ma!"

Jane turned, watched her daughter come through the door from the coop, basket hanging on her arm. A feather was caught in the curl of her hair, and Jane came forward, drew it gently away, then put her hand to Eliza's cheek.

"I'm glad to have yer help," Jane said, "and yer company."

She watched Eliza's eyes fill, watched her lower lip start to shake a bit.

"It's all right, dear girl," she said softly. "Yer John will come home or he'll not; I'll be here either way."

---

Sarah Call handed it to him on the first day of January: a little pocket diary bound in soft, dark leather with a chart of weights and measures on the first page, then a full 1862 calendar, and then page after page of clean space for his writing. And at the back, a list of postage rates—a great convenience for Charlie, she thought, at those times when he might need to figure how many stamps to send a billing for his services rendered, a billing for freight charges for runs up and down the Eastern on the *Ida Belle.*

Charlie sat now at table, just after dinner, holding the diary in his hands and admiring the stitching at the bind.

"Traded eggs for it at Young's Store," Sarah said, smiling, pleased by her own cleverness. "Got it last month, hid it in the pantry behind the flour crock. I knew you'd never look for something back there."

He held it up to his nose, smelled the leather.

"It's fine goods," he said. "Calfskin, I should say." He sniffed again, made a small sound of satisfaction in his throat.

"We can write things in it every day," she explained.

"Things like what?" he asked, rubbing his thumb over the cover, feeling the softness of it, fingering the little strap that held it bound when not in use.

"Things we like to keep a track on," she answered. She swept her hand at some crumbs on the table. "You're always noting the weather, or how many calves have dropped in a season, or how much money you've made cutting ice each winter."

At that they both looked out the window over the snow-covered slope and down to the Eastern; the river ran open even now—even in this dead of winter—the water deep and black and slow-moving.

"Well, maybe not so much for keeping tracks on ice this year," she admitted.

Charlie laughed.

"But what about days when you run the *Ida Belle,*" she went on, "or the day you begin the haying, or how many bales you press?"

He would understand her sense of purpose in this, she knew; he had a great respect for organization.

"For me," Sarah went on, "it's who might come to call, or how many eggs I gather each day—most importantly the eggs, I think."

He looked down at the pages. "I've got the big ledger for my working records," he said, "so there's room for more of the other in this little diary; I could write things of daily importance to both of us."

"You'd do that?" she asked. "You'd share that space with me?"

"I would," he said. "There are some things we both need to keep tracks on around here."

He stood up, went across the room to the corner cupboard and rummaged around until he found his ink bottle. He held it up to the window light to check the supply, then shook it gently, came back across the kitchen and set it on the table between them.

"When the moon's full," she suggested, "or when the children have their birthdays."

He sat back down, scuffed the chair back up to the table.

"Those two are good," he said, looking across the board at his wife. "And the weather—that's surely important to note—and who comes to call."

"All right," she agreed.

"We can add more things later."

She nodded, folded her arms onto the table, watched him set things up—the diary before him, the ink off to his right, just a little.

He uncorked the bottle, dipped the nib and clinked it gently on the inside of the neck. He held his hand over the first blank page.

"What should I say?" he asked her.

She looked out the window again. "Well, 'tis fair enough today," she said. "You could start with that."

The nib scratched across the page; she watched the words form one by one in the little block of space, the black ink tipping off the nib and flowing smoothly onto the paper.

He put the pen down, cleared his throat, read the entry back to her.

> *Wednesday, January 1, 1862*
> *It was a fair day. Sam & Caroline come avisiting in the fore*
> *noon and staid two hours brot us two newspapers.*

"Could you read that again?" she asked, "so I can hear it one more time, get it set in my mind?"

He read it again, then handed the little diary across the table to her; she looked at the writing on the page, then closed it carefully, slipped the strap into the loop to secure the cover.

"Wait," he said, reaching back across the table for it. "I forgot."

"Forgot what?" she asked. She handed it over to him.

"How many eggs did you get today?"

"Only five."

"You could make five tick marks—right here beside the date," he said, opening the diary and pointing his finger to a spot. "You could keep the egg tally on your own; I'll add the writing later when I'm doing my ledger."

He slid the open diary across the table to her, handed her the pen.

"Dip it just a bit into the ink," he said, "then tap the most of it away on the side of the bottle."

"I'll make a blot."

He shrugged. "No matter."

She straightened her shoulders, dipped the pen and tapped it; she gave him one last look, then made five careful slashes, blew gently to be sure the ink was set, reclosed the diary.

"Where should I keep it?" she asked him. "It's so small I fear misplacing it or dropping it about the dooryard."

He thought about that for a moment, tapped his forefinger against his mouth and considered.

"I think keep it in the document box," he said.

"With your ledger?" she asked. "With the mortgage and the will?"

"Best to keep all those paper things together," he explained, "don't you think?"

She moved to his cupboard, brought out the document box, opened the lid, and dropped the diary inside.

"It will be all together," he said. "We'll always know where it is."

She slid the box back onto the cupboard shelf, closed and latched the door.

"The ledger and the diary," he said. "Together, we can make sure it all gets done."

---

"I've two things to say," Isaac said.

"Just two?" Eliphalet Crocker pitched the last forkful of hay down from the loft; it spun in the light from the shed doorway, landed softly in the alleyway. "Usually you got more to say than that." He leaned on the handle of the fork, smiled down at his son.

"Just two," Isaac said. "One I think you're going to like, the other not."

I know them both, Eliphalet thought; I know the one I like and the one I don't, and I know them even before they come out of yer mouth—ye're my son, and I know how yer mind works.

"All right," he said. "Tell me the both of 'em, one after the other."

Isaac took a breath. "The first is that I'm going to marry Hannah Marson—I've asked and she's said yes."

"Well," Eliphalet said, "ye're right to think I like that one."

Isaac leaned back against the shed doorjamb; the sunlight angled across his face, across his nose and chin.

"And what's the other?" Eliphalet asked, his breath tight inside his chest.

"The other," Isaac said, "is that I'm going to enlist."

———————

They started haying in early July. They ran two full gangs—one starting at the south end of the road at Alfred Stilphen's, the other at the opposite end at Joel Thompson's. They worked to the middle, and ten days later, when all was done, they figured they'd cut and hauled about one hundred sixty tons of good English hay.

Joel needed most all of his for his own stock; the others, though, would have some to spare, especially if the second cutting in August yielded even a third of the first tonnage.

"A third's most likely," Alfred said. "We've gotten that much before, so I can't see why we wouldn't get it again this year."

Charlie Call planned to press a few tons, stack the bales in the riverbarn, and store them until the army's supplies got low, then ship them down to Portland for sale when the prices were highest.

He worried about the risk of it, though.

"All it would take," he said, "is a couple of hot spots in those bales—pressed and stacked tight like that—and we'd get a burn, maybe lose the whole lot to fire."

They talked about it some; decided to store the hay loose in the riverbarn over the winter, press it just before running the scow in the spring.

Safer that way, Charlie thought.

———————

*Pittston Town Meeting*
*East Parish*
*November 11, 1862*

*Marriages in the Town of Pittston, Registered & Recorded by*
*me, Benjamin S. Jones, Town Clerk*
    *Miss Laura Stilphen & Mr. Leander Crocker, both of*
*Pittston, December 12, 1861*
    *Miss Hannah Marson & Mr. Isaac Crocker, both of*
*Pittston, September 3, 1862*

# Chapter Twenty-four

Cast twenty-six stitches on each needle. Rib two inches two and two. Commence the thumb by taking two stitches as seam stitches...

Army Mitten Directions
*Gardiner Home Journal*
Gardiner, Maine

"MARY?" he said.

She smiled at him, nodded her head, but kept counting. "Twenty-two, twenty-three," she intoned, casting stitches onto her needle, "twenty-four, twenty-five, twenty-six."

She dropped her hands to her lap, looked over at him.

"What's that thee's working on, then?" he asked.

"Mittens for the soldiers," she said. "We all are—even our Victoria, though she's got a ways to go yet to get up to quality." She reached down into her bag, pulled out a piece of paper and slid it across the table to him. "Here's the pattern of it."

He reached for the clipping; the light from the lamp pooled on the table.

"Mittens with forefingers?" he asked, resting the paper on his knee. He looked at her.

"Yes," she said, "so the boys can pull their triggers."

She knitted and rocked in the warm kitchen.

Alfred held the book up to catch better light; she heard the pages slide across each other as he lifted and turned them, heard his voice dip and rise.

Mittens and socks and scarves and vests for the 21st Maine, she thought; caps and shawls for the Sanitary Commission—every twist of yarn I have is going off to war, and I could find use for more.

She finished a row, switched her work and empty needle to her opposite hands, started in again.

And uniforms—all those wool pants and jackets, winter capes and coats—mills all over New England, even over to Gardiner, are shaking and rumbling with the run of the looms inside, using up all their wool as fast as they can get it, looking hard for more.

She stopped rocking, put her work down to her lap, thought about that for a moment.

"Alfred," she said, pushing for his attention. "Alfred?"

He stopped in midsentence, surprised; he closed the book on his finger, leaned forward in his chair to see her better in the lamplight.

"We need more sheep," she said. "There's good profit to be made; we need as many as we can manage."

The spring rains pushed hard up the Eastern.

Joel Thompson stood in his barn doorway in late March, looked straight down his drive and across the road, sloppy now in mud and heaved stones, looked down the slope to where the fog sat thick and gray in the valley, all swirly on top of the Eastern.

He couldn't see the river, but he knew it was there—he could hear it, full as it was with upriver snowmelt—still there, still there, he thought, patiently turning tide after tide.

Alfred Stilphen worked the numbers. He stacked all his ledgers on the kitchen table, then got scratch paper from the writing box in the front room for his figures; he got a pen and a bottle of ink, then set himself up.

When he was ready, he sat, pulled his chair up close to the edge of the table, rolled up his right sleeve to keep it out of the smears, started in.

Thirty years, he thought. I've been keeping numbers on our sheep for thirty years of breeding and lambing—how many dropped live or born dead, and how many kept within the flock; how many butchered or sold or lost in pasture to scavengers; how many tons of timothy and clover, bushels of beets and carrots, how many kegs of dried herring.

And thirty years of Mary's careful tending to cuts and sores, of her help at lambing; her good hand at shearing, her quick sorting and bundling of fleeces, her knowledge of weight and grade.

Thirty years, the two of us, together.

When Mary Stilphen came back in from the workroom, his ledgers were spread all over the far end of the table; directly before him, three sheets of careful, round figures. His hair was untidy where he'd dragged his fingers through it, his collar loosened, top buttons undone; his hand, despite his care, a bit dirty at the side where he'd dragged it across damp ink on the paper.

"Thee's all in disarray," she said, and stood behind him, combed out his hair with her fingers.

"True enough," he said, leaning his head back into the comfort of her hands.

"Well?" she asked.

"We can double this year," he said. "We've got the acreage for grass and feed, the pasture for grazing; we've got good sheds, we've got the labor—we can double."

———

He took the letter from his coat pocket, placed it on the table before her.

"From Isaac?" Lydia asked, her hand already reaching for it.

Eliphalet nodded. "It's addressed to me," he said, "but it's as much ours as mine alone."

"You haven't read it?" She pushed her thumbnail under the flap, pried it loose.

"No," he said. "I wanted to read it together."

*Port Hudson, Louisiana*
*21ˢᵗ Maine Co H*
*June 10ᵗʰ 1863*

*Dear Pa I thot that I would write to you & let you know that I
am all of one piece & in good health after several days of fighting
after we left New Orelans & they started us up the Miss. River up
to here to Port Hudson. We got into it some at Plains Store, aint
that a funny name for a town. We are laying siege at Port Hudson so it is on & off again fighting & not fighting I got caught
in a crossfire yesterday forenoon with another man & there was
so much shot flying overhead, so we lay down flat in the gully &
waited it out finally crawled out the end now we are getting a few
days to rest. The 28ᵗʰ Maine is nearby tell Mr. Thompson that
Laura's husband Seward is there we had a visit yesterday & he is
fine. The weather here is all right it can get hot & thick at midday
it is fogy on the Miss. in the early morning it looks just like on
the Eastern except it is a lot bigger river. We should be starting to
home early in August for our tour will be up. I am getting mostly
enough to eat. Give my love to Ma & tell her I am so dirty she
would not know me. From your son, Isaac*

———

It rained for three days to start July, a steady but gentle rain that left
the timothy heavy with water, left it leaning, bending in the fields. When
the sun broke out on the morning of the fourth, the green slopes of the
Eastern river valley steamed in the new warmth.

Two, maybe three, days to dry out, Alfred thought, and then we'll
start haying; in the meanwhile, we'll run over to King's Mills, buy us
some more sheep—some Cheviots, maybe, they make such a good, solid
fleece, medium grade.

He turned on the stoop, stepped up into his shed and headed for the
kitchen to find Mary.

Or more Shropshires; we'll see what Mary decides.

She bought four Shrops and ten Cheviots at two dollars per; they
drove them up the ramp into the heavy wagon, raised and pegged the

tailgate to keep them from leaping out into the roadway, and got back home by late afternoon.

They marked them on the wagon bed. Alfred punched and notched their ears, Mary spread salve from her tin, soothed their wounds, then pushed them down the rampway into the near shed, where they huddled and bleated, confused and worried by their new surroundings.

"All's right, all's right," she sang to them; she stayed in the pen with them, touching their faces, their shoulders, until they quieted, then came out again, turned to Alfred.

"So now we got three breeds," she said, latching the gate behind her. "Shrops, Scots Blacks, and Cheviots."

"That's quite a mix," he said.

"'Tis, but I think a good one," she said. "My bets are on the Cheviots—I think they'll outdo both the Shrops and Blackface, but we'll give it a few years, make sure."

"I'll turn that decision over," he said. "Thee has a far better eye for that kind of thing."

———

Joel Thompson cut the grass in his apple orchards; he worked a scythe in the open rows while young George followed with a hand sickle, cutting away the growth around the trunks of the trees.

"Keeps the bugs down," he told the boy, "and keeps them away from the fruit."

———

Sarah Ann Thompson sat in the bittersweet at the base of the wall. She stretched her legs out in front of her, leaned her back against the warm stones and listened as they worked the orchard—the broad *whoosh* of Pa's scythe, the quicker *schop-schop-schop* of George's sickle.

She liked them working together; it was much easier to watch them when they were in the same space. When they were apart, there was no time all day for her to be still; she was always moving back and forth between their two places to keep them both in sight, always trotting along the rears and sides of buildings to spot first one and then loping back to the other, trying to keep their places—and the distances between them—fixed in her head.

But when they were together, she could do what she was doing now—she could sit in the bittersweet and watch flies land on her skirts and on her hands, crawl along her fingers and arms; she could try to not move against the tickle.

———————

Isaac Crocker came home in August.

He got off the train on Monday, spent one last night in camp there, then collected his pay and mustered out on Tuesday morning. He was dirty and tired; he hungered for his wife and a month in a real bed.

———————

Four days later, Lydia balanced a blueberry pie on her left palm, trimmed the edge away with her paring knife. She set the pie in the oven, gathered and rolled the cuttings, made twists, sprinkled them with cinnamon, and put them in as well.

There, she thought, treats for the children and a pie for Liph when he comes in for his tea.

She thought she heard a horse in the road, the squeak of harness and wheel; she turned to the window and saw the buggy come up the drive, saw Isaac beside Hannah in the seat.

She whirled in the kitchen, ran through the shed and out onto the stoop; he was out of the buggy and she reached for him, found his sleeve with her fingers and pulled him near; she held him to her for a long time.

## Chapter Twenty-four

I further proclaim that if any State shall fail to raise the quota assigned to it by the War Department under this call, then a draft for the deficiency in said quota shall be made on said State, or on the districts of said State, for their due proportion of said quota; and the said draft shall commence on the 5th day of January, 1864.

Abraham Lincoln
October 17, 1863

BENJAMIN APPEARED just before noon.

He came alone; he rode up the drive, tied his horse to the hitch post and loosened the girth, came in through the shed and opened the kitchen door.

"Just about to serve dinner," Lydia said. "I'll put down another plate."

"Got enough?" he asked.

"Always enough for one of my own," she said.

———

"Did you know?" she asked.

Eliphalet shook his head. "I didn't," he said.

"I knew something was coming from him," Lydia said. "He don't appear here at dinnertime too often, so I knew something was coming, but I didn't expect him to enlist."

"Well, there's the draft to worry over," Liph said. "He gets a bigger bounty if he enlists—three hundred dollars, I think."

"Three hundred?"

Liph nodded. "That's a good enticement, I'd say," he said, "though I don't think three hundred dollars is fair trade for his life."

Lydia burst into tears.

---

In no time, Benjamin was gone; two months later, Lew and Isaac, too—Isaac for the second time.

Doing their duty, Lydia thought, responding to the call.

She felt struck hard in her stomach and her chest; it hurt to breathe when she thought of them. At night, she climbed into bed with Eliphalet, and while he slept soundly, she lay on her back and stared into the darkness, wondered where her sons slept each night—in which state, which town, by which river, under which stars?

And not just her boys; she knew that well: Laura Thompson's husband, Seward McKenney; Sarah Call's two brothers, Fred and Jimmy; Eliza Blodgett's husband, John Buckman—everybody on the road had somebody, it seemed; only the Stilphens remained unscathed, and only because their boys were too young.

"I've made a list of all of 'em," she told Eliphalet, "so we don't lose count on who's gone."

She tacked her list to a kitchen cupboard door and read it at least once every day—while stirring oatmeal or beating eggs, kneading bread or cutting up pieces of meat for the pan.

*Llewellyn Crocker*
*Benjamin Crocker*
*Isaac Crocker*
*Frederick Goud*
*Jimmy Goud*
*Seward McKenney*
*John Buckman*

A list isn't much, Lydia thought, but it's the best I can do.

---

*East New York, New York*
*21ˢᵗ Maine Co H*
*December 26, 1863*

*Dear Ma & Pa Seeing that it is one day after 25th I thot that I*
*would write to you & tell you I hope you had a happy Christmas*
*day yesterday We had a big feed with beef & potatoes & turnips*
*there was a barrell of peanuts that we could eat all day I am*
*doing a lot of gard duty we are working in pares & two on a side*
*of the building at the same time We get up at about half past five*
*in the morn. then do a drill before we eat break fast then inspec-*
*tion then drill drill & drill some more We have free time after*
*dinner for washing and writing letters & for cards & chekkers.*
*All of us need a new pare of socks. Tell Mrs. Stilphen I got them*
*mittens she made me they are some fine and warm & I thank her*
*very much for making them for me. From your son Isaac.*

---

That February, most everybody on the road had a cold.

Polly felt all right, overall—she had a short headache and a bit of stuff in her nose, yet worked her way through it. Sarah Ann had but one day in the house; Joel took to his bed for four, coughing and hacking, blowing his nose into the rags she kept by the bed.

George had neither sniffle nor sneeze, but Polly kept him home to help with chores while Joel was laid up; he didn't like missing school—the winter term was short enough—but she needed him to feed and water the livestock, milk the cow, keep the woodboxes full.

He's but twelve years old, Polly thought as she went out the kitchen into the workroom to get a string of onions, and we'd be holding a short stick without him.

She peeled and chopped four of the onions, her eyes smarting and water-ing a bit. She slid them off the end of her board into a pot and added some water and a few mashed juniper berries, put the pot on the stove to boil.

George came in close to noon, carrying a load of firewood.

"Well, yer timing couldn't be better," she said, smiling at him.

He dumped the wood into the box, clapped his hands together to drop the bark and chips from his palms, turned to her.

"What can I do?" he asked.

"I need another pair of hands," she said, "to hold the straining cloth."

She stretched the cloth over a clean bowl; he put his hands to it to hold it in place as she poured the liquid.

"Cold syrup?" he asked.

She nodded. "Some for yer grandpa, some for Grandpa Crocker—I hear he's terrible sick with it."

"He is," George said. "Charles Henry told me."

She wrapped the onions and berries in the cloth, set it aside. She poured the liquid back into the pot, added a little butter, and set it back on the stove, stirred until the butter melted, then filled six old glass bottles, set them in the pantry to cool.

"I'll cork 'em when they're cool," she said, "and then maybe you could walk a bottle down to the Crockers."

He nodded.

"Tell them to give him a couple of spoonfuls morning and night," she said. "It'll help relieve that congestion."

"All right," he said, and sat down to his dinner.

———

Eliphalet slept as much as he could. When he was awake, he coughed a lot. His throat burned when he breathed; his rags grew soft with phlegm and blood.

It was easier to sleep, and so he did, slept long and hard and woke up between his quick dreams, unaware for just a moment before he opened his eyes and found himself propped up in the downstairs bed. He was cushioned in several soft pillows against the backboard; his chest was warm under the quilt, his shoulders wrapped in a shawl.

And Lydia was there, sitting still in a chair beside the bed.

"Want some soup?" she asked, reaching out, patting the back of his hand. "I made new this forenoon; it should be ready by now. I'll bring in a cup if ye'd like."

He nodded at her.

"I'll be right back with it," she said, and stood, kissed him on the forehead, and turned away, walked through the door into the kitchen.

The sunshine streamed in through the south windows.

Eliphalet felt it on the side of his face; he brought his hand up to his cheek, felt the warmth of it on the backs of his fingers. He turned his head to look outside, to look at the buds on the tips of the maples, at some crows winging across the pale spring sky up over the cattle shed, at the soft roll of his land as it fell down the slope to the Eastern.

He heard Lydia puttering in the kitchen, heard the scrape of the soup pot sliding off the stovetop, the rattle of a cup against a plate. He heard, too, a calf somewhere outside bawling for its mother, his other cattle calling for hay.

Chores to do, he thought, so he pushed himself away from the pillows and rose—light as a leaf now—up out of the bed and across the floor to the window and through the glass, somehow; he soared out over the dooryard and then high up into the April sunlight.

---

The *Ida Belle* bumped gently against the pilings.

Up beyond the dock, beside the riverbarn, the struts and braces of the haypress groaned under the pressure of the screw as the horses—Alfred Stilphen's paired blacks and Charlie's own roans—plodded around the capstan; they'd pressed ten bales already, and five more would do.

Eliphalet two days gone, Alfred thought. Knew him most of my life, and now he's gone; with him or without him, time to make the first run, get those high prices.

"It's pretty tight!" Alfred called out. "Maybe tie it, turn the horses and back that screw off."

Charlie Call looked up. "Let's give it another couple turns," he said, "get it good and firm."

"All right, but not much more."

The horses kept on; the screw pushed harder on the plate, the frame of the press shook and quivered with the force of it; the guy ropes sang with the tension and one began to fray near the top—Alfred saw it go, saw it spin and split.

He tried to call out, but there was no time. The rope snapped, whipped back between two of the horses, caught Charlie Call across the neck and took him down.

The horses jumped, whinnied in fear; dust rose in a cloud from beneath their flashing feet, drifted up the slope in a murky cloud. Alfred scrambled to calm them, to back them off; he took a quick look at Charlie, flat on his back, eyes open—he looked surprised, Alfred thought—and backed them off some more.

He held the reins bunched in his hand; he heard birds singing in the bushes on the riverbank, heard Sarah Call shouting and looked up toward the house, saw her—hugely pregnant, one hand holding up her belly, the other lifting her skirts—lumbering down through the meadow, bare legs showing in the spring sun.

---

Sarah Call knew exactly where to find the will—in the black document box inside the cupboard, underneath the mortgage and the business ledger and the diary.

She retrieved it, took it back outside and handed it to Alfred Stilphen, who read it out loud to her on the front porch. When he was done, she turned away from him, looked out across the dooryard and down the slope where the top shaft of the haypress was golden in the late light and the small wagon was stacked with pressed bales, ready to move down to the wharf and load on the *Ida Belle.*

"It's mine, though, isn't it?" she asked softly, worrying a strand of hair from the loose braid she'd fashioned that morning, when Charlie was still a live man and moving in the house with her and the children.

"What?"

"It's mine—the farm, I mean."

"It is," Alfred said, turning on the step to face her. "All of it: house, outbuildings, land, animals. The lot."

She twisted her hair around her finger, then loosened it, leaned her shoulder up against the porch column.

"Are you certain?"

"That's what this will says; even without that, we would make sure of it."

Ida Belle and Charlie pushed up against their mother, eyes wide, mouths tight, silenced by the suddenness of it all. She ran her hands down over her huge belly, slipped her palms over their heads; they turned their faces into her skirts, made small fists against her thighs.

"Now what?" she asked, looking down at her children, wondering what she might do without Charlie, how she might get along, especially with a new baby any day and the hay still stacked in the riverbarn.

"Nothing," Alfred said, "right now."

She lifted her head.

"You'll have to inventory," he explained. "Make a list of all he owns." He looked down at his boots, shifted his weight, looked up again. "Owned," he corrected, changing the tense, "a list of all he owned."

She slumped, defeated. "You know I don't write," she said bleakly. "Charles did all of the writing for the both of us."

Alfred shrugged. "You needn't bother yourself," he said. "I can write it up, then deliver to the court up in Augusta."

"It has to go that far?"

He nodded. "To probate." He ran his hand over his chin. "The court will be sure it is all in order, then can sign it over to you."

She watched the sun drop; the tops of the trees were brilliant points of green against a mass of dark sky.

He touched her shoulder for her attention, and she turned to him.

"It's setting to rain," he commented. "I'll help John and Daniel get those bales into the riverbarn."

She looked at him, square on, her eyes gray and vague.

"It's no matter to me," she said, pushing helplessly at stray ends of her hair. "Do what you will."

KILLED. On Tuesday forenoon, Mr. Chas. M. Call of Pittston was killed in that town, by the rope of a hay press striking him and breaking his neck. He lived only about fifteen minutes. He leaves a wife and two children.

*Gardiner Home Journal*
April 21, 1864

Mary Stilphen stepped out of the shed into the dooryard, crossed the drive, and slipped into the east shed. She stood in the alleyway and breathed in the smell of the sheep, that sweet mix of feed and manure, lanolin and hay.

And Alfred, she thought; that's the scent of Alfred, too.

"What's this?" he said, moving in the near pen, shaking clean straw to the clean floor. "I'll be in shortly for tea and a good read—or is there something thee needs now?"

She shook her head. "Just need the sight of thee," she said.

He stopped, tipped his head and looked at her.

"Lyd's lost her husband," she said, "and Sarah's lost hers, too." She picked up his broom from the corner, turned and twisted it in her hands, then put it back, looked back at him. "And I find that I can't let thee out of my sights."

He was still, quiet; she heard the rustle of sheep in the straw, the soft bleats.

"All's right, Mary," he said gently. "All's right."

Alfred went to town meeting on Thursday.

"I must," he told Mary in the morning. "It's my obligation, thee does see that?"

"Reluctantly," she said, "but, yes."

*Pittston Town Meeting*
*East Parish*
*April 28, 1864*


*School Agent*
    *Eastern River District*    *Alfred Stilphen*
*Surveyor of Highways*    *Samuel Crocker*

*Births in the Town of Pittston, Registered & Recorded by me,*
*Benjamin S. Jones, Town Clerk*
    *John Crocker, to Samuel & Caroline Dudley Crocker, May*
*10, 1863*
    *Willis L. Call, to Sarah Goud Call & Charles M. Call,*
*April 21, 1864*

*Deaths in the Town of Pittston, Registered & Recorded by me,*
*Benjamin S. Jones, Town Clerk*
    *Eliphalet M. Crocker, husband of Lydia, April 17, 1864 at*
*74 yrs of age*
    *Charles M. Call, husband of Sarah, April 19, 1864 at 32*
*yrs of age*

# Chapter Twenty-five

None genuine without the words "Dr. E.G. Gould's Pin Worm Syrup" blown in each bottle, and his portrait and a fac-simile of his signature on the wrapper.

*Gardiner Home Journal*
1864

SPRING, FINALLY.

Caroline Crocker warmed a half-pint of milk, poured it onto her yeast cake, and left it to sit a bit in her smallest bowl. She beat up a couple of eggs, melted a teacup of butter. She scooped the flour into her best bowl, then poured all the liquids on top, mixed it with a wooden spoon.

She added a little more flour to get the texture right, kneaded it in with her fingers.

There, she thought, biscuits for dinner; she covered the bowl with a fine cloth, left it on the counter to rise.

---

*Maine 6th Light Artillery*
*Near Chancellorsville,, Virginia*
*May 9, 1864*

*My dear brother Samuel I am not sure where we are but we are near Chancellorsville that is all I know I thot I would write to you whilst I have got a chance before I try to sleep some before we get on the move again tomorrow although I would rather not We come down here five days past & camped in a woodsy place near*

*the Rapiden River where year old dead were laying thick in the*
*ground & at night the wind sang & moned in the old trees there*
*in a place they call the Wilderness & that is a good name I can tell*
*you. I seen things I do never want to see again We are chaseing Lee*
*south trying to cut him off but he keeps one step before us each time*
*Would you please share this letter with Ma & Pa & Cal & please*
*look in on Eulalia & share this letter with her for I do not know*
*when I will next have a chance to write Your brother*

*Benjamin F. Crocker*

Samuel Crocker folded the letter, then leaned it against the base of
the lamp on the kitchen table where Lydia and Caroline would find it
when they came in from taking the washing off the lines.

He does not know Pa is dead, he thought, and went out to the sheds
to start evening chores.

---

The Stilphens sheared in the middle of the month.

It was good weather—not a breath of wind to stir up the chaff in
the holding pen; it was still a bit chilly outside, but warm enough on the
shearing floor, what with all that sunlight pouring in the doorways.

Alfred sent the sheep in to Mary from the holding pen, kneed them
through the gate and onto the shearing platform, where Mary brought
them down, one after the other, brought them to ground and dragged
them up against her shins, started in. Her shears flashed in the light, sang
in the sheep shed.

Augustus sat back on his heels, watched his mother work, listened to her
voice sing out the patterns; he knew them by heart, but he wanted to be sure.

"Across the belly," she called out to him, as she made four passes.
"Keep her head tucked under yer arm…"

She handed Gus the shears.

"Give it a try," she said. "We'll start you on one of the younger ones—
they're smaller and will give you good practice."

She coached him from the side. "Watch her teats," she said. "Move
careful across there—good, that's it!—and then lift the fleece to the side a
little bit, keep a little tension on that skin…"

The lamp spilled yellow light over the table, reflected a starburst in the glass in the front window, dark now with night.

"How much did we get?" Mary asked. She leaned against the counter to ease the ache in the small of her back; she reached up and pulled the pins from her hair, fingered it through as she watched Alfred work the numbers.

Gus tapped his fingers on the table, edgy for the answer. "Well, Pa?" he said. "How much?"

Alfred looked up, grinned. "I think about one hundred pounds," he said. "That's near double from last year—and the yearlings will give more as they grow."

"Well done," Mary said, looking first at Alfred, then at Gus. "I say, well done for the Stilphens."

The following Tuesday, shortly after the sun broke over the valley ridge and pushed through the river smoke curled along the Eastern, Mary and Gus Stilphen walked up the road to Sarah Call's.

"She's just had that baby," Mary said. "She can't do her own clip this year."

Her shearing clothes were rolled into a bundle and tied with a piece of string; she looped her fingers through the twine and carried it easily at her side. Gus shouldered a small sack with shears and stone, a rag damp with oil.

"Yer first clip off farm," she said. "Does it seem all right?"

Gus nodded. "It does," he said, "especially if ye're there to keep me on tracks."

They crossed the plank bridge, passed through the short stand of woods, then moved out of the shadows into the spread of Sarah Call's lower fields. The grass shimmered in the breeze; below the boathouse, the Eastern turned and glinted in the sunlight.

They paused, took a long look.

"I'll never tire of that," she said. "It somehow gives me hope that this war will soon be over; it gives me hope that everything here might go back to what it was."

She turned her head to Gus to gauge his response; she found she had to tip her head back to catch his eyes.

He's taller than I am now, she thought, surprised by the notion.

———

Sarah's shed was in minor disarray—no man about the place, Mary thought—but her sheep were bright-eyed, clean enough for shearing.

Sarah came out to greet them. She had Willis, wrapped in a clean flannel, on her shoulder, and Ida and Charles close alongside.

"Brought my new lead man to run the operation," Mary said, tipping her head toward Augustus. "I've got my shearing clothes; I'll be working the holding pens for him."

Gus moved his sack from his shoulder, rested it on the ground near his feet, looked at Sarah Call. "I'm not yet as good as my mother," he said.

"You will be, soon enough," she said, and smiled.

———

"They're all scratching at their bottoms," Caroline said. "They've got their fingers in their pants, up their skirts—all of 'em."

Lydia looked at her daughter-in-law, shook her head. "It's the pinworm," she said. "Saw Polly Thompson yesterday; she says George has it."

"They getting it from school?"

"Probably—and if that's so, every house on the road's got worms."

———

Polly Thompson went out at midday, carried her basket across the road and down the slope to the Eastern. The early field grass was heavy with dew—both her shoes and stockings were soon wet through—but the sun was warm on her face and shoulders and the breeze smelled sharp and clean after the long months spent cooped inside the house.

She found it soon enough: a thick cluster of pussy willow she remembered growing along the shoreline near the north property line. She cut a basketful of stalks, choosing them carefully, thinning the patch rather than cutting away whole sections. No sense destroying the whole for the use of a few parts, she thought.

She sat on the shed stoop, her basket by her side, and stripped long tendrils of bark away from the stalks, collected them in a pan of water resting on the ground between her feet.

She heard the outkitchen door shut, heard Joel's boots on the shed floor behind her.

"What's up, then?" he asked. He lifted her basket to make space, then sat beside her on the stoop.

"They've all got the pinworm," she said, and pulled another long sliver of bark from a willow. "All of them—from George all the way down the road to Freddie Stilphen."

"Oh, Jesus," he said. "Does that mean we're all in for gallons of willow tea?"

"It does," she said, and reached for another piece.

———

"I'd almost rather the worms than Polly's tea," Samuel Crocker said. "It's dreadful."

Caroline put her hands on her hips, looked at him across the kitchen. "You can make that choice if you want," she said, "but you'll be sleeping in your own bed; you'll not be sharing mine."

———

In the end, it was Dr. Gould's Pin Worm Syrup that made the difference; Samuel picked up a few bottles when he made the market run over to Gardiner on Friday.

He and Caroline set their children in a row, then went down the line with the bottle and a loaded soup spoon.

"It's not bad," Charles Henry said, puckering up just a little after he swallowed. "And it's sure better than that willow tea."

"It works pretty quick," Caroline told Mary Stilphen a few days later.

"We dosed all of us Friday after supper; spent all that night meeting up in the privy, fighting over the seats, but it cleaned us all out pretty good."

*Company C, Maine 31st*
*Cold Harbor, Virginia*
*June 1, 1864*

*Dear Brother Samuel We are resting up tonight & they say they can get a mail out so I thot I would write you a few lines & please forgive me, I cannot tell Hannah for fear she might be frightened but I must tell someone all I am seeing & doing here I think I shall never forget the site & the smell of battle I seen dead lying side by side & upside down with feet & hands & legs missing & sometimes a head or all of everything I do not know what we have done to get things to come to this terrible war but I do not want to ever see this again & when I am finally home I will try to put it to rest They tell us there will be another battle tomorrow & so we have all wrote our name & town we live on paper and pinned it to ourselfs so somebody will know who I am should I fall Please see to Hannah if I cannot I am your brother*

*Isaac Crocker*

# Chapter Twenty-six

They have responded nobly for the defence of their country's integrity and honor, and they carry with them the hopes, the pride and the prayers of every citizen. May they all return, having won imperishable laurels.

*Gardiner Home Journal*
Gardiner, Maine

SARAH CALL pinned the last of her washing on the line—her other everyday skirt, two waists, Ida and Charlie's small clothes, some linens—then went back up the line, smoothing wrinkles from the tablecloths and napkins, tightening a pin here and there in case the breeze came up.

The Crockers have letters, she thought. Their boys send letters home pretty regular, while Fred and Jimmy send none at all to me—they can't write well enough for letters, and even if they could, I can't read them.

She pulled one of her kitchen towels straighter, reset the corner pin, then leaned down and picked up Willis, sleeping soundly in his basket. She turned, started back across the yard to the shed door.

It will be different for my children, she thought; all three of my children will read and write, I'll make sure of it.

---

He tucked the newspaper under his arm, headed out of the kitchen. "I'm off to see Sarah," he said. "Back in an hour."

"All right," Mary said. "Remind her I'll be up tomorrow, mid-forenoon to carry her up to Polly's—we're rolling bandages for the Sanitation Commission, I think."

———

Alfred Stilphen sat at Sarah's table, sipped his coffee. He added a spoonful of sugar, poured in some cream from Sarah's little pitcher, stirred, took another sip.

"Good," he said, wiping his mouth with the back of his hand. "Mary's not got the hang of coffee yet; we're still strictly tea."

"I don't suppose it matters much which one you drink," Sarah said. "I think it's more about keeping good company while ye're drinking it."

Willis stirred in his basket, and Sarah left the table to check on him; she pulled his flannel up around his shoulders, brushed her fingers on his cheek.

"He's fine," she said, and came back to the table, to her chair.

"All right, now," he said, picking up the *Home Journal*, turning the pages for the war news. "Let's see where Fred and Jimmy are these days."

He found a colored map of the United States in Ida's geography; it folded outward from the middle on both sides, spread out like wings on Sarah's kitchen table. The states were tinted pink, light blue, yellow.

"Maine's blue," he said, and put his finger down on it.

"Where's Virginia?" she asked, and he showed her.

"That's a fair way off," she said.

"It is," he agreed. "And here's where Fred and Jimmy are," he said, pointing, "near Mulberry Run, Gravel Springs Run."

Sarah Call looked at the map, nodded a few times. "What do you suppose a 'run' is?" she asked.

"Well," Alfred said, tapping his fingers on the folded newspaper, "it must be a southern word for a brook or a creek."

"Well, whatever it is," she said, "it sounds like poetry to me."

———

They lost part of Nathaniel Blodgett's upper mowing to a week of terrible wet weather.

Samuel Crocker and his son George, Daniel Blodgett, and Gus Stilphen scythed the lower field on Wednesday in a clear, fine sun; they turned the hay on Thursday morning, got it up onto the wagons and into the barn by evening.

On Friday, they worked the upper field from wall to wall, finishing the last few rows as evening fell. When they woke the next morning, thinking to turn the grass and leave it to dry for the day, the valley was overcast, dim and wet with mist and fog. The timothy lay in swaths for five days in a steady drizzle; by the time the sun poked through on Wednesday, it was beyond saving.

"We'll dry and turn it anyway," Nate said. "We can use it for bedding in the barn."

———

Lydia Crocker wrapped the bolt of white linen in light paper. She folded over the ends and pinned them, tied a piece of string around the center to keep the paper closed, protect the roll.

"All set to go?" she asked her daughter-in-law. "Mary will be here any minute to carry us up."

"Just need my other scissors," Caroline said. "I've got those different sized ones, and they might be handy—can't do good work without the right tools."

Lydia cocked her head, let her eyes roll. "If I had one penny for any time Liph said that, I'd be the richest woman on the road."

"Well, I'd be a close second," Cal said. She took her scissors from her sewing basket, put them in her bag. "Samuel says it all the time; it used to annoy me something fierce." She headed for the kitchen door, her heavy hips swaying underneath her skirts. ·

"But not anymore?" Lydia asked.

Cal turned her head, spoke over her shoulder. "I stopped being annoyed when I figured out he was right," she said, and went into the shed.

Mary and Victoria Stilphen came clattering up the road in the cart.

They stopped in for Sarah Call, who carried two baskets—one full of sewing supplies, the other full of Willis; they stopped again for Lydia and Caroline Crocker, who slid her John's basket in beside Sarah's.

"No Jane?" Victoria asked, turning on the board seat and slipping over into the back to give Lydia the better place in front.

Lydia shook her head, climbed up next to Mary. "She's got work in Gardiner now," she said, "in that shoe factory on Water Street—where Eliza Buckman's working, earning her own money." She settled herself, arranged her skirts, tucked them in, away from the spokes. "She started last week."

The horse started off; Lydia looked over the stone wall, down the run of the fields to the river.

Off the farm, she thought. I never had outside work in my entire life, never had money of my own.

They set up in Polly Thompson's outkitchen, put her two worktables end to end down the center of the room, then unrolled the linen down the full length.

"What's the measure?" Polly asked. "Aren't there two different bandage lengths?"

Jane Blodgett picked up the *Home Journal,* turned the page back, folded the broadside into quarters. "I'll read it," she said.

"'Using all linen…4 inches wide and 6 yards long, or 3½ wide and 4 long, 2½ wide and three long, 2 inches wide and 3 yards long or 1 inch wide and 1 yard long, to be rolled very tight and pinned, labeled with a gum label describing the character and length of the bandage. Packages to be formed of five bandages, one of each kind.'"

"So, four lengths," Polly said. "Six, four, three, and one yard."

"And five different widths," Mary said.

They all stood still and looked at each other, caught up short by the complexity of it all.

"You'd think a bandage is a bandage," Victoria said. "Why all those different lengths and widths?"

Somewhere outside, one of Joel's horses blew, shook its head, blew again; the farm wagon came down the drive, the bed piled with a mix of manure and straw bedding headed for the fields. Polly looked out the window, watched George in the driver's seat, hands full of reins; saw Joel walking beside, fork over his shoulder.

"I guess it depends," she said, "on what part of a man gets shot—big bandages for body, smaller for legs and arms, smaller still for hands and fingers."

———

Later, when Pa and Polly and George were through with outside chores, when they were still at supper and there was still some early evening light coming through the glass in the shed windows, Sarah Ann slipped in from the barn, saw the different piles of cut linen on the tables.

She saw, too, the bandages—the baskets of rolled bandages in the center—rolled tightly and pinned, sorted by width, by length.

"*Nnnnnn*," she whispered, reaching out to touch, to lift the little rolls in her hands, turn them back and forth in her palms. "*Nnnnnnn.*"

She took one of each, put them carefully into her skirt pockets, then went back outside and loped across the dooryard, headed for the chicken coop.

———

George Thompson wrapped his hands around the rails and pushed his body closer to the rungs—chest and knees pressed to the wood, just as his grandfather had taught him—and pulled himself higher into the tree, tipping his shoulder up under the branch.

The ladder bounced with the shift in his weight, and George felt that combination of fear and exhilaration swoop through his belly as he dipped and swayed on the rungs.

Like barn swallows when they fly, he thought, when they swoop down from the loft doorway and rise up again over the roofline; dip and sway, swoop and rise…

He adjusted the sling around his neck, moved the bag to his side; he reached out to his right, twisted the Baldwin lightly against its stem and, as it released and fell, trapped the apple in his upturned hand, dropped it into the folds of the bag.

He reached out for another.

He preferred picking Baldwins to Winthrop Greenings—they were easier to hold onto, smaller, more compact than the Winthrops—and so he and Grandpa had made an agreement: George worked all the Baldwins while Grandpa did the other orchard by himself.

George moved up a couple of rungs, settled again, reached out for another apple.

He wanted to learn to pack his own barrels this year—Grandpa could pack an apple barrel so tight that nothing moved inside, nothing bumped or bruised; he set stones in the bottom to soak up the moisture, then packed the apples tightly, hammered down a lid. Those apples went by wagon to Gardiner without a single damaged fruit, and two grocers in town paid high cash for them, no questions asked.

Maybe I could start making my own money, he thought, buy some of my own trees, start my own operation. There was that corner of the old north meadow sitting idle now—I could ask, at any rate; I could ask.

"The corner up near our north line?" Joel asked. "The angle made by the road and that tumbled stretch of wall?"

George nodded.

Polly clanged the grates of the woodstove, then opened the side door and pulled out the ashpan, headed out to the dooryard to dump it into the compost pit.

The shed door banged shut behind her.

"Well, I don't see why not," Joel said. "What are you thinking to start in there, anyways?"

"Well," George said, "I thought more Baldwins—Gram says they make the best pie."

Joel Thompson smiled into his teacup, then took a few sips. "Good a reason as any," he said. "Let's go up to see Jim Carpenter—he starts the best seedlings; we'll see what we can do for next spring."

———————

In the middle of October, they closed the school until the start of winter term.

They roused their children early, fed them bowls of oatmeal, and sent them out into the potato fields each morning at sunrise, fed them twice more in the field during the day—once at late morning, once at early afternoon. Later, just before sunset, one of the older boys took a team down, helped the children—their noses smeared and runny, their hands dark with dirt—load their full baskets and burlaps into the wagon, then drove them home to a warm supper.

———————

*Company H, 1ˢᵗ Maine Light*
*Cedar Creek, Virginia*
*October 25, 1864*

*Dear Samuel I am writing you a few short lines to tell you that*
*I am alright after a battle here when we was surprized by rebels*
*we lost some ground but then Sheridan rallied us all he is a small*
*man but he is fierce I can tell you I am on light duty now for a*
*fortnight I caught a ball in my ankle & it bled something awful*
*but it went clean thru & did not brake my bone but tore apart*
*my mussel I might have a limp for my life but at least Maggie*
*will have a whole husband after this war & that is more than a*
*lot of wives will be able to say Please call on her for me and give*
*my love to Ma & Caroline & all the others to home your brother*
*Llewellyn Crocker*

———————

The snow came in December.

On Tuesday morning, Lydia Crocker stepped outside for just a moment to watch her grandchildren amble down the drive and across the road to school. She pulled her shawl close around her shoulders, shivered in the cold breeze.

Here it comes, she thought.

She turned on the hard ground, came back in through the shed, back into the warm kitchen, closing the outkitchen door behind her.

"Smells like snow," she said, and loosened her shawl.

Caroline wrapped her hand in a towel, tipped the bread out of the pan; she rapped her knuckles on the bottom of the loaf, listened for the muffled thud.

"Done," she muttered, and turned the loaf onto the rack to cool, opened the oven door to pull out the other loaves.

"Cal?" Lydia said.

"What's that?" Caroline said, her face pink in the heat. "I missed what you just told me."

"Snow," Lydia repeated. "It smells like snow."

The first flakes drifted down past the windows at noon. By the time the children came home from school, the road was covered with it; by nightfall, the dooryard was aswirl.

It snowed at least once every week for the next two months—quick squalls, mostly, and a few mild storms—but in mid-February, a dark gray front moved in from King's Mills in the early afternoon, pulled a storm in behind it that lasted all through that night, brought a heavy fall.

In the early morning, the branches of the trees were thick with it; firs and pines sagged.

Alfred and the boys spent most of the forenoon clearing pathways from the doorways—from the big house to the road, then from the kitchen to the well, from the backhouse, sheep sheds and barn to the dooryard.

Alfred paused once to catch his breath. He leaned his weight on the handle of the scoop and watched his sons work their shovels, watched them throw the snow easily over their shoulders.

How did I ever do this alone? he wondered. How did I ever get it all done?

After dinner, he harnessed the blacks and they all climbed on the pung, went up to Sarah Call's to break her out, too, to clear her yard and pathways, to free up her well and her shed doors.

Livingston and Fred filled her woodboxes.

By the first of March, the stone walls on both sides of the road were buried. The landscape flattened into a smooth spread that ran from the back of Samuel Crocker's cattle sheds all the way down to the lower fields and over the Eastern; beneath the glaze the tides moved in and out, over and over.

He spent some time piling and packing snow around the open back side of the privy to keep the wind from blowing underneath, blowing up through the holes in the seat.

"The cold's problem enough," he said to Caroline, "without the wind freezing your ass off every time you sit."

She grunted. "Not to mention blowing everybody's business back into my face whenever I empty all the house pots."

———

There was a break in early March. The sun lifted high enough in the sky each day to heat the shingles on the main roof, and by noontime, water started to drip from the eaves. It dripped all the afternoon, but when the sun went down it slowed, then stopped again—froze solid each night, started up again the next day.

"I'm glad this weather's broke," Joel said. He rolled over in bed, snugged up to Polly, dropped an arm across her hip. "Time to tap the maples."

———

After supper, after the dishes were washed and wiped and tucked into the cupboard, Lydia Crocker carried the washpan to the shed door, tossed the graywater out to the dark of the backyard. The sky was full of stars, the light of the moon threw the sharp shadow of the barn across the snow.

She stood there a moment, the cold air biting her nose and throat. The moonlight danced across the snow; foxes barked somewhere in the river valley.

Sometimes I think my boys are never coming home, she thought, then turned and went back inside the warm kitchen.

Sitting in the kitchen rocker near the stove, she worked a short while on her knitting—a new vest for Samuel, a green one with a ribbed bottom—but when she reached the end of a row, she wound her yarn around her needles, tucked the whole thing into her bag.

"I'm off to bed," she said to Caroline. "I'm a bit gurmley—a headache I can't seem to shake off."

"All right," Cal said. She licked her thread, put it through the eye, pulled a length from the spool; she watched her mother-in-law shuffle down the hallway to the back room.

The logs shifted in the firebox.

"Need a lamp?" Cal asked.

"Goodness, no," Lydia called back. "It's bright as day with that pretty moon."

———

Cal Crocker went down the line, dished heavy spoonfuls of oatmeal into their bowls—one each for Samuel and Amanda, two for Charles Henry and George; there was butter and cinnamon to add, or thick maple syrup.

She sliced some of yesterday's bread, smeared it lightly with lard, then dropped the pieces onto the skillet to toast; she looked out the window while they browned, then flipped them to toast the other side.

"There's strawberry jam in the pot," she said, placing two slices on her husband's plate. "I'm going to check on Mother—be right back."

She slipped down the hall and opened Lydia's bedroom door a bit, tipped her head inside and saw her there, propped up against the headboard, hands tucked underneath the bedclothes, the quilt spread neatly across her chest. Strands of gray hair wisped across the pillow, her head was turned to the window; the morning sun fell in through the glass, bright on her face, her vacant eyes, her slack mouth.

Caroline Crocker closed the door, heard the drop bar click in the latch; she went back into the kitchen to feed her family.

They tended to Lydia Crocker, the three of them.

Polly Thompson, Jane Blodgett, and Mary Stilphen readied her, washed her with pieces of worn flannel, cleaned the loose skin on her face and neck, her freckled shoulders and arms, her spotted hands; they wiped her long breasts, her soft belly, her back, her veined legs, her twisted toes.

They poured lavender oil into their palms, spread it slowly along her body, over each muscle and bone, each curve, each rise and fall.

They wrapped her in fine linen.

---

Alfred and Gus Stilphen stayed the night in the sheep sheds.

They draped blankets over their shoulders and sat in the hay, leaned back against the walls, and settled in. They eyed the ewes, watched carefully for the start of discharge, then kept close watch on each one as her labor intensified, alert for signs of distress.

The ewes dropped their lambs into the clean hay, then circled about and cleaned them, licked away mucus and membranes from nostrils and mouths, pushed against their ribs, nudged them into breathing, encouraged them to stand, to nurse.

Only once was there trouble, and Alfred made the call.

"Grease up," he said to his son. "Yer hands are smaller than mine, and she's stuck."

Gus pulled off his coat, pushed up his sleeves and greased his arm. He leaned over the ewe, slipped his hand, his wrist, and the first part of his forearm into the hot, wet inside; he felt two legs, then a shoulder.

"What's up?" Alfred asked.

"Head back, far as I can tell," Gus said. He closed his hand, pushed at the lamb with the flat of his knuckles, pressured it back out of the birth canal; he felt the neck turn in that larger space, guided the head forward.

"All right," he said, "she's all right now; here she comes!"

---

The ice started moving at the end of March, started to crack and split along the course of the river. Sheets of it snapped and dropped every day; the water showed black and moving in the open channel.

In the faint dawn, Samuel Crocker watched the shadowed humps of geese moving along the shoreline in the lower meadows; heard them call as they lifted from the snow, headed north in the early light.

I'm head of household now, he thought.

———

Nathaniel Blodgett sat just inside the shed doorway, out of the chilly breeze but still in full April sunlight, such warmth welcome on his face and chest, on his legs and arms.

The breeze came out of the north, just right to carry sound down from Joel Thompson's, and he heard a commotion of sorts up there— young George's dog barking, a shouted exchange—he recognized Joel's voice, but couldn't place the other; he couldn't make out the words.

It grew quiet again, then came the rattle and bang of an empty wagon coming down the road at fair speed.

He pushed up out of his chair, grabbed hold of his cane, and eased down the step, headed out into the dooryard to take a look; down below, the wagon pulled up at the end of the drive.

"War's over!" the driver shouted. "War's over!"

The man's horses blew, jumped and twitched and stepped in the roadway; he held them firm, the reins taut in his fingers.

"Lee surrendered!" he yelled. "War's over!"

Nate forgot himself, started forward, felt the pain leap through his hip. "Go tell Crocker!" he called, pointing down the road, "and Sarah Call just below that—they've got boys in; they'll want to know!"

The man flicked the reins to the horses and they set off with a start; the wagon bed clattered against the frame, the wheels bumped in the ruts.

Nate turned, started back to the house.

Oh, glory, glory! he thought, propping his cane to the ground, hitching up his hip; then, out loud, hollering now, "Janey! Ho! Janey!"

Within the week, Polly Thompson's snowdrops poked through the last of the snow along the rail fence; there were three bright yellow ones clustered at the bottom of the far fence post, and Joel couldn't keep his eyes off them.

"From the surrender to this," he said. He looked down at the *Home Journal* in his hand, at the black funereal border around the columns of type. He could hardly read it; the words blended together, swarmed over the page. "It's too much to swallow all at once," he said. "I'm feeling kind of straggled."

"We all are," Alfred said. "We're all going up and down with it; there's too much space between those extremes to take it all in." He sat down next to Joel on the bench just outside the shed doorway, stretched his legs out, crossed them at the ankle. "How's Polly holding up?"

"She's beside herself," Joel said. "She's all unsettled, weepy."

"Mary, too," Alfred said, "and wearing black, from head to toe, as if Lincoln was one of our own." He tapped the toes of his boots together, leaned his head back against the shed wall.

"Maybe he was," Joel said, watching the breeze push at those yellow snowdrops. "I never thought of it like that until now, but maybe he was."

The *Eastern Queen* inched up to the dock in Gardiner at four in the afternoon; Isaac Crocker stood at the rail and looked out at the backs of the buildings along Water Street, all fine brick and slate, with whole chimneys and solid glass in all the windows—no rubble, no scarred ground.

It's a different country, he thought. I hardly know where I am.

He picked up his pack and his rifle, stepped down the gangway to the pier, then walked down the length of it into the sunlight in Depot Square; he crossed Water Street to the livery for a horse to hire.

Two hours later, when the August sun was just lowering over the back of the western ridge, Isaac Crocker rode up his own drive. He stopped in the dooryard, sat very still atop the hired roan, and looked around at his barn, his shed, his chicken coop, and finally, his own house.

Hannah opened the door.

He tried to say her name, but his breath was stuck fast in his throat; he slid off the horse, let go the reins. He looked at her again—Hannah, standing whole and straight and clean there on the front step—then put his hands to his face and started to weep.

———

They all came home in the middle of August, all came home when the aster and goldenrod grew thick along the roadways, along the stone walls, against the back sides of the barns and sheds.

They wore their brass buttons and battered boots; they carried their rifles, their packs, their tin cups and plates; they carried, too, their dysentery, their pounding hearts, their night sweats and terrors; they carried their pride and their guilt.

All of them came home—Isaac, Llewellyn, and Benjamin Crocker, Fred and Jimmy Goud, John Buckman, Seward McKenney—all came home by second haying.

———

One evening in late September, Jane Blodgett went out to feed her chickens; she pried the lid from the barrel of cracked corn and scooped some into her pan, replaced the lid, pushed it down with her palm.

She stood for a long moment in the doorway, looked south down the slope of the road. She saw smoke rising from Samuel Crocker's kitchen chimney, rising straight and white up into the evening sky.

Oh, Lydia, she thought; there now, Lyd, just look at that now—it's all over and everybody's back home and everything looks the same as it was before.

She watched the sun slip down over the western ridge of the valley, watched the last of that golden light run along the river; the trees on the shoreline were sweet with early color.

It happens so quick, Jane thought; the turning happens so quick. Everything on the Eastern is green, green, green until suddenly it isn't anymore, and the next day the tips of the hardwoods all along the water are gone to orange, red, and yellow.

She stepped down onto the stoop, scanned the width and length of the dooryard for wayward chickens. She saw a few Barred Rocks scratching in the dirt beside the shed, so she started across the drive and shook her pan of corn at them—gently, now, gently—encouraged them back up the drive to the safety of their coop for the night.

"Chick-chick-chick!" she sang, "chick-chick-chick!"

# Sources

Bury, Charlotte Campbell. *The Lady's Own Cookery Book*. London: Henry Colburn, 1844.

Child, Lydia Maria Francis. *The American Frugal Housewife*. Boston: Carter, Hendee, and Co., 1832.

Child, Lydia Maria Francis. *The Mother's Book*. Boston: Carter, Hendee, and Co., 1831.

Hanson, J.W. *History of Gardiner, Pittston and West Gardiner*. Gardiner: William Palmer, 1852.

North, James W. *The History of Augusta*. Augusta: Clapp and North, 1870.

*Eastern Chronicle*, Gardiner, Maine, 1824–1827.

*Christian Intelligencer & Eastern Chronicle*, Gardiner, Maine, 1827–1834.

*Cold Water Fountain*, Gardiner, Maine, 1844–1849.

*Fountain and Journal*, Gardiner, Maine, 1851–1853.

*Northern Home Journal*, Gardiner, Maine, 1854–1858.

*Gardiner Home Journal*, Gardiner, Maine, 1858–1865.

Probate Court Records, Kennebec County, Maine.

United States Federal Census of 1850, 1860.

Selected United States Federal Census Non-Population Schedules Schedule 4: Productions of Agriculture in Pittston in the County of Kennebec, State of Maine, 1850, 1860.

Town Records of Pittston, Maine.

## Acknowlegments

Thanks to: David Bellows, David B. Chittim, Ann Costello, Barbara A. Desmarais, Howard Gould, Gwen Hinman, Jude Maloney, Guido Romano, Mike Rosenzweig, Lisa Schinhofen, Tom Settlemire, Pam Burr Smith, Dawn Thistle, Deborah Ullman, June Vail, Pam VanVolkenburgh, and Amy E. Waterman.

## About the Author

Deborah Gould has lived on a dairy farm, owned a graphic arts business, and worked in educational interpreting/English language acquisition for students with cochlear implants. She lives in Brunswick, Maine, where she belongs to a small unprogrammed Quaker Meeting and volunteers for a domestic violence agency.

Visit her website: www.debgould.com
Contact her at: debgould12@gmail.com